I0523594

WORKS BY THE AUTHORS

KELVIN WHITE:

From the Spencer Marlowe series:

The Singapore Saga
The Hawaiian Intervention
The Manhattan Sting
(forthcoming)

BRUCE RUSSEL:

Jacob's Air
The Chelsea Manifesto
Channelling Henry
Reunion

ALSO IN COLLABORATION:

The King of San Francisco
(forthcoming)

BIRTHRIGHT

KELVIN WHITE

BRUCE RUSSELL

Printed by:
Ingram Spark
https://www.ingramspark.com/

(PB) ISBN: 978-0-6489109-8-5
(EB) ISBN: 978-0-6489109-7-8

Interior design by: Red Room Editing
Cover design by: Aspire Book Covers

ACKNOWLEDGEMENTS

I would like to acknowledge the role my friend and collaborator, Bruce Russell, played in the creation of this novel. We met in a class he was running at Maylands Library. He seemed to be interested in the time-travel novel I was writing at the time. Perhaps it was merely part of his role as a teacher of creative writing, I thought.

Months later we both decided to go and have a beer after class. Bruce wanted to know more about my past – musician, taxi driver, businessman. I was certainly interested in his life as a writer. The next morning, he called and suggested we collaborate on a fiction project. Had I planted this idea in his head by autosuggestion? We soon got to work on a novel titled "The King of San Francisco". We disagreed about almost everything. I wanted to write like Lee Child. He wanted to write like Dostoevsky. Somehow, we worked it out, completed the novel (which we are hoping to publish in 2024) and then went to work on "Birthright".

The differences continued, but throughout the year we swapped drafts of chapters, met over numerous coffees, edited, trimmed, and augmented the text. We remained friends and collaborators over every bump in that long road.

What follows is the result of that collaboration. I would like to express my gratitude to Bruce for his mentoring and the many hours he spent devoted to the project.

ACKNOWLEDGEMENTS

I would also like to acknowledge the excellent work of my editor, Janet Bayliss of Red Room Editing, whose expertise and knowledge have been invaluable in the production of this novel.

I special thanks to my wife Jenny for her ongoing support, literary perspective and practical advice.

A big thanks to the Armadale Writers Group for their interest and encouragement along the way.

Kelvin White
December, 2023.

PROLOGUE

Lidice, Bohemia. 1942

Hauptmann Franz Wagner sat up tall in the noisy *Volkswagen Kubel* and pulled at the stiff collar of his uniform. The Opal Blitz trucks ahead of him belched black diesel fumes as they rumbled across the roads, quaint country lanes and farmlands of Moravia en route to the village of Lidice, population five hundred.

At the head of the procession was *Obersturmbannführer* Werner Bohme, no doubt enjoying the plush leather of his gleaming black Mercedes 770 saloon, the clean air and the prospect of continuing the *Führer's* work.

Franz Wagner knew what was coming, and he dreaded it. He was due some leave. His farm in Freiburg and his wife, Jutta, beckoned; but first he must assemble the townsfolk of the village in the town square.

As the convoy pulled up outside the town hall, the sun's rays cast a rosy glow on the old stonework embracing the square. A cock crowed in the distance. Closer, a dog whined. Wagner climbed out, pulled his jacket straight and began barking orders. His men fanned out and went to work. It took time. Terrified residents did as they were told, spilling out of houses and forming into ranks eight lines deep; the children in front, then women, then the men.

Wagner watched as a tiny girl, still in her summer nightdress, desperately clutched at her mother's skirts. A sad stain of urine soaked her nightdress and dripped on to the ground. He and Jutta had already named the girl they were sure they would one day conceive, the merciful God willing: Marion. He felt nauseous now. He was a farmer. He had slaughtered pigs and chickens, reached inside his cows when they were having difficulty giving birth, but nothing in his former life had prepared him for this.

The officer with the clipboard separated out the children of Aryan blood, to be bundled off to the fatherland and assimilated into the right sort of German homes. Another group, swarthier women and children, were destined for the death camps. Smoke was now rising from the town hall and beyond that the shops that lined the square.

Hauptmann Franz Wagner prepared his MG42 for firing. This is work, he said to himself. Forget Jutta and the farm. Forget pigs and cows and the taste of fresh sauerkraut. He looked along the line where his men had taken up positions on the cold flagstones of Lidice. On the signal from *Obersturmbannführer* Bohme, they opened fire. The citizens crumpled as they were hit. None fell at exactly the same time. Wagner could hear the sounds of their anguish, cries and screams and the plop of bodies hitting the ground. This was work. Just like any other work. In the corner of his eye, he saw the tiny girl in her stained nightdress make a run for it. Wagner swung his machine gun, squeezed the trigger and she dropped like a stone, blood spurting from her head.

Wagner gazed at the litter of bodies. The *Unteroffizier* barked orders at his men, who then drenched the three hundred and forty corpses in gasoline. Three men were designated to detonate the ordnance. The smell of charred flesh meshed with the pungent odour of gunpowder and high explosive as the whole desolate obscenity of it went up in smoke.

The town of Lidice was levelled to the ground, as if it had never existed.

PART ONE

CHAPTER 1

Northbridge, 18 September 1998.

Trung Nguyen was enjoying a lunch break in his brother's restaurant, in Perth's Chinatown. Bao had made a good life for himself. His business was thriving, and his three children were all successfully launched in life, two of them were lawyers and the third had enrolled in a master of business at the University of Western Australia (Murdoch University). And Trung? He was happy enough.

The soup arrived, *bánh canh*, Trung's favourite. He stirred the thick noodles with his chopsticks, soaking up the sauce of crab and snakehead fish. Happy enough, he thought. If he wanted to make himself happier still, he would go visit Lily. Lily could make any man happy. Or if he wanted to make himself miserable, he would head up to the corner of Brisbane Street and sit in the park where the community was planning a memorial to the boat people, the hordes of refugees—he had been one—who managed to escape South Vietnam at the end of the war. Hundreds of thousands had perished in the long conflict that engulfed Vietnam. He was not interested in commemorating that part of his life.

He was lucky, he supposed. The Vietnamese community was strong. They helped each other out. He had a regular job as a taxi driver, working for Jack Sprague, a generous man with a gentle disposition. Trung had scrimped and saved enough to buy a small flat in Maylands. He'd survived a marriage and a messy divorce without putting a cleaver through the head of his first wife, Truuc. One day soon he might have enough to invest in a taxi plate for himself.

From his window seat he looked out on William Street, which was filled with people, many of them Asian. The Chinese had done well. Most of them had shiny cars and all the trappings of wealth. They owned butchers shops, fish shops, gift shops, and of course restaurants. His brother predicted a swing away from Cantonese food—the 'Chinese restaurant' food Australians were used to—in favour of more exotic cuisines, including his own. But the Chinese would always thrive, Trung thought. It was in their blood.

He looked idly across the street to the Chinese butchers. A black Mercedes van had nosed into the laneway, waiting for the way to be cleared. Strange really. As a taxi driver he was used to strange sights. But something about this van held his attention. He finished his soup, waved to his brother as he left—the soup was on the house for family—and crossed the road. The lane cleared and the Mercedes nosed in further, taking a tight turn and stopping half way through an open roller door. The driver got out of the van, opened the rear doors wide and watched while two men wearing heavy pvc butchers aprons and gumboots unloaded a heavy bundle wrapped in stitched sailcloth and hoisted it onto a trolley. The driver slammed the cargo door shut and followed the bundle into the gloomy interior of the warehouse.

Trung moved in closer to get a better look. He noticed a piece of adhesive tape at the bottom of the cargo door. The tape had been sprayed the same colour black as the van. He lifted the edge of it, peeled it back. 'Satinwood Funerals', he read. 'Private Transfer Vehicle'. What could that mean? Trung heard the thud of approaching footsteps, and a curse.

Oh shit, now I'm in trouble.

As he turned to run, a muscular arm grabbed him in a head lock. The foul odour of meat and blood on the apron made him retch. There was no chance to defend himself as his attacker dropped him to the ground and someone else kicked him in the ribs.

'Fucking slope. You should mind your own fucking business.'

'Give the little bastard another kick from me.'

Trung heard the crack as the delicate bones gave way, one by one. He could feel his feet bouncing off the rough bitumen of the alley way as he was dragged along and dumped on top of a pile of stinking offal. He heard the rumble of the diesel engine as the van backed out, and a clunk as the roller door found bottom and was locked from inside. He rolled over and vomited warm noodles into the gutter.

Every fibre in Trung's body felt like it had been smashed to pieces. How long had he been lying there? He groaned as he slowly lifted his arm and peered at his old Seiko. It was 2 pm. Time for work. No time to visit Lily; no time for coffee. Sometimes he wished he'd been born incurious. It was possible that what he'd witnessed had an innocent explanation. That was something he could ponder while he was driving. Sunday night was likely to be slow. That thought arrived like a guest bearing fragrant flowers. He sighed, dragged himself painfully to his feet and headed slowly back to his car.

CHAPTER 2

1998

'*Point Eighth Avenue.*'

The despatcher's voice took Trung's mind off his aching ribs. He jabbed the microphone button. 'Don 82,' he responded.

'*Heaven help us. If it isn't Trung, the Vietnamese bandit.*' Barnsey, the cheerful Swan Taxi despatcher, seemed to know every one of the eight-hundred-night drivers by name or nickname. He had a soft spot for the wiry Trung, who never complained and never cheated.

'*Go to 122 Peninsula Road and pick up Mr Edwards and take him to Qantas at the domestic. M11 on pick up please Trung. You do know where the airport is, don't you Trung?*'

'Me not know boss. Where is please?' Trung responded in fake pidgin English. He laughed, wincing as a dagger of pain tore through his chest.

It was a typical quiet Sunday night. Trung turned the key on the battered million-kilometre 1994 ED Falcon. Slipping the transmission into drive, he glanced at his rear vision and side mirrors. The differential whined. As he settled into the sagging bucket seat, his thoughts flashed back to the violent encounter in Northbridge. What had all that been about? The goons' reaction seemed out of proportion. The pain strengthened his resolve. They *will* pay, he thought.

The house in Peninsular Road was a newish, semidetached brick bungalow with a yellowing front lawn and a letter box stuffed with old newspapers. Not a tidy person, Trung thought. An athletic-looking man dressed in a lightweight suit emerged from the front door, a travel bag slung over one shoulder and a briefcase in hand. He opened the back door, threw his gear onto the seat, and sat next to Trung in the front.

'How's things, Don 82?' he said.

'How you know my call sign?' asked Trung.

Robin Edwards looked at Trung, then back to the road. 'I know a lot of things,' said Edwards. He wanted Trung to be impressed by his knowledge of Taxi call signs; but it wasn't his police training that informed him. His father had been a cabbie and taught him all about the numbering system the taxi networks employed. He was fond of cabbies, ready to take their side. Like the cops, they had to deal with their fair share of drunks, drug addicts and general trouble makers. Not only that, he valued the sheer number of hours these guys spent on the road, hours when they absorbed a great deal of intelligence, to give it a fancy name, about criminals.

The cabbie shrugged. 'Qantas Domestic, is it?'

'Thanks. What's your name?'

'Trung. Trung for short. Trung for long. Ha ha.'

'You start early today?'

'Night shift,' said Trung. 'I was late starting. Got mugged in Northbridge.'

For the rest of the trip Edwards listened to Trung's account of the attack. He probed for details and noted the location. He was particularly intrigued by Trung's description of the thugs who'd waylaid him and the van they'd used.

'You say one of them was dressed in butcher's clothing, apron, that sort of thing.'

Trung thought back. It had all happened so fast. 'Yeah, I guess. He looked like a regular Chinese butcher. The driver was dressed in a plain black suit, white shirt, thin tie. Like the Blues Brothers, you know?'

'And the van?' said Edwards. 'Any markings?'

'Yeah,' said Trung. 'The back door had tape on it, sprayed black like the van. I peeled it back and it said Satinwood Funerals, Private Transfer Vehicle.'

'No kidding,' said Edwards.

They had reached the airport and Trung pulled up behind the other cabs queuing to drop their passengers in the marked zone outside the terminal building. Trung grimaced as he climbed out of the cab and retrieved his passenger's bags.

'It's been great to meet you, Trung.'

Trung smiled and took the other man's hand. In it was a business card, which he read before he pulled away. *Detective Sergeant Robin Edwards. WA Major Crime Squad.* 'Holy shit!' he said out loud. 'A friendly copper.'

In the early hours Trung decided enough was enough and he would return to base. The garage served as a depot for what Jack Sprague called his fleet. It was more like a litter, thought Trung. Seven cars and none of them new. Sprague was doing well if he kept five on deck at the same time. Trung filled up, noted the mileage, counted his takings and pocketed his share.

Sprague was in the corner office labouring on his accounts. Jack had that look about him. The look of a life well lived. His lined face peered out from under a wedge of blue hat bearing the Swan Taxi logo.

'Aha,' he said. 'If it isn't comrade Nguyen.'

'G'day Jack,' said Trung. 'I think I'll call it a night. You driving today?'

'Yeah, I'll give it a run. What's it like out there?'

'The usual thing Jack. Plenty of drunks in Northbridge.'

Jack frowned at Trung. But Trung knew he was Jack's best and most consistent driver. He realised, Jack, brought up in the days of the white Australia policy, found his alien ways at times a little confronting. Trung made sure he worked harder than any of the Australians and was happy to nurse his taxi through all its tantrums and breakdowns. But now he knew he looked like he'd picked a fight with Bruce Lee.

'You ok?' Jack asked. 'You're all bent up like a wounded alley cat. Did some moron have a go?'

'Nah,' said Trung. 'Slipped on the stairs at my brother's place.'

Jack was gathering his things: street directory, change dispenser, his notes wallet, and the heavy spanner that he kept for self-defence, hidden within easy reach under the driver's seat.

Taxi driving was a dangerous profession. The year before, a group of hoons on a night out had locked a cabbie in the boot of his taxi and set it alight. Maybe living was dangerous—period! thought Trung.

'Have a good one, Jack,' he said.

CHAPTER 3

1998 September, Hanoi

The Six Pub was a ten-minute walk from home. Kim negotiated the curved concrete steps unsteadily; he knew he'd consumed too many Tiger Beers, but as he often did, he forgave himself. He had a stressful job. A man needed a way to relax and recharge. It was a pity his girlfriend didn't get that.

He turned left down a narrow side street. It was way past midnight, and even in his befuddled state, he knew Lo would greet him with a barrage of accusations. He breathed deeply, oblivious to a couple of rats that scurried past. The city was still ablaze with lights. Down at ground level, Kim loved the quiet, empty streets. The battered Volkswagen Kombi, parked at an angle, did not disturb his meditation.

A young man in tattered jeans appeared, as if from nowhere.

'Hey, you got a light?'

Kim fumbled in his trouser pocket for his lighter, then gasped in surprise as another man appeared. He was covered in tattoos, his head shaved bald apart from a ponytail.

'Have a look at this, pal.'

Kim glanced down just in time to see a flash of silver as the long-bladed knife slid into his chest, piercing his heart. He grunted, dropped to the ground. Since his heart had stopped beating, the blood loss was minimal.

'Give me a hand to get him into the Kombi,' the tattooed man muttered to his companion. He flung open the side door and both men grabbed Kim's warm corpse, hurling it into the van.

'Twenty dollars US, right, Johnny?' the young man asked.

Johnny produced the banknote from his back pocket, grinning. 'Happy?'

The young man grabbed the money and saluted. 'You bet. Let me know when you need me again.'

Johnny Ho was a simple man with simple pleasures. The German paid him good money for fresh corpses. Why? He didn't dwell upon the 'why' of things. That was none of Johnny Ho's business.

The Volkswagen clattered to life. Johnny Ho lit a Marlboro and headed off into the city, his day's work done.

CHAPTER 4

Late September 1998

The Killing Floor, a new novel featuring Jack Reacher, had Trung completely engrossed. A good way to brush up on his English was to read novels, and this one had him completely absorbed. So absorbed he missed the first call as he laboriously struggled with new, unfamiliar words. What the hell does 'jurisdiction' mean? he wondered.

The operator's voice broke through. *'Point car on the Broadway. Is there a car on the Broadway?'*

The cab behind Trung's angrily blasted his horn.

'Sorry base. Don 82.'

'Well, if it isn't beef with black bean sauce!' The operator chuckled.

Larry had a sense of humour and never intended to be offensive, but Trung was nonetheless puzzled. 'What's with the beef and black bean?'

'Number 82 on the menu at Viet Hoa. You should know that!'

The five cabs lined up behind Trung on the Broadway rank all honked their horns in appreciation of Larry's scintillating wit.

'Fifty-six Jutland Parade Dalkeith, Don 82. Pick up Mr Duffy and take him to the Air Force Memorial Estate in Bull

Creek. Oh, and can you check number fifty-four Jutland on the way? I may have left my sprinklers on.'

Trung smiled. They all wished they lived in Jutland Parade, Dalkeith: Perth's most prestigious address. 'Sure thing, Larry. Do you want me to check on the Rolls at the same time?'

Trung reluctantly placed the paperback under the centre armrest of the Falcon and turned the key. The tired motor clunked and rattled. Checking the rear vision mirror, he carefully executed a U-turn on Broadway and turned right into the Avenue. It wasn't the shortest route, but he loved the stately homes with their glimpses of the Swan River. At moments like this he would reflect on his life. This was the lucky country, wasn't it? More for some than for others, obviously. Sure, he was lucky to have made it out here on a leaky boat. His brother was luckier. And these bastards with their big mansions were the luckiest of all.

He was still mulling over 'Fate' and his lot in life as his cab swung into the driveway of 56 Jutland Parade. The mansion was all concrete and tall glass windows. The uninterrupted vista of the wide blue river was spectacular. And yes, there was a maroon Rolls Royce squatting importantly on the broad drive. A tall, muscular man was carefully wiping it down with a chamois. Trung stared hard at the man. Wasn't he the bastard who'd kicked the shit out of him a week and a half ago and left him lying in garbage? The man glanced in his direction and turned away. Trung realised he probably hadn't been able to see him properly through the sheen of his taxi's windscreen.

A spritely older man stepped through the double-embossed metal doors of the mansion and walked past the Rolls, heading for Trung's taxi. Clad in a houndstooth tweed coat, grey flannel trousers and highly polished tan brogues, Alan Duffy was the epitome of the English gentleman. His waxed moustache added to the image.

'You don't mind if I sit in the front, son?'

Trung recognised the voice of Australia's ruling class: smooth, paternal, with just a touch of English polish. Announcers on the ABC had the same voice. Nobody Trung knew talked like that. Perhaps he could learn to speak that way? He thought of the schools he'd attended, the pressure from his parents to learn the language. He'd picked up everything he knew in the schoolyard, including the obscenities. His parents had struggled with English and still spoke their native tongue at home.

'Which way would you like to go, sir?'

'Any way you like son, I'm in no hurry. You know where we're going?'

'Yes, sir. RAAF Bull Creek.'

'You've got it. I'm going to address a group of youngsters about Lancaster Bombers and their role in the big one. Hell, you probably wouldn't know a whole heap about our little stoush with the Jerries, would you?'

Trung was confused. What in hell was a stoush? And what was a Jerry? And why was this guy talking about it with school kids, filling another generation's minds with war bullshit? 'No sir, I know nothing about that,' he said.

'I'm talking about the Second World War son. I was a bomber pilot in a Lancaster. We dropped bombs from one end of Hitler's Germany to the other.'

Duffy turned towards Trung and stroked his moustache. 'You're Vietnamese?'

'Yes sir. From Hanoi.'

Duffy whistled. 'Well in that case I'm guessing you know all about air raids. What's your name, son?'

'Trung, sir.'

'Well, let's drop the *sir* bullshit, ok? My name's Alan.'

The old man gazed keenly at Trung and paused for a moment. Then he held out his hand. It was wrinkled and covered in liver spots. Trung took it, as he was expected to.

'As I said, I'm giving a bit of a chat to some youngsters. Then I'm going to head back into Perth for a bit of grub. If you think it's worth your while, you can wait at Bull Creek and take me back when I've finished my talk. We might just have something of interest to discuss. My business success is all down to making sure I have the right man for the job, and my gut feeling is you could be just who I'm looking for. But no promises, eh? Not just yet.'

Trung was confused. 'Sure, thing Alan. I'm interested, but apart from that, I'm wondering why you don't use your own drivers? The guy who was polishing the Rolls at your place. He is your driver, isn't he?'

'A long story, Trung. To be honest, I love cabs. Having a chauffeur is not really my style. It's good for show, when I need to impress a client, but otherwise ... well, I'm a people person. And the man you saw working on the car ... let's just say I'd rather be talking to you. So, will you wait for me? It could be worth your while. It's not just a driver I'm looking for; it's more than that.'

Trung gave a thumbs up, his thoughts racing at a million miles an hour. Was this one of those once-in-a-lifetime opportunities, or ... He checked his battered Seiko. Jack had no other shift scheduled for him. He was a free agent.

'Sure thing, Alan.'

CHAPTER 5

Malignant and threatening, the Supermarine Spitfire stood guard over the Bullcreek Airforce Museum, a silent sentinel poised ready to engage the enemy. It was the aircraft that stymied the Nazi invasion of Great Britain during the Second World War, and was as relevant to the coming century as whale oil. Trung had only sketchy ideas about the war that had consumed the world in his parents' time. The Japanese had become the new colonial masters of Vietnam. His understanding of those events was from watching old movies on television. He had seen *The Dam Busters* and *The Guns of Navarone*, but apart from knowing who the protagonists were, and more importantly, who had won, he knew little about it. If Alan Duffy had been a dam buster, or at least known one of them, then perhaps he could forgive him for being so old and so white. As he quietly cleaned his taxi, he wondered what on earth the old fossil had in mind for him? He climbed back into the driver's seat and took out his Jack Reacher novel.

An hour later Duffy arrived, his face wreathed in smiles.

'Thanks for waiting Trung, that was fun. The little blighters were full of questions. And I might add I was happy to oblige with all the answers. Now, I want to head back to town for lunch. I rather fancy some Vietnamese tucker. I'm sure you know a good restaurant?'

'The Yen Do is very good,' said Trung. 'Take you there?'

Duffy clipped his seatbelt in place. 'How about I buy you lunch and tell you about my little scheme. What do you say?'

Trung had the feeling his fortunes were about to change. And if the agent of change was a funny old fossil like Alan Duffy, so be it. As they turned onto the Kwinana Freeway Trung stifled his curiosity. He would wait for the moment they were sitting across the table from each other and then hopefully Alan would tell him what the hell this was all about. Now in narrow Robinson Avenue, behind the Yen Do, Trung squeezed the old Falcon into a spot vacated by a Kombi.

The Yen Do was in full swing. Noisy Asian families sat at round tables laden with fried rice, beef, lamb, chicken, and seafood dishes. The proprietor, Duong, waved at Trung.

'Busy, busy, Trung. Sit anywhere.'

They managed to find a table at the rear, next to a bubbling fish tank where the patrons' dinners swam listlessly, oblivious to their fate. Alan studied the menu and shook his head.

'Christ, Trung, I've got no idea. How about you order for both of us?'

Trung signalled the boss. Duong was a lean, balding whippet of a man who moved quickly from table to table, schmoozing with the customers but with one eye on his harried staff. Trung proudly introduced Duong to Alan, then ordered two Tiger Beers, a laksa each, and the *bánh xèo*, a crispy crepe bulging with pork, shrimp and bean sprouts.

Alan explained the nature of his business. He had inherited Duffy Family Funerals, now Satinwood Funerals, from his father, who'd inherited the business from his father before him. Trung listened patiently and wondered what any of it had to do with him.

Alan slurped at his *laksa*. 'Bloody hell! Spicy, but damn tasty. Probably pay for it in the morning, but what the hell!'

Trung shrugged.

'To get back to the funeral business. What I inherited is just one part of the operation. Because the funeral business is so competitive, I have expanded internationally. This is where you come in.'

'Ok. But I still don't... '

'You will son, you will. We are contracted to pick up Westerners who have come to a sticky end in Third World countries. No offence. So, for instance, an American has a motorcycle accident in Pakistan, Nigeria, or any other God-forsaken hell hole. We go and retrieve the body, making sure it's transported quickly and efficiently to the US of A, Germany, Australia, or whatever. And let me tell you Trung, it pays bloody well—as it should. At times it's damned dangerous. Retrieving a corpse from Somalia or the Congo is fraught with danger. We have to bribe local officials. Jesus, we earn our bloody money, I can tell you. We even get some contract work from the US military, who are absolute sticklers for procedure. That's the nuts and bolts of it. What do you think?'

Trung was no closer to understanding what the man wanted. He used a lot of words but that's all they were, words. His own business model involved rapid talking, direct speech and a quick conclusion. Also, there was something about Duffy he didn't quite trust.

'I'm sorry, Alan, but I still don't follow.'

'I should have explained myself better. Here it is. Australians, Yanks, Poms etcetera get killed in Vietnam. What I want is someone, and that could be you, to go to Vietnam and liaise with some people I know there. It's simply a new business opportunity. They have established a mortuary, a place where bodies can be held. And you would put in place procedures to transfer corpses to their ... ah ... country of origin. You could be just the man I need, and I guarantee it'll pay a lot more than taxi driving. Well, what do you think, Trung?'

Trung really didn't know what to think. A paid trip back to his homeland was very appealing. And if the money was better, well... 'What sort of money are we talking about, Alan?'

'Initially you would take home a thousand a week. But if things go ok, I can guarantee you a lot more than that. Naturally, the trip to Vietnam is all expenses paid, with a nice hotel and all of that.'

'Alan, there is one thing.'

Duffy's eyes narrowed. Trung told him about following the Mercedes van and the beating he'd received ten days ago.

'My ribs still hurt!' he said. 'No offence.' Apparently, that's what you said when you wanted to soften the effect of your words. Westerners were so strange.

'Not only that, but I saw one of these bastards—no offence—in your driveway today, washing your car.'

Duffy was silent for a minute. He frowned. 'Trouble is, Trung, all Westerners look the same to you, don't they? I mean the same thing works in reverse. We can't tell one Asian apart from another one. As for the van you describe, the Mercedes, it was stolen from our headquarters at Canning Vale two weeks ago. How brazen is that? And these thugs you describe, one who looks a bit like my chauffeur—yes, I employ security ... muscle if you will, but there's a reason for that—you say they were up to something very suss? In broad daylight, in Northbridge?'

'Why do you employ thugs?' asked Trung.

'I told you what happens in some of the countries we do business. I'm not prepared to go into detail just yet, but sometimes we get a jumped-up official or big-headed war lord obstructing the flow of business. They won't release a body, say. Or they get a little too greedy. Then it's no job for pussies. My men get the job done. Christ, even I don't want to know all the details.'

'Hell, Alan,' said Trung, 'Not sure I want to get mixed up in that sort of shit. And we've only just met. We don't know each other.'

Duffy laughed, an easy sound like water trickling down a drain. 'As I said before. My success in business has always been about choosing the right people. And I reckon you're exactly what I need. And Trung, as far as the danger aspect goes. That sort of nonsense only happens in places like Africa or Cambodia. I don't for one minute think you'd have any obstacles in Vietnam.'

Trung emptied the last of his Tiger Beer. Something still didn't quite stack up. They'd only just met and Duffy was ready to take him on?

'One last question, Alan. Do your men like dressing up? Costumes, you know.'

Duffy stared at him. He looked angry. Trung hoped he hadn't blown it.

'Ok, Alan. I'm thinking about it,' he said. 'I must think of my life here, you know? Not sure I can be away for too long.'

CHAPTER 6

Lincolnshire, 1942.

October 23 dawned rainy, with fog covering the runways at Wickenby and apparently little prospect of action that day. Operations detailed the day before had been cancelled due to poor weather, and Sandy had no reason to think that the 23rd would be any different. He tried to read an old paperback for a while but gave up.

'Scramble, scramble!' an orderly shouted down the corridor. Heart hammering against his ribcage, Sandy grabbed his kit and headed for the briefing room. The latest forecast showed the fog lifting and the rain down to a spatter. By late afternoon Sandy had been fed, briefed, and motivated. Tonight, was to be maximum impact. The Wickenby Squadrons, a force of 39, would be joining a massive fleet of Lancasters from the surrounding bases. As usual there was to be absolute radio silence once they cleared the coast and careful timing over the target, since large fleets of bombers crowding to release their bomb loads were inherently a danger to themselves.

As their plane rattled along the runway, gathering speed, he felt the same galloping power in his waters. There was no other place to be, nowhere else to go except to join the charge against the Bosch and drive them into the ground. Everything in his training, the months on the prairies of Canada, the practice flights over Wales, the long days in classrooms, all had led to this point. He was a warrior in full battle mode, ready for the fray, again. Could they survive another op? This one was number 17. Hands shaking, he checked his intercom and oxygen. Sandy glanced out of the fuselage window at a sky crowded with Lancaster Bombers.

Alan Duffy, the pilot, cursed. Although cloud cover was usually a favourable sign, tonight's sky was a massive bank of the stuff reaching as high as 23,000 feet. The navigator announced quietly that they were over Germany, on course for Düsseldorf and Cologne and ultimately Stuttgart. As in a dream, albeit a surprisingly stark one, Sandy performed the necessary preparations for the bombardment. Soon the flak began, bursting around the aircraft, shrapnel pinging the fuselage like hard rain.

Over Düsseldorf the air was thick with smoke, although the cloud cover had dissipated. Sandy yelled to Duffy that he was unplugging his intercom before climbing down into the bombing compartment. As soon as Sandy saw the cones of searchlights ahead, he began to jettison his stock of 'window' reflective strips, the secret new weapon they were trialing, designed to defeat the German radar. On the approach, Sandy stifled a scream as the bomber rocked and juddered in a ferocious flak barrage. He reeled at the bitter smell of high explosive, and was winded as the pitch and roll of the Lancaster slammed him hard into a bulkhead.

Duffy struggled to steady it for the bombing run. The aiming point for the release of the bombload appeared to be sliding up smoothly and into the graticule of the bomb sight. Sandy, now back in position, calm and focused, pressed the tit, releasing the main bomb and a cluster of incendiaries. Even from 20,000 feet above the target, the ground seemed alive with fire and destruction; a version of hell he hoped to forget once the war was over. Somewhere in that inferno was a factory which 'his' bomb had decommissioned in the most brutal way possible. *Herzliche glückwunsche, Herr Hitler.*

As they pulled away sharply to avoid another burst of flak, Sandy counted again the number of raids remaining before they would be finished their tour of duty. What were the odds, really? He wasn't a betting man, and he would rather not guess. He climbed up into the upper turret and tried to screen out the sounds of mayhem around him. They seemed to be in one piece and according to the navigator, were on a south-westerly course away from Stuttgart. Sandy breathed a huge sigh of relief.

The twin engine Messerschmitt Bf 110 first appeared dead ahead. Duffy pulled the plane sharply upwards to avoid it, and then began to corkscrew out of the way of the U-turn the night fighter would undoubtedly make next.

'What the fuck's happening?' Sandy heard Harry the radio operator yell.

Then Johnno yelling, 'Skipper, we're on fire.'

The air was split by a loud explosion and a scream from Bernie Hawke, the rear gunner, 'I'm hit, I'm fucking hit.'

In every part of his being, Sandy wanted to go back and help him, but Duffy abandoned the controls and ordered them to bail out. Sandy screamed impotently into the dead intercom,

'What about Bernie, you bastard?'

The Lancaster began to veer and yaw in a way he had never experienced. It was every man for himself.

Years later, Sandy would try to recall what happened next. He remembered the raid in vivid detail. His escape from the burning plane, the terrifying fall through thin air before he found his ripcord, the sight of the plane going down in a ball of flame; all had been etched on his brain like a nightmare. He'd only seen one parachute; its stark white silk illuminated briefly by the flames of the burning Lancaster.

When he hit the ground, he found himself curled in a ball in a field of stubble. The hair stood up on the back of his neck as he heard the ferocious barking of dogs in the distance. In the near darkness he could hear groaning. Not far away was Duffy, doubled up, with a bleeding wound to his head. Ridiculously, Duffy had still been wearing the football club scarf he wore for luck, originally blue and white but in the semi-darkness, a mottled grey.

'Quickly man,' he said. 'Get up. You have to walk. There are dogs.'

With the thin moonlight for guidance, they managed to find a rutted lane that led to a barn. In the barn they climbed into a hayloft and listened nervously while the barking of the dogs receded. They had been lucky. They laid low, hungry and anxious, until...

And that was where his memory failed him. For the life of him, Sandy could not recall a single incident between that dreadful night and waking up in a hospital in Bern, Switzerland.

CHAPTER 7

Early October 1998

Sandy Tuckwell checked his reflection in the mirror. Not bad for a man of 77, he thought. He wished Mario the barber would do something about the strands of hair that sprung out from his scalp like wild ivy. Other than that, he could probably pass for 70, at least that was what his female admirers told him. Rosalie, Deborah, and Liv all made a fuss of him at choir rehearsals. Today they were meeting at the Guildford Town Hall in preparation for a Senior's Week performance. He had showered and dressed way too early, an aspect of his life he found annoying. He missed having a life of deadlines and purpose. He missed Maisie. He remembered his time in the Air Force, running to make briefings and drills; always running. But that was half a century or more ago, He was so old!

In the hallway he kissed the portrait of Maisie. She had died of cancer eight years ago and he had missed her every day since. They'd met on the train to work. She was a pretty girl and had caught his eye. Like Sandy, she took the same train to the city each day, and sat in the same seat. One morning the carriage was overrun with schoolkids, and they had to stand. The train lurched around a bend, Maisie swayed, and Sandy put out his hand to steady her. By the time they reached the city they were close to an embrace. He courted her fiercely, married her and settled down.

He deadlocked the front door before closing and locking the security screen. He would wait on his front veranda for the taxi to turn up. He loved taxis. They were his life blood, whisking him from one appointment to another and good opportunities for a discussion.

A battered Falcon turned into the driveway. The little Vietnamese driver again. Good, thought Sandy, at least he'd be clean—even if his car was not. They always found something to talk about, ever since they discovered that each had lived through a war. Trung, that was his name. He had survived the war that had turned his country into a nightmare of napalmed forests and ruined villages. Sandy had survived the Second World War, one of the lucky fifty percent of Lancaster men to come out of it alive. Five of his own crew didn't survive. At the time, they were, Sandy thought, as close as brothers. Bernie, the Tasmanian happy-go-lucky rear gunner, was Sandy's best mate. Bert, Johnno, Harry, Clive and Reg were Sydneysiders. Memories of that night—the night fighter, their plane on fire— still haunted him.

'Hi, Trung,' he said as he climbed into the front passenger's seat.

'Hi, Sandy,' said Trung. 'You going to Guildford today? Singing, I guess. And putting the hard word on all those grandmas.'

'No need,' said Sandy. 'They're chasing me.'

The cab turned out of Eighth Avenue and onto Guildford Road, the morning sun already too hot for the Falcon's air conditioning.

'What else is new, Sandy?' asked Trung.

'In a couple of weeks I'm off to Europe!' said Sandy. 'Imagine that.'

'What part of Europe?' asked Trung.

'Germany. A spa town called Baden-Baden. You wouldn't believe it; an archaeological team has found our crashed Lancaster bomber. Isn't that something? Brings back memories.'

'Why would you go there?' asked Trung. 'They were the enemy.'

That's right, thought Sandy. They were the enemy, and we bombed the crap out of them, just like the Americans bombed the crap out of your country.

Sandy wasn't going to Germany in triumph. What happened to him there had been life changing. But Sandy and Trung didn't do big topics like 'life'. The journeys were never long enough, and, in any case, it would be patronising to bring it up. They were in Bassendean already. Soon it would be time to climb out and go sing.

'Let's just say it will be educational, Trung,' said Sandy.

'One more thing,' said Trung. 'You know a guy called Alan Duffy? You were in the Air Force too, yeah?'

Sandy made a noise at the back of his throat which sounded like he was trying to clear some phlegm. 'Why do you ask?'

'He's a customer,' said Trung. 'That's all.'

'Yeah, that's one word for him,' Sandy growled. 'Everyone knows war hero, Captain Alan Duffy.' What were the chances? A beautiful day ruined by coincidence. He had no wish to discuss Duffy, a man who epitomised everything Sandy despised: wealth, privilege, and a ruthless streak that was all about coming out on top, never mind whose head you trod on to get there. Sandy was convinced the DSO gong Duffy had been awarded was the result of a bullshit story Duffy concocted. The hall came into view, and Trung deftly cut through the oncoming traffic to pull up at the side door. Sandy fished around his wallet and pocket for the right money, plus his usual tip.

'You are a champion, Trung,' he said.

'Call me and book your ride the day you're flying out, and I'll look after you.' Trung passed him a Swan Taxi card.

CHAPTER 8

October 1942, Freiburg

War really is hell. Franz Wagner reflected on his last campaign. The stench of burning flesh seemed to cling to him. The harrowing screams from the burning barn, accompanied by the futile hammering of fists on the doors. Children screaming, parents pleading as they were shot. The ghastly moment when he'd machine-gunned the little girl in her nightdress wouldn't leave him. Rivers of schnapps helped, temporarily. The October chill leached through his greatcoat as he strode along the road leading to Freiderjes, the family farm.

The troop carrier had dropped him two kilometres from home. He thought a walk through the Black Forrest he loved would settle his nerves. The crisp resinous scent of the tightly packed conifers and spruce was just as he remembered. His eye caught sight of a reddish nut-brown squirrel as it scampered up a wide girthed oak tree. How he loved this beautiful place. Was this stroll through the woods only about his love of nature, or was it something else? Did he want his arrival to be a surprise? His thoughts turned to his wife Jutta: a beautiful woman. But one heard so many stories of infidelity. He remembered discovering one of his corporals in tears recently. 'What is it, Dieter?'

The corporal handed him a letter. *I am so sorry Dieter, but I have found someone else. You have been gone too long. Best regards, Hannah.*

Best regards. Franz stared. The ridiculous formality of it.

That night Dieter Muller held the muzzle of his 9mm Walther P38 to his head.

But not his Jutta.

Franz remembered Jutta's rich auburn hair, her willing ways in bed. But try as he might he couldn't picture her face. He remembered she was pretty, with a sprinkling of freckles. A woman has needs, just like a man. *Has she been a good wife? I wonder?* That *dummkopf* Hans from the next farm, Hogenkamp, seemed to always find a reason to sniff around. *Heaven help any man who's had designs on my wife.*

Franz threw back his head and roared with laughter at the memory of how he'd pulled strings to have Hans Meyer sent to the Russian front. That sure fixed the bastard. Anyway Meyer, sounded Jewish if you asked Franz. But that lovely wife of his, Helga; beautiful blonde Helga. Perhaps he should look in on her sometime, she might need a hand ... perhaps more than a hand ... eh? Franz Wagner paused, realising he was approaching the Meyers' farm, Hogenkamp. *Just look at the big apple tree; neglected. It's a disgrace.*

'Should I knock on the door? Say hello. Jutta wouldn't be happy. How those two women hate each other.'

***

'*Kaffee, das omelett, Ja?*'

'More you, *Liebling*. He grabbed the woman roughly,

pulling her on to the bed. She laughed, pulling her night attire up, exposing her full breasts.

'You are gorgeous,' the man whispered.

Their passion was swift and brutal, the man thrusting into her until she screamed with pleasure. Then came a knock on the door downstairs. They froze. A voice called out. 'You there Duffy?'

The man, Duffy, rolled his eyes. '*Der kamerad*,' he said, and yelled, 'piss off, Sandy.'

Duffy sat up, grabbing the petite fleur coffee cup in his big hand. He gently stroked the woman's face. 'I will never forget you, Jutta.' He slid a photo from his flying jacket lying at the end of the four-poster bed. 'Now, *der fuller, bitte*?' he said in halting German.

The room had a slightly musty odour, evocative of his granny's old house. A room that made you feel safe, cosy, and horny as hell, Duffy thought. It was dimly lit by a tall lamp, the shade, a pale mauve decorated with undulating patterns. An old four poster bed rested on a rug featuring a hunting scene. The floor was fashioned out of wide oak boards polished to a dull lustre. On a dresser, a large photo of Hitler scowled menacingly. A gilt-framed photo of a man in an SS captain's uniform sat beside it.

Duffy idly wondered how long he could stay. Jutta's husband was away fighting, hopefully dying for the Fatherland. If there were police and soldiers scouring the forest and surrounding countryside for him or any of his crew that had survived the crash, the longer he stayed here the greater chance things would die down. But for how long? What about Sandy? Pathetic Sandy. What a weakling! He'd probably been captured by now and on his way to a prison camp. Best place for him. Would he keep silent about his captain's whereabouts?

Jutta opened the drawer on the bedside table and removed a black Pelikan Fountain pen, engraved with a gold Swastika. Duffy quickly scrawled a few words. Jutta, smiled, as she took back the photo, placing it reverently into the top drawer of the cabinet. She wrapped her arms around Duffy and murmured in English, 'I love you, Alan.' The couple drifted into a dreamless slumber.

Bang, bang, bang. Someone was thumping on the front door.

'*Jutta, offne die tur. schnell.*' The man's guttural command needed no translation.

'*Hinter tur,*' Jutta whispered, pointing to the rear of the house.

Duffy gathered trousers, flying jacket, shirt, underwear, socks and boots, and his scarf, flew down the stairs and through the animal stalls. A curious cow watched phlegmatically, chewing its cud, as Duffy frantically dressed.

SS Kapitan Franz Wagner pounded again on the door. '*Jutta, schnell.*'

CHAPTER 9

Early October 1998

Lily smiled as she greeted Trung from the curtained alcove that formed the entranceway to her establishment. The brothel was housed in an old two-storey dwelling on William Street. The house had survived the growth spurts and recessions which hit Northbridge like so many seasonal cyclones. Lily knew there would always be a market for pleasure and so she held on during the bad times and celebrated the prosperous.

'Hello, my Trung. Come in please. Would you like a drink?'

'Yeah, the usual please, Lily.'

Lily poured a scotch on the rocks and handed it to him. 'You like to sit first, or get straight into it?'

'Mmmm. How about sit and fuck at the same time?'

They both laughed. Trung had been a customer for a long time, and he could take such liberties. A woman who called herself Alicia Zee emerged from the front bedroom and flopped onto the lounge. Her customer had apparently taken the back door exit—probably a judge or a politician, thought Trung. Alicia Zee was young, lithe and exotic looking. Trung supposed he could ask for her next time, but that would disrupt his long connection with Lily. No, if he wanted to play around, it would need to be somewhere else.

They disappeared into Lily's room and emerged an hour later, both laughing. Jack Sprague had once asked Trung what the hell they did in there for an hour (his business with an old whore called Molly had taken about ten minutes) but Trung had merely smiled. Later, when they were in the pub, Sprague asked him again and Trung began to sing, the Charlie Rich song, 'Behind Closed Doors'.

Trung handed over a bundle of notes.

'You're too generous, Trung,' said Lily. 'How many cab-hours does that represent?'

But Trung kept mum about his financial dealings, just as he kept mum about most other things. Australians liked to think Asians were something called 'inscrutable'. Ok then, he would be that. He kissed Lily on the forehead and headed out the door and down William Street towards the city. It was Monday; his day off. Perhaps he would catch a movie, maybe *Saving Private Ryan*.

William Street always disappointed Trung. His parents had told him about Hanoi before the war, with its wide boulevards and vibrant atmosphere. What happened here, he wondered? It was as if the energy to create something of note ran out around James Street. There was the CBD and then you crossed the railway line and there was Northbridge. Really racy: really dangerous. Except it wasn't. Northbridge was tame, Trung thought. More reason to value what Alan Duffy had offered him. But why put excitement ahead of certainty? Here, he had Lily. He had Jack Sprague, a good boss. And he had his routines.

In Aberdeen Street some backpacker hostels had established themselves. Trung always enjoyed the sight of pale Europeans revelling in the sunshine and open spaces of Perth. There were

Americans too, along with a sprinkling of Japanese. Outside Fair Dinkum Backpackers he studied the noticeboard. Cut-price tours of the Pinnacles, Margaret River, Monkey Mia, Broome jostled for attention. There were cars for sale, clapped out station wagons that had done the lap around Australia. A cut out sepia picture of a man in uniform drew his gaze. On the lapel of his jacket was a set of wings, over the initials RAAF. The war theme seemed to be coming at Trung from all angles. First Duffy, then Sandy, and now this.

The man looked distinguished, upright. He had a jet-black moustache just like Alan Duffy's white one. He had piercing eyes, just like Duffy. It could be Duffy as a young serviceman. Written below the picture in ballpoint was an appeal. *Do you know this man? He served in WWII as a Lancaster pilot. Please apply within and ask for Renata Schmidt or call the number below.* Trung tore off one of the reminder tabs – her name and the phone number of Fair Dinkum Backpackers – and strolled off towards the city.

Back at his flat in Maylands Trung opened the balcony door and looked out at the city. Who was Renata Schmidt and what was the connection to Duffy, if the man in the photo was Duffy? Was this coincidence or a sign? Did he want to be a cabby all his life? He wasn't the only taxi driver in residence. His mate Duncan lived two floors down, although their shifts rarely coincided. Duncan had lived here for years. Trung looked around at the cramped balcony and back into his small living room. The block had once been public housing. Now it was managed by a strata company and had been tarted up accordingly. Among the Commodores and Falcons, a BMW and two Mercedes graced the parking lot with their upmarket presence. A swimming pool had been installed, along with a new lift and carpet in the hallways. Indian families had moved in and the spicy scents of cumin and curry leaves wafted along the corridors and out into the open air of the fire escapes. Despite the improvements, the place retained a faint aura of poverty.

In his modest kitchen he put together a stir fry from what was left in the crisper. An egg to top it off and an Asahi beer to wash it down—heaven. He turned on the news. Clinton was still trying to wriggle out of the Monica Lewinsky scandal. Why didn't he just fess up? Trung wondered. *Yes, her flesh was young, and she had no ambitions for me.* That would be preferable than the spectacle of such an important figure being brought to his knees by gossip. It was pathetic. Bored, he opened another beer, turned off the TV and emptied his pockets. He found the chit he'd torn off the notice at Fair Dinkum Backpackers. He dialled the number of the hostel.

'Yeah, Fair Dinkum,' drawled the voice at the desk.

'I'm looking for Renata Schmidt,' said Trung. 'She there?'

'Hang on.'

Trung heard the bellowed summons and tried to imagine what living in a backpacker's might be like.

'Hello, yes. This is Renata.' Her voice was cultured, with just a trace of an accent.

'Hello, Renata,' said Trung. He wanted to sound more like her, less like the slack bastard at the desk. He explained his reason for calling. 'I'm not completely sure if it's him,' said Trung. 'Maybe just coincidence. The guy I'm thinking of gives talks about the war to schoolkids.'

'One minute, please,' said Renata. 'These details I am wanting to write down.'

Trung heard shuffling and then she was back on the phone. As he talked, he could hear her writing down every word. Trung told Renata about Duffy's fine house. About the Rolls Royce, what little he knew about his business interests. It did cross Trung's mind that his curiosity had already gotten him into trouble with Duffy's goons. His aching ribs were testament to that. Maybe his curiosity wasn't such a good thing. But, what the hell.

'If he is my grandfather, he would surely look different from the old photo?'

Trung sensed Renata had some doubts. Did she think he was perhaps an opportunist with another agenda? 'The Mr Duffy I know looks older. But the resemblance is … um … I'm not sure exactly what the right word is, but it definitely looks like him. He's a little heavier. Not much. Grey, definitely grey. But the same moustache. It's him all right.' The more Trung thought about it, the more he realised it simply had to be Duffy.

They arranged for Trung to pick her up next day, at 11 am at the hostel. Renata would pay the normal fare, she said, plus a 'good looking tip.' Even Trung knew she meant 'handsome'.

CHAPTER 10

'Higher *Opa*, higher.'

The little girl squealed with delight as her grandfather pushed the swing ever higher. She was the apple of her grandfather's eye. No school for her this warm summer's day even though her recovery from a bout of bronchitis appeared to be complete. 'One more day at home, just to be safe,' *Mutti* had said. Clad in blue jeans, sneakers and a T-shirt with a picture of Sweden's super group, Abba, she could have been any little girl in America, Sweden, or Australia even. But this child lived in southern Germany, in the fabled Black Forest; the land of Hansel and Gretel, Rapunzel, and the cuckoo clock. Her life was a fairytale, a *gemütlich* bubble with a backdrop of trees and snow-covered peaks, with a father, mother and grandparents who cherished her. She was too young to realise it was an illusion.

Her home was a shingle roofed, eighteenth-century two-storey house with a long overhang, sweeping right down to the ground floor, shading the walls in summer and protecting them in the frosty winters. Freiderjes had been in the Wagner family for more than a hundred years and had survived wars and turmoil; a picture postcard farm with cows, sheep, pigs and a boutique vegetable garden. Restaurants paid top dollar for the produce, including their own brand of Black Forest ham, much sought after by tourists and merchants alike.

Her grandfather sweated as he pushed the swing. *Opa* insisted they dress in traditional attire. Like everything else about the farm, it was an elaborate pantomime in which Franz Wagner played the German farmer to perfection.

'Tourists, ja?' he would say, 'they love all this bullshit.'

Life indeed was good. Along with tractors and farm machinery in its spacious garage, the latest Mercedes 450 SL and a convertible BMW3 series, both meticulously waxed and polished, announced that the former *Hauptmann* had made a good recovery from the trauma of the war and was making a go of things.

The child, Renata, seldom thought about the future. If she did, it might stretch as far as the weekend. At six years of age, she imagined nothing more than life as it was now. In her mind, parents and grandparents lived forever.

Soon it would be her birthday. There had been talk of *Opa* and *Oma* taking her to Berlin, or perhaps Munich. She had already visited Freiburg and had gazed in wonderment at the canals, the old cobblestoned streets, and the baroque architecture.

'Don't stop, *Opa*. C'mon,' she cried.

Two vehicles quietly entered the grounds of the farm; a klunky silver Mercedes Benz Sprinter van and a Mercedes 420 SE sedan, with its distinctive green and white livery. *Polizei!* Two uniformed police and two plain clothes officers marched grimly to the swing where her ashen-faced grandfather stood.

'Franz Wagner? You are under arrest for atrocities committed in Lidice, Bohemia, in 1942 and other war crimes. Anything you say will be recorded as evidence and used against you in the tribunal.'

CHAPTER 10

The moment would remain forever imprinted on Renata Schmidt's mind. Serenity interrupted by harsh reality. The ugly officials in their stupid uniforms and drab suits. The amplified voice of the arresting officer, drowning out the bird song and the distant mooing of a cow. A pig squealed in its pen beyond the house.

CHAPTER 11

Early/ October 1998

Robin Edwards looked at the pile of papers in his in-tray. Some people thought police work was all high-speed chases, arrests, and interrogations. 'Not so,' he sighed to himself. At times he wondered about the relevance of his Bachelor of Criminology. The air conditioning hummed away in the corner of the long room his squad had occupied forever. The room was about half full of officers doing what he was doing; catching up on paperwork. Tomorrow, the 7th of October, was circled in red on his desk calendar. A major review day—with meetings, case reviews, allocations—all the Major Crime Squad squeezed into one room with the chief berating them for various failings Police Commissioner Len Bruce had brought to his attention. But today he was stuck with office work and would remain so unless a new case burst through the bubble of paper industry.

He turned over the first file—domestic violence ending in murder. He hated those cases. Halfway down the stack was an insurance claim for a Mercedes van, allegedly stolen from Satinwood Funerals. *Satinwood Funerals*—the name sounded familiar. Robin read the details. The van had been found dumped in an old quarry in the Swan valley, and the insurance company was refusing to pay. The insurance sleuth considered the claim to be a cover-up and wanted the police to examine any records for hold-ups or other crimes involving the van.

That rings a bell. Robin flicked through his notepad. *September, Trung. You little beauty. There's no such thing as a coincidence.* He closed his notepad.

He picked up the phone and dialled the records registry. The WA Police were in the process of putting all their records on computer and arming every cop with his own terminal. Robin preferred the old way.

'Julie?' he said. 'D S Robin Edwards from Major Crime.'

'Hello, Robin, how can I help?

'What have we got on Satinwood Funerals?'

There was a delay, then Julie's voice, 'Are you and Batman ready for this Robin?'

'We are, Julie. Want to come over to the Batcave after work?'

Once past the preliminaries, Julie was able to recite a string of minor traffic infringements involving Satinwood vans and hearses. There was nothing unusual in this, except perhaps for the frequency with which they seemed to be caught speeding. Edwards also noticed the times of the offences were unusual— late at night or early hours of the morning. He located a photo of the missing van's personalised licence plate—Satinwood 6— and asked if there was anything more serious connected with it.

'Nah,' said Julie. 'Just like all the others: speeding, a red light. And that's about it. Nothing after July this year.'

He thanked her, ended the phone call, folded his notebook and headed out. *Maybe, just maybe, the taxi driver had been on to something.*

The head office of Satinwood Funerals was a sleek, modern building in Canning Vale. In the car park were several sedans and one black Mercedes van, licence plate Satinwood 1. A large roller door in the corner of the building was closed. He opened the sliding glass doors. The receptionist, a middle-aged woman pretending to be 30, offered her standard greeting.

'How can we help you, sir?'

A box of tissues sat prominently on the counter. Robin imagined that she was ready to comfort the bereaved at the drop of a hat. He flashed his badge at her.

'Who is the principal of Satinwood Funerals?' he asked.

If she was impressed, Jane Cooper didn't show it. 'We don't have a principal, sir. We're not a high school. The owner is Mr Alan Duffy, DSO.'

Edwards gave her his best 'good cop' smile.

'Let's start again. Who's in charge today?'

'That would be Hugo. Grantley and the others are all at a funeral, a big one over at Karrakatta. An Italian family. The patriarch, Frank Portaro, died. Perhaps you know the name?'

Everyone knew the name. The media had seen to that. Frank Portaro was from one of the big Melbourne crime families. When he moved to Perth and started a seafood chain there was consternation in both the underworld and the fishing industry. But last week, only a few months after the move, Portaro had suddenly died of a heart attack. Or so it was said.

Edwards smiled his good cop smile. 'Where can I find Hugo?'

Jane stood up and led him to a side door. Edwards guessed that she had been working out. She really looked very good when she walked. 'Head down the corridor. At the end is the garage. He should be there.' She smiled. 'I hope you find what you're looking for.'

The garage was cavernous and dark. Edwards headed

towards the far corner, where a gleam of polished metal caught his eye. Closer in, he could make out a Holden muscle car. A bulky man wearing stovepipe jeans and a white T-shirt was leaning against the fender, talking into a cordless telephone. Behind him a small glassed-in office was in darkness. The man fixed Edwards with a hostile stare and kept talking.

'Yeah. Got it. Friday night. Don't forget bring the goods. Ha ha. Cold, they reckon. Rain. Yeah. You seen Joey? Tell him, Hugo said to get his arse in gear.'

Hugo rang off and walked back to the office to replace the phone. When he returned, he looked over Edwards from head to toe. Robin wondered if he was measuring him for a coffin, or a body bag.

'Yeah?' was all he said.

Edwards flashed his badge. 'Nice car. Hugo, is it?'

'Yeah,' said Hugo. 'Help you?'

'One of your vans went missing,' he said. 'Know anything about that?'

'Not really,' said Hugo.

'Interesting. A van goes missing? I would have thought that was a pretty big deal?'

Hugo shrugged.

'I mean, you're the man here, right?'

Another shrug.

'You, know what? I'm a little confused. A van goes missing. You seem to be in charge. You don't know anything about it. Have you worked here long?'

'Long enough.'

'I'd like to have a look at your employment records'

'Got a warrant?' Hugo sneered.

Robin didn't answer. 'What about Joey? Maybe he could help me?' asked Edwards.

'Whadda you know about Joey?' asked Hugo. 'The fuck?'

'We all know about Joey,' said Edwards.

'Listen,' said Hugo. 'Joey was in charge of the van. The drivers sometimes take them home after a funeral instead of bringin' them back to the depot, 'specially if a funeral is across town. He took it home, came out the next morning and it was gone.'

'Gone, eh? It's not gone any more, Hugo. It's up on blocks at our laboratory. Police are going over it with a fine-tooth comb. Whatever Joey did with it will come out, know what I mean?'

'That it?' asked Hugo.

By way of an answer, Edwards removed a compact Minolta from his jacket pocket, aimed at the muscle car and clicked.

'What the fuck?'

'Don't worry,' said Edwards. 'It's for my grandson. He collects pictures of performance cars. You don't mind, do you? Relax, I'll let myself out.'

Hugo looked like he wanted to obliterate Edwards from the face of the Earth.

CHAPTER 12

Sandy studied the diagram in the seat pocket. The aircraft he had boarded was an example of what the aviation industry could turn out in peace time. He gaped out of the window at the sheer bulk of the thing. Each engine more powerful than all four of the Rolls Royce Merlins that had powered the Lancasters he'd flown in. As the plane became airborne, he had a brief panic attack. He remembered the flak, the screams of terror from his late comrades. The moment passed and he forced himself to relax. 'More like a city than a plane,' he muttered.

Sandy sat back with a whisky and soda and asked himself what was it all about? Why had he decided to accept the offer to fly to Germany? Was it about Duffy? Was he seeking answers? Or was it just that it appealed to the ego of an old man wanting to remain relevant?

Prompted by the announcements, which were offered in Arabic and English, Sandy reached for the safety information in the seat pocket and discovered that the Boeing 747 could seat a maximum of 410 people, fly 12,200 km at a cruising speed of 980 kph and on and on. It made the Lancaster, the plane he had loved, feel like a mosquito; although of course it wasn't at all, it had been a behemoth when it first came into service. Its most impressive statistic was the fact it carried 1000kg of bombs, all destined to wreak havoc on the enemy. Sandy put the card away and fiddled with the plastic package containing the headphones. There were more announcements, some heavy thuds and a conclusive thump before the great whale lurched backwards to begin its crawl to the runway. Sandy looked sideways at his neighbour; a young woman encased in headphones. He closed his eyes and went to sleep. It had been an exciting morning and the day had only just begun.

The hotel in Baden-Baden was modest. Sandy stretched out on the bed. It had big puffy covers the Germans called duvets. He'd noticed the change in seasons as soon as he arrived in Germany. Perth had been warm but here, in late October, there was a chill in the air. The rest of the room was chintzy. There was a distant view of a park, which he thought led to the ornate gardens and the spa palace which was now a casino. In the morning he hoped to wake up fresh, or was it already morning? The light in the sky might have been dusk or it might have been dawn. He tried to get his head around the time change from Perth, and gave up. Whatever time it was, he needed to rest. When his brain woke up, he would speak to the receptionist and arrange a car to take him to Freiburg, near where his Lancaster had crashed. There he would contact Jules Whitechurch, the British archaeologist who had contacted him about the dig they were conducting on the edge of the Black Forest.

Whitechurch had found Sandy's name in the war records and was confident that the Lancaster they were uncovering was WX796, the plane Sandy and his mates had gone down in on that fateful mission. Whitechurch had been lucky to access funds from the Imperial War Museum, and now he had recruited a team of student archaeologists to help with the painstaking work of recovering the wreckage. They had already found a cap badge which had been traced to the tail-end gunner, Bernie Hawke. Of all the horrible deaths that a tail gunner might suffer, crashing in a burning plane was possibly the worst. Sandy had shuddered when Whitechurch had told him the news, and he'd wondered if he could bear reliving the catastrophe. He still remembered the cry from the back of the plane when the night fighter first struck. Bernie may have died instantly, Sandy hoped so, a blessing if anything about that horrible war could be called a blessing.

A larger mystery was what happened after he had bailed out. He had discussed it with Duffy once, at an RAAF veterans' reunion in Perth. Duffy had been dismissive and arrogant; Sandy had avoided him at the annual RAAF get togethers. Their paths had diverged since returning to civilian life. Duffy's family business was waiting for him. All he had to do was step into the seat his father had vacated. Sandy, on the other hand, had gone back to school and studied architectural drafting. He had worked his way up—polished up the handle of the big front door—and all that.

Sandy disliked Duffy; always had. Something about his sense of entitlement, the 'air force brush' he had cultivated on his top lip, the way he wore his cravat—and the suspicion that he had deserted his bomb aimer when they were both in trouble, stranded airmen, injured and trying to avoid capture in enemy territory. He had a memory of Duffy's back, heading in the direction of a forest road. Sandy had twisted his ankle when he hit the ground and was limping badly. Duffy had a minor head wound. After an uncomfortable night in a hayloft, they had set out, starving and anxious, in the direction of the

Swiss border. After a morning dodging German patrols, they had argued. Duffy had refused to slow down.

This flashback took Sandy minutely further than he'd been before. Had they walked through a forest? Yes, into a dark forest, the trees beetling down at them like ogres. It was if the forest had swallowed his memories.

***

Jules Whitechurch's room at the Black Forest Hostel in Freiburg was basic, as befitted a man on a mission. Each year, he stepped back from his academic commitments at the University of Winchester and hosted a student dig in Germany. War archelogy was a rapidly growing field, becoming more crowded each year. Like divers in search of sunken treasure, his students and those from a sister institution in Germany, the University of Cologne, were highly motivated if not always handy with a trowel. His plan was to spend a week setting up and then move to the camp on the hill where some local children had stumbled across a rusty air speed indicator, which they had carried home in triumph to show their grandfather. This morning he was meeting Sandy Tuckwell, the bomb aimer, one of only two survivors of the Lancaster crash. Every year the veterans of Bomber Command dwindled in number. Some of the living weren't able to travel, others were demented. It was a rare opportunity to revisit history. And the history of this Lancaster was of particular interest.

The Freiburg railway station was a modern cathedral of a place, built of steel and glass and offering a vista of the old city, or at least those parts of it that had survived the 1944 Allied bombing. The train from Baden-Baden arrived on time and Tuckwell stepped out, a slight man, instantly recognisable from his photographs.

Whitechurch stepped forward and held out his hand. 'Mr Tuckwell,' he said. 'I am very glad to meet you.'

'Just a minute, son. Got to get my stuff sorted.' He folded a cream raincoat over his arm, extended the handle on his suitcase and then returned Jules's handshake. 'Where to?' he asked.

'I've got a room for you at the hostel next to mine. Tomorrow we'll drive out to the dig, and you can decide if you'd like to camp with the rest of the team or stay here in Freiburg.'

The old man grunted. 'Any chance of a coffee?'

In an airy coffee shop on the gallery level, Jules tried to bring his guest up to speed. 'We hope to find some larger parts of your aircraft over the coming weeks,' he said. 'The wings, for example. Engines. Farmers may have souvenired things over the years. Nature has a way of burying the smaller things. There's been more than fifty years of snowstorms, rain and wind. Finding Bernie Hawke's cap badge was sheer luck.'

Tuckwell grunted again. He seemed less interested in the project than Jules had hoped.

'Is there some aspect of the excavation that particularly grabs you, Mr Tuckwell?'

'Sandy, please.'

'Maybe you need some time to get over the flight,' said Jules. 'We're a long way from Perth.'

'I'll tell you what I'm interested in,' said Sandy. 'I'd like to find where I fell to earth, so to speak. Me and Duffy—our pilot. If possible, I'd like to retrace our way out of the forest and into farmland and find out how I ended up in a hospital in Switzerland.'

Jules' heart sank. There was no predicting how veterans would react to the discovery of a wrecked plane, the scant evidence of what must have been the worst moment of their lives. I'm afraid that's way outside the scope of our project, Sandy,' he said. 'You could spend years reconstructing your rescue, if you could do it at all. As for the place you fell to earth, as you put it, I'd say without coordinates that's impossible.'

The old man was staring into space. Jules tried to imagine what it was like for the other man and whether Sandy was reliving the horror of the mission. Tuckwell wasn't the first airman to have come down in the vicinity. His escape to freedom had been nothing short of a miracle. Perhaps such memories should be left intact, he thought. His own interest was academic. What could be gleaned from examining the wreckage of a war plane? There would be reports on every aspect of the dig and then journal articles. None of it would help this man and what haunted him. They drank their coffee in silence. Jules picked up Sandy's suitcase and found a taxi rank.

'Hostel Schwarzwald bitte,' he said when they were settled in the back seat. Sandy spoke in a whisper, 'They were bloody noisy, you know. Christ, they were noisy.'

'What was that, Sandy?'

'Those bloody Merlin engines.'

CHAPTER 13

October 1998

Sandy walked along the trail through the pine forest. On either side of the track moss grew. An earthy smell permeated the air, strong enough to make him sneeze. With Jules's help he had found a holiday apartment on the outskirts of Freudenstadt. It was Jules's way of brushing him off, Sandy thought. Let the old man wander around the Black Forest and we'll get on with the serious stuff. Jules had no idea. He would not have lasted five minutes in Bomber Command.

On his second day in Freiburg, Jules had taken him out to the dig in a Mercedes off-road vehicle. At the dig site a group of German students were sitting around a long table in the open air, heads bent over a small device they said was a Blackberry—a sort of pager, capable of sending messages to others who had the same device. They seemed more interested in this small piece of equipment than the dig itself, which consisted of a series of long trenches where the rich black soil had been excavated. Jules gave them a pep talk, which made little impression. They were volunteers, after all, enjoying a break from their studies. Sandy could understand their reluctance to crawl down into a ditch and sieve the soil looking for the charred ruins of what must to them have seemed as ancient as a dinosaur.

In the tent where unearthed treasures were being examined and catalogued, he'd met Jules's assistant, an English woman called Monica. The prize find so far was a bomb sight, the very instrument through which Sandy had lined up the targets far below, shouting his readings to Duffy who trimmed the plane accordingly until Sandy released the ordnance on its mission of death. Sandy had never had any illusions about what he'd done—dealing out death. Like all wars, it was dirty.

'You recognise this, Mr. Tuckwell? You'll need to put on some of these if you want to take a closer look.' Monica passed a pair of lab gloves to Sandy as she held out the cumbersome prized instrument, miraculously still intact.

'Of course,' Sandy replied. 'It's a Blackett sighting head, Mark X. I spent far too many hours squinting into the wretched things. To pass our test in Canada, we had to achieve seventy percent accuracy. Not to mention all the homework, trigonometry and so on.'

'It's marvellous that you remember it so clearly,' said Monica.

Sandy sensed that she had not intended to be patronising. And why quibble if she had? He carefully took the instrument from Monica and weighed it in his gloved hands. The manufacturer's mark was still visible on the underside. He handed it back to her. He didn't want any part of the exercise. Let them dig up what they wanted. He was after gold: the gold of recollection. He remembered the sense of relief when his parachute deployed. The air moving against his face had felt like a caress. The fear he'd smash into a tree. That maybe guns were trained on him?

The track cut deeper into the forest. One part of him agreed with Jules. Finding the place where he and Duffy had landed and set out to save themselves would be impossible. The Black

Forest was the setting of some of Germany's darkest folk tales. He thought of Hansel and Gretel and could hear the theatrical voice of his mother as she read the fairy tale to him and his sister, Ginger. If he was Hansel, who was Gretel? For that matter, where was the candy house and the Wicked Witch? He sat down and ate the sandwich he'd packed for himself before he left. He had shunned the organised tours of the forest advertised in the town and instead, picked up a map of walking trails. The map was about as useful as the silk maps of Germany the RAAF had issued, along with emergency rations and a potassium cyanide pill to be taken if he was captured. But he was still confident that even as an old man he could retrace his steps back to the dig site.

What was it all about, that war? They had believed in the war, all of them. It was necessary to believe if you were going to go out and kill people. But what if the story of a 'just war' had been a fairy tale? The 'peace' at the end of it merely a candy house? Bomber Command was the witch. It offered the fable of peace, but in fact was all-devouring. It had eaten all the Hansels and Gretels and Duffys and Sandys that it could.

He thought of Maisie, and the times she had comforted him when he had woken up covered in sweat and shouting. This wasn't even a nightmare; it was the vivid memory of his plane being ripped apart from under him and the miracle of his escape.

He finished his sandwich, upended his water bottle and stretched out on the grass in the sun, which at this time of day, had found its way through the pine trees to the forest floor. It was an effort to find the ground but eventually, propped up by one arm, he found a resting place. Doglike, he squirmed around until he found the right hollow for his old bones to settle in.

Something woke him with a start. *What the hell's that?* A red deer was looming over him, curious and remarkably tame. He rolled onto his front and pushed himself up into a squat and then painfully stood up. The deer sprinted off. There was no more sun and the light was fast disappearing from the trail. In the gloom, moss covering the rocks took on an evil-looking shade of green. Sandy thought of what would happen if he didn't turn back now. Getting lost in this forbidding forest didn't bear thinking about. Better to return to the trail, and go back the way he'd come. If he wanted to relive his ordeal, then this was as close as he was likely to get. His water bottle was empty. The salty salami on his sandwich had dried out his mouth. Or was that fear?

He recalled their printed silk maps showed a road that cut through the forest. If they could reach it, then there was hope, as well as danger. They found a road, perhaps *the* road they were looking for. Duffy forged ahead, ignoring Sandy's pleas to slow down.

Sandy saw in his mind the top of a rise. A farm truck stopped. He saw Duffy climb in. The truck then drove straight towards him. He rolled into a ditch, his head up and staring. Duffy would look out for his mate. Wouldn't he? Sandy watched as the truck roared past, gathering speed. The driver was a woman in a head scarf. She was laughing. Heart racing, he was acutely aware of his predicament; injured, without food or shelter, and facing another cold night alone in hostile territory. His mind zipped from one unrelated thought to another. *Where are the rest of the crew? Do I wait for Duffy to come back for me? I haven't paid my mess bill. Mess bill?* Memory after memory surged through his mind. Why on earth had he worried about an overdue mess bill?

Why couldn't he remember the important stuff? The escape from Germany?

As the day's light began to dissipate, he quickened his pace and was glad to recognise the forest trail markers that had guided him earlier that day.

CHAPTER 14

October 1998

In the morning Sandy asked the receptionist if she had any brochures about the Black Forest. She obliged with an English language booklet. On the first page was a geological history of the South German Scarpland followed by a description of the Black Forest, its history, the various sites of interest, and its fauna and flora.

He considered the idea of staying inside and reading all day. There was no hurry. In Baden-Baden he had intended to chase up the therapist his friend Liv had recommended. The counsellor specialised in recovered memory therapy. Sandy harboured a deep mistrust of such things. He knew too many air force men who had lost their minds to really believe in the efficacy of talking cures. He would much prefer to continue his self-imposed walking cure.

After breakfast he spoke to the concierge, who so far had treated him like something out of Madame Tussauds Wax Works.

'I'd like you to contact Jules Whitechurch and tell him I need a car for the day, with a driver,' he said. 'I would prefer someone who can speak English. And if you could arrange a picnic lunch for the two of us?'

The concierge sneered but with brisk efficiency made the necessary phone call. At 9 am a smartly-turned-out driver appeared driving a Mercedes diesel saloon. She introduced herself as Hettie—about 25 years old, Sandy guessed, with blonde curls and a lively manner.

When Sandy explained his mission, she pulled out a detailed map of the forest, which included walking trails and minor roads. Sandy retraced what he thought were his steps from the day before.

'*Ja*, that is good *Herr* Tuckwell. You see this road here? That will get us close to your finishing point and we can take it from there.'

From her crisp transatlantic accent, Sandy surmised Hettie had been educated in America. He felt reassured. They made their way through the forest, stopping at Sandy's bidding, checking the map, then moving on. They turned onto a narrow dirt road, which in turn criss-crossed other dirt roads.

'The roads all look the same,' he said. 'It's hopeless.'

Hettie found a roadside clearing. A wooden table and sturdy oak benches were an invitation for travellers. With a backdrop of aged trees and rustling grasses, it could have been a photo for a tourist brochure. In the hamper the hotel had provided, they found a thermos of coffee and some almond biscuits. Hettie spread out the map like a tablecloth. On an impulse, Sandy walked further into the forest. Hettie watched as he disappeared into a patch where the pine trees seemed to close ranks against the outside world. A few minutes later he emerged again, looking defeated.

'This is where I got to yesterday,' he said. 'I've found the hollow where I fell asleep.'

Hettie smiled. 'And from here?'

'Needle in a haystack,' said Sandy. 'I have no idea. But if I had to guess, I'd say keep going on this road and see where we get to. But drive slowly if you would, Hettie.'

After their coffee they motored along the uneven surface, Sandy pictured again the memory he'd recovered yesterday; the scene of Duffy's betrayal.

'Just stop here please, Hettie.' All the side roads looked the same. He was wasting his time. But what if he could recall the events, in order, as they happened? Then he wouldn't need to find the place. It was the memory that counted. He just wanted to remember.

'Ok, this is far enough, I think. Can we drive back to the excavation site where Jules and his team are working? Back roads, all the way, if possible. And can you zero the trip meter so we know how far it is?'

Hettie looked surprised but did what she was asked. On the way he closed his eyes. His breakfast reading had given him the dimensions of this part of the forest, where the densely-packed dark green conifers loomed close to the road's edge. Only now could he picture it as a distinct region, a place he had traversed all those years ago, but in an exhausted condition, his nerves worn thin from fear and sleep deprivation, cold and hunger. He remembered following what had seemed to be a network of narrow, winding roads. He and Duffy had cautiously edged by the occasional small farm cleared out of the forest, where pretty brown and white cows had gazed at them with disinterest. And then he remembered. They'd been trudging along the side of a long road—he couldn't remember for how long. Duffy marched on ahead, leaving him far behind.

'Keep going please, Hettie. Very slowly.'

There was a ditch at the side of the road. He remembered it now. He'd cowered in it while the truck roared past. What then? He seemed to remember running after the truck, like a lost boy.

After a time, they came to an overgrown driveway, hidden behind a farm gate. A faded sign announced the name of the farm: Freiderjes.

'Hettie, look over there. That's it. Has to be. It's like time has stood still.' Hettie crept along now. With his eyes closed, Sandy played the scene out in his mind.

The gate was unlocked, and there were signs of a truck's progress up another slope, at the top of which stood a farmhouse. Sagging now from his walk, he helped himself to water from an ancient pump. Around the back was the truck that had picked up Duffy. He pounded on the door, which was locked. He pounded again. Duffy's head emerged from a bedroom window on the first floor.

'Piss off, Sandy. There's only room for one. Leave now! It's unsafe for the two of us to be in the one place.'

With that the window slammed shut, and no amount of hammering on the door made any difference. He slumped on the doorstep, unbelieving. Animal sounds were emerging from the first floor above. Human animal sounds. The laughing woman was having an orgasm. That was it, the final insult that told him he had only himself to depend on.

Sandy opened his eyes, pleased with the morning's progress. He imagined returning to his house in Perth, opening the note book from his trip and drafting a map of the forest on his old drawing board in the spare room where Maisie had set it up for him when he retired. He'd illustrate it, like a map in a children's story book. Except that the story he had to tell was less innocent; the story of a man who walked and hitch-hiked his way to freedom after his leader had left him for dead.

Hettie had reached the main road to Freiburg and picked up speed as they headed back to the dig site.

CHAPTER 15

October 1998

Trung awoke in good spirits as golden fingers of sunlight crept across a cloudless sky. The birds on his balcony were alive with song. The days were becoming warmer, summer was just around the corner. Life was on the improve and in the light of a new day, he was favouring the prospect of working for Duffy. Every driver knew that driving a cab for someone else was the road to nowhere, even if the someone else was as friendly as Jack Sprague.

At 5:30 am he slid into the still warm seat of Don 82. Fuel tank, check. Enough change, check. Seat adjustment, check.

The tired voice of Barnsey crackled over the radio. *'Car for Shaftesbury Avenue going to the International. Is anybody out there working? C'mon guys, regular customer. Do I hear the Don car? Trung, you're a bloody lifesaver! Go to 29 Shaftesbury Avenue Bayswater and pick up Mr Vaughan, M11 on channel six.'*

The early morning ran smoothly with good fares, nice people and good tips. He checked the time. He was picking up the intriguing German lady, Renata at 11. He still had time to slip home for a late breakfast of noodles and coffee before his appointment at Fair Dinkum Backpackers.

Northbridge was busy as Trung reversed into a bay in Aberdeen Street at the front of the popular backpackers. A chubby man with dreadlocks was fast asleep on the verge, curled up like a discarded croissant outside Salty Towers Seafood. Fast food wrappers and empty beer cans overflowed from a green wheelie bin. Trung stared disdainfully at the man. He could never understand why Australians drank until they fell over. He slammed the door of the old Falcon and pressed the key fob to lock the door. Nothing. *Why doesn't anyone ever replace the batteries in these things?*

A blonde woman in designer jeans and a Gucci T-shirt sat alone at one of the tables on the verandah. She had a rucksack at her feet with what Trung thought was the German flag sewn onto the flap.

'Trung, is it?'

Trung couldn't help grinning at the German lady as she smiled warmly, appearing to take stock of his cheap black trousers, worn Nikes, blue shirt and a faded blue polyester bomber jacket with the Swan Taxis logo.

She held out her hand. 'Renata.'

Trung shook her hand, then grabbed her rucksack, carried it to the Falcon and placed it on the back seat. 'Do you want to sit in the back or with me ... in the front?'

'I sit with you, ok?' Renata slammed the door shut. Trung hesitated before he started the car and put the meter on.

'I'm not sure what you want. I'm not even sure the guy I know is the man you want.'

'How about we go to his house,' said Renata. 'I'm not sure if I will have the courage to approach him.'

Renata chatted about her trip, Germany and her family, as she gazed at the sights of Perth. 'I have been talking too much. Tell me a little about Perth, please Trung.'

Trung gave a running commentary until they reached Dalkeith. As the cab swung into The Avenue and then into stately Jutland Parade, the conversation faltered.

'This man is very rich, yes?'

Trung winked assent. The maroon Rolls Royce was in the drive. It made Trung's taxi look like a piece of junk. 'You want me to stop? Are you going to knock on the door?'

'Just ... I don't know. Keep driving, yes? Take me back to the hostel please.'

They drove back in silence, following the Swan River into the city and then on to the hostel. There was thirty-one dollars on the meter. Renata smiled as she handed Trung two twenty-dollar notes He noticed her eyes had filled with tears.

'There's very good coffee on the corner,' said Trung, acting on impulse. 'How about I buy the coffees, and you tell me what's wrong'

They made their way to the Bar Italia and took a seat in the window, looking out on busy William Street. Renata dabbed at her eyes with a paper napkin while they waited to order. Trung thought about the beating he'd copped in the lane up the street; the customers who wanted to tear him apart because he was Asian; and the charming and powerful Duffy with his funeral business and decidedly shady employees. Renata could cry all she liked. He didn't mind. In fact, he enjoyed it. It was like rain in the desert.

'I grew up in a beautiful part of Germany, the Black Forest. We lived on a farm. Oh, Trung it was beautiful. My family owned a traditional farmhouse with a steep roof and shuttered windows. We had snow in winter. It was like a fairy tale.'

'I've never seen snow.' Trung leaned back in his chair.

'Our home was very big. My grandparents lived there, as

well as my father, mother and brother. I was a happy child. I had a wind-up dancing bear, my favourite toy, and I used to dance with him all around the kitchen.'

Trung's childhood memories were dominated by the image of their leaky boat, his frantic mother, his worried father. And the sea, everywhere you looked, the sea.

'Then one day my opa, my grandfather, was hauled away by the police,' Renata continued.

'How come?' asked Trung.

'*Opa* had been in the war. He was a *hauptman*, a captain. As far as we knew, he had done his duty, been a good soldier and survived. He showed us his medals sometimes, and a scar on his shoulder where a bullet had passed right through it. I was only six when they took him away, I didn't understand.

'Oh, sad story,' said Trung. 'How does Mr Duffy come into all this?'

Renata stared out of the window. 'If we have the right man, I will confront him with some facts he probably doesn't want to hear. It is such a nice city, Perth. I'm not sure why, but I'm finding this difficult. You are the first person I have told. The man I am looking for was a bomber pilot in the war. You know that. His plane crashed near our house in the Schwartzwald, the Black Forest. *Opa*, my grandfather was away fighting in the Wehrmacht, the German army.'

Trung said nothing. Renata well and truly had his attention.

'My *oma*, my grandmother, was alone in the house. She found this man on a road that ran through the woods. He was exhausted and a little *fetzig* in the head, you know?' Pointing at her own head, Renata made a twirling motion with her fingers.

Trung laughed. 'Oh yes, fucked in the head.'

It was Renata's turn to laugh. 'Well, maybe not fucked. How about delirious?'

They tucked into the cannoli they had ordered and called for more coffee.

'I'm not sure exactly what his injuries were. My *oma* was on her death bed when she told me, and it came out a bit mixed up. I did ask her, "why *Oma* did you pick up an enemy flyer?" but she wouldn't answer.

Trung tried to smile, his mouth full of pastry.

'Oma told me she nursed the man back to health and they ... and they. Well, they had sex. Together.'

Trung almost choked on his treat. 'Yes, people do it together.'

Renata glared at him. 'Do you want to hear the story or not?'

'Yes, yes. Great story. Sexy! Mr Duffy, who would have thought?'

'We don't know if it's your Mr Duffy yet. Whoever he was, he left, never to be heard of again. My *oma* seemed to think he escaped out of Germany. I think she was a little confused. In her mind it had become quite a love affair, it was as if it had been days or weeks, but that simply doesn't make sense. She said she'd nursed him back to health, suggesting he'd been at the house for some time. But I think it was really nothing more than, what do you call it?'

Trung shrugged, 'What do you mean?'

'It's, you know? Like a fling, a...'

'You mean a one-night stand?'

'Exactly, a one-night thing. I think as the years went by; she'd convinced herself that this man, this flier was the love of her life. She'd even managed to get the scarf he'd worn, back from the *polizei*.'

'I still don't get it. This is why you want to find the guy? Because he did it with your grandmother? I mean, so what?'

'Nine months later my mother was born.'

'And you think...?'

'The very next day, my grandfather returned home on leave from the army. Even so, *Oma* was absolutely positive the Australian airman was the father. My mother looked nothing like her supposed father, the *hauptman*. Apparently, my grandfather was very suspicious. But the doctor told him it was normal, it happened all the time. Genetics, you know. Very strange, but the baby looked more Aryan than expected. You know, the sort of German Herr Hitler preferred. Many South Germans were dark, more like Italians.'

'But you are blonde,' said Trung. He didn't know what genetics meant, not really. He slurped up the last of his cappuccino.

'A girl can do a lot with a bottle,' said Renata.

'So, you think this airman is your real grandfather?' said Trung. 'I understand why you would want to see him. But what made you think he was from Perth? Australia is a very big place.'

Renata reached into her rucksack and pulled out a moth-eaten blue scarf, worn thin from use. She turned it over a few times until the words Old Easts showed. 'Do you know anything about Australian football?' she asked.

'Of course,' he said. 'It's a game played by mad bastards who can jump very high in the air. Like kangaroos. And the people who go to watch it are even crazier, believe me.'

'When my *oma* showed me this, I did some research. At first, I thought it meant Eastern Suburbs, in Sydney. They play rugby leg, yes?'

'Rugby league,' said Trung.

'But this scarf is from East Fremantle Football Club. Right here in Perth.'

Renata gazed out of the window again. The hustle and bustle of Northbridge seemed to hold her attention. 'There's a little bit more to the story,' she said. 'It's not nice. You want to hear it?'

Trung nodded. For a young woman, Renata had real depth. He hoped that her new *opa*, wherever and whoever he was, would not disappoint her.

CHAPTER 16

At home, Trung found it hard to relax. Renata's story haunted him, not least for what it told him about Alan Duffy. He was sure Duffy was her man. According to Renata, the old goat carelessly impregnated her grandmother and then left without another word. Or maybe he left because Hauptmann Franz Wagner arrived home from the war. Around the same time, their neighbour was found murdered at her farm. In 1982, when they arrested Wagner for war crimes, the police pinned the murder on him. It was all very strange. The airman would have been desperate—for money—for a safe way out of Germany. What did he do when he left Renata's grandmother? Where did he go? Renata wanted to settle the questions, so she could love her opa as a romantic war hero, not as a criminal. Yes, he had been careless with his wiener, Renata said, but he was an airman, and it was wartime.

Renata was clearly hoping that Duffy would prove to be the good grandfather she was looking for. And Trung was hoping he would be the man who would deliver him from poverty. He'd driven Duffy a few more times since he'd taken him out to the Air Force Museum. Duffy had asked him if he'd thought about the job offer. Trung still wasn't sure. He had no illusions. The guy was probably crooked. As long as he wasn't violent. Trung had suffered enough violence in his life. No more, he thought.

Trung popped a beer and turned on the television. The Clinton-Lewinsky saga was still making the news. Trung laughed. He would call his mate Duncan downstairs and see if he was up for a game of chess.

****

Morning announced itself in the form of a fierce, dry wind from the east; not Trung's favorite sort of weather. But he was feeling triumphant. He had trounced Duncan in chess last night. Maybe he would go in to work early today and attend to some of the irritants that plagued him every shift: the windscreen wiper blades that needed replacing; the driver's seat that seemed to have sagged even further and refused to adjust; the glove box full of crap left by the weekend drivers.

At the base, Sprague greeted him with unaccustomed reserve.

'Someone to see you,' he said, signalling with his eyes.

Detective Sergeant Robin Edwards was walking amongst the empty cabs, all of them washed and ready for the day shift drivers to claim. He looked as if he owned the place.

Trung's recall was instant. *The friendly copper.*

'Mr Trung!' he said.

They shook hands and Trung walked him around to the kitchen. The filthy sink was an embarrassment, but what could he do?

'Coffee?' he asked.

'Sure,' said Edwards.

Trung scrubbed the cups and made two coffees, which he set down on the stained brown Formica table.

'What brings you here, Sergeant?' he asked. 'A social visit maybe?'

Edwards laughed. 'Yeah, I just love taxi bases. Used to hang around them all the time when I was a kid. But no, not a social visit. What do you know about a Mr Alan Duffy? Swan Taxis records show you dropped him out at the Air Force Memorial at Bull Creek recently.'

Trung was conflicted. He knew way too much about Alan Duffy. But surely the police wouldn't know anything about Renata's story?

'What is it you want to know?' asked Trung. 'He seemed ok. Maybe a bit slippery.'

Trung thought of the octopus his brother Bao served in his restaurant. and what it took to prepare. Once he had taken Trung fishing with him, a rough trip on the ocean around Fremantle Harbour. Bao had reached out the back of the boat to net the octopus he'd caught on his squid jig, before hauling it in. Maybe Duffy was like a giant octopus with deadly tentacles? And yet he had offered Trung an exciting job in Vietnam.

'Slippery?' asked Edwards.

'He's an old air force guy,' said Trung. 'Reminds me of the navy guys who tried to stop us landing our boats, back in the day.'

'What day was that?'

'My family were Vietnamese boat people. Are boat people.'

'Yeah, I get that. Incredibly brave,' said Edwards. 'Yeah. Wow.' He waited a beat. 'Are you in touch with Duffy at all?'

'Oh yeah,' said Trung. 'He gives me a call if he wants a cab. I pick him up when he calls. I've picked him up two or three times, I guess. I think he's still keen on me working for him,'

'I saw that in the records, that you'd picked him up. So, he's still interested, obviously?' said Edwards.

'He seems to like me. Thinks I'm his chauffeur.'

'And are you?'

'No, he's got big muscle heads to do that. And a purple Rolls Royce.'

'So why would he want to ride in your old Falcon?'

'You'll have to ask him,' said Trung firmly.

'Tell me Trung, now the dust has settled can you tell me any more about the thugs that belted you? Any thoughts about why exactly they picked on you?'

Trung thought for a minute 'Duffy sort of brushed it off, you know the sort of thing? To an Asian, all white people look the same. That sort of bullshit.'

'So, he's saying it may not have been his guys?'

'I don't know really what he thinks, but it could just be that these blokes just hate Asians. We cop a lot of that, all the time in the cab. I guess I could give him the benefit of the doubt.'

'I've got a favour to ask you Trung,' said Edwards. 'We are keeping an eye on Mr Duffy's activities at present. If he calls you again, would you be prepared to wear a wire and record what he says? We would pay you something for your trouble, of course.'

'How much?'

'More than chauffeurs get paid, put it that way,' said Edwards.

The offers were coming thick and fast.

CHAPTER 17

October

Back at the hotel, Sandy left a message to be faxed to Jules Whitechurch at the dig.

Dear Jules,

Thank you for your hospitality and assistance. I wish your excavation every success and will be interested in anything else you learn from the wreckage.

As I told you, my reason for coming was primarily to recover some memories of the night our Lancaster came down and how the pilot, Alan Duffy and I were able to survive.

I believe I am having some success. My walk in the forest was the prompt I needed. Just as you are putting together the shattered parts of our bomber, I am putting together fragments of my survival story as they come to mind.

Please keep in touch.

Yours sincerely,

Sandy Tuckwell.

From the hotel he caught a cab to the railway and was soon on his way to Baden-Baden. He booked into the same hotel he'd found on his arrival. The bed was soft, the linen snowy, the pillows deep.

He woke to a crisp morning with overcast skies and snow predicted. After breakfast he spent the morning exploring the Altstadt, the old town. The place spoke of old Europe: cobblestones, fountains, and in the park, a wonderful rotunda where summer concerts were staged. The famous casino loomed up at the end of a picturesque walkway. Had the Allies bombed Baden-Baden? If so, there was no evidence of it now.

He returned to the hotel to find a message from Jules Whitechurch: *Hi Sandy, before you leave, I have someone you should talk to. Can you meet us at the Café Koenig at 12:30 pm for lunch? My treat.*

Sandy gazed around the square with its old, terraced buildings. He'd spent the last few hours exploring and his stomach was growling. The café was hard to miss. A riot of colour with cream slatted tables and chairs placed with Germanic precision at the front with matching umbrellas advertising Grolsch beer. The expansive front awning was a slash of vivid pink, while the ancient brickwork was painted bottle-green with reddish orange shutters. The window boxes were filled with vibrant blooms.

Sandy wandered inside and was met with the aromas of lunchtime dishes; big chunks of *knackwurst* slathered with a sauerkraut seemed to be favoured. He spotted Jules and a young intense-looking man in coveralls and work boots chatting earnestly in one of the booths. Sandy assumed he was one of the young German students assigned to the dig.

'Room for one more?'

'Sandy! Have a seat. I know you don't have a lot of time. I'd like you to meet Horst Weber. How about a beer?'

Horst, a lean beanpole with an outpouring of wiry black hair, sprang to his feet, shaking Sandy's hand, rather too vigorously Sandy thought. Jules flagged down a waitress and ordered another beer. The two men still had half-finished *steins* in front of them. Sandy noticed a pile of old newspapers in front of Horst.

'How did the rest of your walking go?' asked Jules. 'Did you discover anything?'

Sandy hesitated. He was still putting it all together in his mind; the night he'd spent on the cottage doorstep. He remembered waking early, hungry and with the smell of coffee wafting from the kitchen. Had Duffy appeared, he would have choked him.

'Anything at all?' prompted Jules.

'Ok,' said Sandy. 'I remembered a farm gate with the name *Freiderjes* on it. The Dutch sound of it rang a bell. A loud bell. Not much else, really. I gave up trying to find it, but my memory is pretty clear.

'We spoke to your driver, Hettie. She told us you were very happy with how it came out, and that you'd shared the memory with her,' said Jules. 'That's why I've brought Horst along. He has something of interest to share with you.'

'*Ja*, Sandy. I couldn't believe it when Hettie said Freiderjes. That farm is quite famous, or ... what is the word in English? Infamous. Well anyway, my father was with the *polizei*, and some years ago he arrested the farmer who owned the house. Franz Wagner. Herr Wagner was in the SS and a war criminal.'

Sandy stared blankly, a little disappointed. The story held no particular interest for him.

'Well, here's where the pot thickens,' Horst said.

'You mean the *plot*, Horst,' said Jules. 'The plot thickens.'

'Ja. Anyhow, when Wagner came back to the farm in '42 on furlough, he murdered—or so the *polizei* said—a woman who lived on the next farm.'

Suddenly Sandy was interested.

Horst opened one of the newspapers. 'When the story came out in 1982 it was followed all over Germany. Everyone wanted to know how the crime had gone unpunished for so long.'

'How had it not?' Sandy asked.

Horst shook his head 'My father had no idea. He thought— you know—the war. The *polizei* were busy. Wagner was SS, and nobody messed with the SS.'

Horst spread the newspaper out on the broad oak table. 'See here? There are photos. Wagner readily admitted to the war crimes but said he had nothing to do with the murder. He said he found the woman when he went to her farm to ask for some eggs. She had been strangled. If you look, there's a photo of the scarf that was used.'

Sandy felt a thrill of horror run down his back. The scarf was described as being royal-blue and black wool stripes. The words *Old Easts* were visible in the picture.

'I'll be damned!' said Sandy. 'That's Duffy's. What happened to the scarf?'

'It's been lost,' said Horst. 'The police were careless in those days. But it didn't stop them putting Wagner away. I had a look at the case and I thought the murder charge was a bit flimsy but the world had changed. War criminal SS. As you say in English, the deck was stacked against him.'

'He probably deserved it if he was SS,' said Sandy

CHAPTER 17

Horst shook his head, 'Quite so. But it doesn't mean he's guilty of this particular crime. And this is why we're so interested in this particular Lancaster. We think your Captain Alan Duffy may well be the murderer. The local people are very interested in every aspect of this story. Look, it was war so there's no way charges could ever be brought against your pilot. But maybe Franz Wagner could be exonerated. For what it's worth, I've spoken to some of the locals and they're convinced the airman killed the lady.'

'I knew he was a proper bastard, but this...' Sandy shook his head in disbelief.'

'It sounds like you have some business with your old pilot,' said Jules

Sandy stared briefly through the window at the new Germany. He wasn't sure what he wanted. Uppermost in his mind was a quiet life. That's what I deserve, he thought. A quiet life.

CHAPTER 18

Mid-October 1998

It's only October, thought Trung, and Perth was already warming up for the long, hot summer. Renata stood outside Fair Dinkum, looking fresh and eager.

Trung grinned as Renata climbed in. 'You ready for this?' he asked.

'*Ja*, I have had to build up my courage. But now, yes, I am ready.'

Under the uniform blue shirt that all full-time drivers were issued with, Trung was wearing the wire and the activating switch hidden in a fake cigarette lighter that Edwards had rigged up earlier in the morning. To distract from the slight bulge of the activating device, he had clipped three extra pens in his top pocket. 'Let's do this,' said Trung, and turned west.

Renata seemed mesmerised as they followed the line of the silver river. At the university, he turned left into Hackett Drive and skirted Matilda Bay before crossing Broadway and up the hill to Dalkeith.

'It is so beautiful here,' said Renata. 'I might have to stay.'

They reached Jutland Parade ahead of the appointed time. Trung parked a little distance from the house while Renata applied lipstick and bunched her blonde hair into a ponytail.

'What will you say to him?' asked Trung. 'Grandpa, give me all your money!' Trung cackled, but Renata was not amused.

'I didn't come for his money,' she said. 'I came for family reasons; to get the facts of *meine erbschaft*, my heritage, sorted out.'

'Fair enough,' said Trung. He was losing his confidence about the wire and wished he hadn't agreed to it.

At the front door they were met by Hugo, bulging out of his shirt and on alert.

'You are Mr Duffy's ten o'clock?' he said to Renata. She smiled hesitantly. He turned to Trung. 'Arms above your head.'

Trung pretended he didn't understand.

'I said arms above your head, you little slope!'

Duffy emerged from an inner room. 'That won't be necessary, Hugo,' he said smiling generously. 'Mr Nguyen and I are well acquainted, aren't we, Trung?'

Trung tried to smile at Duffy's exaggeration. He could feel the sweat building in his armpits.

'Show them into the conservatory,' Duffy said.

Hugo led them past a formal dining room and a library to a beautiful glassed-in space filled with casual furniture and glossy pot plants. Trung took a seat without waiting for an invitation, glad to be out of Hugo's reach. Renata sat next to him. A young woman in a white apron took their drinks orders. Hugo disappeared and Duffy took a seat opposite Renata.

'Trung called me and said you were visiting from Germany, and you would like to meet me,' he said. 'I can't imagine why you would want to spend time with an old man like me, but here we are. Are you enjoying Perth?'

'Yes. Thank you.'

Renata sounded tongue-tied, thought Trung. No wonder, with all this carry on. Renata cleared her throat.

'I will come to the point of my visit, the reason why I have travelled all this way from Deutschland. I believe you are my grandfather. When your plane was shot down, you were rescued by my grandmother, Jutta Wagner. You had a … I will call it an encounter with her. The outcome was my mother, Marion Schmidt, nee Wagner. And here am I—your granddaughter!'

There was a long, awkward silence, broken by the appearance of the maid, who set out tea and coffee things and some pastries. Duffy sat pinned to his chair. He recovered and waved his hand at the spread. 'Please,' he said. 'Help yourself. The pastries come from a patisserie on the Broadway. Very European, don't you think?'

Renata didn't move. She looked expectantly at Duffy, and then, cast a puzzled look at Trung. Trung shrugged.

'Tea or coffee, dear?' he asked Renata. 'How about you, Trung?'

Trung stood up, poured himself a coffee and then loaded one of the delicate plates with a croissant and a blueberry Danish. Renata sat still, waiting.

'I'll tell you something,' Duffy said, finally. His face had reddened and his breathing had thickened. 'I parachuted out of a burning plane with my bomb aimer, Sandy Tuckwell.'

Sandy, thought Trung. I know him!

'Tuckwell lives here in Perth and he will testify that we did nothing but make for the Swiss border as quickly as we could. We were in no condition to do anything else. We were both injured, and what you say is impossible. I'm sorry if your trip has been in vain, but you're barking up the wrong tree.'

'Barking what?' asked Renata. Reaching into her handbag, she pulled out the same sepia photograph that Trung had spotted outside the backpackers. 'You are wrong. I am barking up the *right* tree. This belonged to my grandmother.'

'Let me see that,' Duffy demanded. He examined the photograph of Duffy standing by a Lancaster Bomber, his face one big smile.

'This proves nothing,' he said. 'This could have come from anywhere.'

'Turn it over,' said Renata. Duffy turned it over. He looked stricken. 'Read it, *bitte.*'

'I can't,' said Duffy. 'The writing is ... indistinct.'

'It says, *To my darling, my hope, Jutta. Love from Alan,*' Renata recited.

Duffy was looking at his watch. 'Look, I'm sorry. I've got a partners' meeting over at Canning Vale and I'm going to be late. Thank you for bringing this to my attention, and thanks to Trung for putting you in touch with me. I am going to be talking to my lawyers and I will ...'

'Your lawyers?' Renata said. 'Your *lawyers!*'

Duffy reached down next to his chair and pressed a buzzer. Hugo appeared immediately. 'Hugo, please show my guests out.'

Trung automatically reached for the cigarette lighter in his pocket. Fuck! He hadn't even switched it on. He grabbed the unfinished pastries from his plate and held them in front of him, like a shield. Very soon he found himself on the front step, facing the river, with Renata sobbing quietly by his side. There is something off about Duffy, he thought. Decidedly off.

They walked back to Trung's taxi and sat for a few minutes staring at the river.

'I am so furious with that man,' said Renata. 'How could he be so insensitive?'

Trung said nothing.

'What should we do, Trung? I am at a full stop.'

Trung made a sympathetic noise, put the car in gear and took off. A little way down Jutland Parade an unmarked sedan came up on them fast from behind, a flashing blue light clamped to the roof. He pulled over and in the rear-view mirror watched Robin Edwards climb out of the car and approach his open window.

'Trung! You've got a passenger. But the meter's not on. Hello there.'

'This is Renata,' said Trung. 'She has a family connection with Alan Duffy.'

Renata smiled.

'Just need a quick word, Trung,' said Edwards. 'Would you mind stepping across the road to the park with me?' He flashed a winning smile at Renata. 'Won't keep him long, darling.'

A few minutes later Trung was back in the car and Edwards had sped off.

'Who was that nice man?' asked Renata. 'He was very handsome.'

Trung handed Edwards' business card to her. 'He asked me to pass this on.'

Renata examined it carefully. 'Why would I want to contact a detective?'

Trung chuckled. 'Maybe he thought you were very handsome, too.'

They drove back along the river and through the city to Northbridge. Renata was still smiling.

'My *oma* Jutta, had a saying. I am trying to think how it

would come out in English. Something like, "handsome is as handsome does". Is that correct?'

Trung chuckled again. 'I guess we better wait and see.'

CHAPTER 19

'Renata, you have a visitor.' A lilting Irish brogue alerted Renata as she reclined in the day room of Fair Dinkum. She placed a book mark in the detective novel she was reading and ambled into reception.

'Miss Schmidt. Nice to see you again. Thought I'd drop in and speak to you in person.'

Renata was surprised at the sight of a beaming Robin Edwards. She half expected him to be offering flowers and chocolates.

'Yes, Detective Edwards. You're not here to arrest me I hope?' she said with a smile. He really was an attractive man.

'No, but it's not really a social call either. Can we talk, please?'

'*Ja*, sure.'

'Well, it's, it's delicate. How about we go to the Regent and I buy you a coffee?'

Renata liked his manful gritty stubble, his twinkling ocean blue eyes and his faintly musky scent.

The unmarked police Falcon slipped anonymously through Perth's CBD.

'Now, here on the right you can see the Supreme Court Gardens, and at the end of Barrack Street, the Swan River.'

'It's a beautiful city. 'Renata admired the delightful park and its lush foliage with the sleepy river in the background.

She cast a surreptitious glance at the good-looking cop as he took her on the guided tour.

'And here we are. Adelaide Terrace.' The Falcon slid into a vacant bay at the front of the hotel.

Renata found herself admiring the Regent's polished steel and brass double doors and the sleek, modern lines of glass and décor. They took seats at the quieter section of the dining area.

The restaurant was busy with the lunch trade. A smiling, pony-tailed waiter in designer jeans handed them menus. Enticing scents drifted from the kitchen, reminding Renata she'd skipped breakfast. She'd been nervous about meeting her Australian *opa*.

'Just two coffees please, pal.' Robin handed back the menus.

'So, Detective. This is very mysterious.'

'Please, my name's Robin.'

'Yes. Robin. I'm Renata.'

'I know people are often nervous when a cop turns up on their doorstep. But I want to assure you that you're not in trouble. I'd really just like to clear the air...'

'I didn't realise the air was unclear. The sun's shining, the birds are singing' Renata laughed.

'Ok, I'll ask the usual questions. Are you enjoying Australia?'

'Lovely. Thank you,'

'Umm, do you come here often. Bloody hell, did I really say that?' Now Robin laughed.

'Detective Robin Edwards. Yes, I had a good flight from Germany. It's my first time in Australia. Yes, I think it's a nice place. Now, how about you tell me exactly what you are up to? You've already said it's not a social call.'

'It's about Alan Duffy, your grandfather. I'm going out on a limb telling you this. But I feel as if I don't have a choice.'

Renata's stomach lurched. Yes, Alan Duffy was her grandfather not her opa.

'Go on, please.'

'I need to tell you; he is under investigation.'

The smiling waiter appeared again, holding menus. 'Everything ok, folks? Can I get you anything else?'

Robin gave a thumbs up. 'Great. Perfect.' And waited until the waiter was out of earshot.

'I think he would like us to order lunch. Anyway, the first thing I have to tell you, is we're a long way from making any arrests. Police work is about lots of things. It's about joining dots?'

'Dots? I'm not sure I follow.'

'That's just an expression, essentially it means putting various facts and ideas together in order to see the whole picture, or to understand something globally.'

'So, you just have ... what, theories?' Renata wished she had worn something more upmarket than jeans and a black halter top.

'There are many things that are of a concern. The men in your grandfather's employ are career criminals. They have never done an honest day's work in their lives.'

Renata recalled the large, not-so-friendly Hugo, who'd opened her grandfather's door this morning. 'But that's not a crime. Maybe my grandfather ... he's helping them to turn over a new leaf?'

Robin laughed mirthlessly, 'believe me. That's not very likely. These two crims have made several trips overseas while in your grandfather's employ.'

'Why is this important?'

'To tell you the truth, I don't know for sure. But there is something very odd about it. And the countries they go to are not the usual holiday destinations. Congo, Nigeria, Somalia. Nobody, I mean nobody, goes to these places unless it's something off. You know what I mean?'

'So, what do you think? You obviously have an idea.'

'Everything about your grandfather points to one thing?'

Renata knew what was coming.' And that is?'

'Drugs. It simply has to be drugs.'

'But surely if his men are bringing drugs in from these countries you mentioned, they would be searched at the airport?'

'No, they're not bringing them in through the airport. Customs tear everything apart when anyone comes from the countries these clowns go to. No, there's something going on. But what the hell it is, I don't know. There's something else... Your grandfather is involved in a number of businesses that traditionally employ some, shall we say ... colourful characters. Tow trucks, porn shops, even a damn gambling joint. But my gut feeling is that somehow the real action is connected to the funeral business.'

Renata realised all of a sudden everything made sense. Hugo's attitude—acting like a club bouncer—attempting to frisk Trung. Robin Edwards pulling Trung over after they'd left Alan Duffy's house. *Why didn't I see it?*

Renata brushed away a tear. She knew the pain she felt was the pain of loss. The same pain when her *oma* died, but this time it was for her grandfather; the grandfather she'd hoped would be the white knight she'd been looking for since her childhood. There had to be an innocent explanation about the scarf, surely? Her grandmother, she realised, had been blindsided by a dashing young airman. Even though he was old, Duffy was still good-looking, with a sophisticated air about him. *Oh, oma, you drew the short straw in your choice of men.*

She looked at Edwards. 'And your reason for telling me all of this?'

'Very simple. We want you to wear a wire the next time you see ... if you meet with your grandfather again ... if you're willing.'

'What! A *wire*? Is that what I think it is? You want me to ... the word ... the word is ... eavesdrop, *ja*? You want me to eavesdrop on my own grandfather?'

Robin frowned and mumbled, 'Sometimes I hate this bloody job.'

'What was that?'

'I have to tell you, Renata, I know we've just met, and it's a lot to ask. But ... the fact is, grandfather or not ... as I've already explained, we have good reason to suspect what we do, and ... well, we have no-one else who is close to Duffy, so you're the obvious choice. I'm sorry.' Robin glanced at his watch.

Renata grabbed her bag, 'That's it then?'

'Well not necessarily. It's almost one o'clock. Can I buy you lunch? A glass of wine perhaps?'

'Detective Edwards, I do watch crime shows on television. This is where you soften me up. Go for the kill.'

Robin gave a chuckle 'No, nothing like that, honest. But even cops get a lunch break sometimes. And no talk about crime and grandfathers. I promise. Ok?'

As if by magic, the designer jeans and ponytail reappeared, and with a flourish proffered two menus.

'I recommend the barramundi,'

'So, Detective Edwards...'

'Robin.'

Renata laughed. 'So, Detective *Robin Edwards,* why did you become a cop?'

It was Robin's turn to laugh. 'The answer to that one sounds a bit silly even to me.'

'Now I'm intrigued.'

'When I was a kid, I used to watch an Australian TV show called *Homicide.* It featured a lot of lantern-jawed detectives fighting crime in Melbourne's mean streets. The cops all wore fedora hats. They drove cars very fast. It was in black and white of course. I just couldn't get enough of it. And well ... like I said, silly but there I was, I don't know nine or ten I guess, and I knew that's what I wanted to do. Now Miss Renata Schmidt...' Robin daggered a finger and laughed. 'I need to know the truth, the whole truth and nothing but the truth.'

'Yes officer.' Renata grinned and rolled her eyes.

'Tell me all about you.'

'Ok, where to start? Born and raised in the Black Forest, in Germany. My mother and father are just the loveliest people. They grew up in the shadow of the war. But they believed in the new Germany. And they worked so hard but they loved the life, as did I. I had a wonderful childhood until my world fell in and my *opa,* my German grandfather was arrested. Then to further compound things, my grandfather was accused of also murdering the next-door neighbour, a lady living alone when her husband was fighting for Germany on the Russian Front. After that my *oma* eventually told me about her affair with Alan Duffy—if you could call it that.'

'Jesus,' Robin gasped. 'This is bloody awful. It's like a movie.'

'As far as the murder of the neighbour is concerned, my *opa* readily admitted his war crimes, but he strenuously denied being involved in that particular horrible crime. And frankly, I believe him. Meanwhile he rots in jail.'

Robin listened without comment.

'I don't think you agree, Mr Policeman?' Renata glared at Robin.

'Hey. How could I possibly know? I wasn't there. But I have to say, I'm very familiar with people simply not accepting that their loved ones have committed some heinous crime.'

'We'll, what is it you say? We'll put it in the 'too hard basket' for now. This leads me to the next part of the Renata Schmidt story.'

'Go on.'

'As tragic and as awful as it all was, I realised there must be hundreds of such stories. Stories that would remain untold unless someone like me ... well...' Renata leant into the table. 'Someone needs to investigate and put pen to paper.'

'You mean, like write a novel?'

'Well, eventually. Maybe. But, no, I decided to become a journalist. And that's what I've been studying.'

'Two barramundis.' The waiter descended, bearing two plates piled high.

Robin grinned. 'If you've never tasted this Australian delicacy, star reporter Renata Schmidt, you're in for a treat.'

After her second glass of the chilled Margaret River Chardonnay, Renata realised that subterfuge or not, Robin was not only an attractive man, he was a good man.

Renata felt her resolve faltering. She had almost resigned herself to going back to Germany and forgetting all about her

Australian *opa*. But Robin's story was compelling, and if the allegations were true, grandfather or not, justice needed to be served. She hesitated; a forkful of the succulent fish poised in midair. 'My Australian *opa*, he could go to prison?'

She remembered her fear and dismay when the police arrived at the farm to arrest her German grandfather, the man whom she'd adored and looked up to all her young life. And again, when she was older, the horror and sense of betrayal washing over her in waves, when she forced herself to read about her German grandfather's involvement in the Lidice massacre in 1942. The Lidice reprisal, authorised by a vengeful *Führer* on hearing about the assassination of Reich Protector Reinhard Heydrich, was swift. And it was the SS who did the killing. *Opa* was a *hauptman* in the SS. Not a humble private who could claim he was only following orders, but a captain, a card-carrying, fanatical Nazi. The same opa who played with her, and bought her presents. Over and over, she read the court transcript: *Innocent men women and children, slaughtered.* And her utter disbelief that her *opa*, the grandfather she adored, was a mass murderer.

Robin put down his knife and fork. 'The fish is good, isn't it?'

'Just tell me.'

'I thought the grandfather thing was off limits? If I'm right ... and Duffy's heading a drug operation ... if we can prove... Yes, he's going to jail.'

'He'd probably die there, wouldn't he?'

Robin shrugged, 'Yep, I reckon so. But It's not your problem. Move on. Go back to Germany, or continue your holiday. You don't have to be involved.'

Renata's gaze locked onto those deep blue eyes. 'I don't see how I can help you, Detective Edwards—'

'Call me Robin, please. And I understand—he is your grandfather, even if you've just met him.'

Renata gave him a bitter smile. 'You don't understand. My grandfather—Mr Duffy, the man who I think is my biological grandfather—he doesn't acknowledge our relationship and he doesn't want to see me again. He made that very clear at our meeting today.'

CHAPTER 20

Trung sat out on his fifth-floor balcony and let the cool evening breeze play across his face. He could see the Swan River meandering east. His beer was cold and the crisps he was eating helped soak it up. To the west was the city. High rise office blocks had risen up since his family first moved to this country. He wasn't convinced they were permanent. They seemed at odds with the desert and the endless ocean. To the north he could see miles and miles of suburbs. Somewhere up there in Kalamunda his brother, Bao, was splashing in his pool after a day of serving up noodles and rice. To the east were the hills, dark shapes in the gloom. Above him, a new moon and some stars.

Earlier that afternoon the radio operator had relayed an urgent message: 'Call Mr Duffy ASAP'. When Trung phoned, Duffy was filled with remorse. He wanted to meet with Renata again, to apologise for his behaviour the previous day. He should not have denied her claim. Could Trung pass on that message as a matter of urgency?

Trung had dropped in a note on his way past Fair Dinkum later in the afternoon. It was up to her. He wasn't sure she would give Duffy a second chance. As for Trung, he had decided to throw in his lot with the man. It was quite likely the cops had something on him, and Robin Edwards would be investigating. But the funeral business, once he had got his head around it, sounded like good old-fashioned money-making behaviour—and he was following the same instinct that had made so many of his countrymen wealthy.

In December he would be heading for Vietnam. Jack Sprague had reluctantly granted him three months leave, on the proviso that he must return after that time and claim his cab. Sprague had warned Trung of the dangers of solo travel in Asia.

'But Jack,' Trung said, 'I am Asian!'

Sprague had merely shaken his head. 'Your funeral, mate.'

What the fuck? Did Sprague know about Satinwood? Then he realised that it was an expression, one of those stupid Australian expressions which meant *you are on your own*, something he had known since birth. He walked back to the fridge to claim another beer. I will miss this place, he thought. But in the pit of his stomach, he felt an excitement to be breaking away, carving a new path. And if there was any truth in Sprague's warning to be careful, he had a powerful ally back home, DS Robin Edwards.

In the park, with Renata waiting in the car, he had told Edwards of his failure to activate the wire. Also, how close he'd come to being caught out. Edwards asked him about the meeting. Had Duffy said anything incriminating? 'Not really,' Trung told him. Renata had shown him the photo with its message, proof of the connection between herself and Duffy. Duffy had denied any association.

'Most interesting, Trung,' said Robin.

'One more thing,' said Trung. 'He wants me to go to Vietnam to smooth the way for his funeral business over there. Thinks I'll be able to help because I'm a native.'

Robin thrust an envelope at Trung and clapped him on the

shoulder. 'Good man,' he said. 'This is a down payment. You need to come into my office to pick up the rest. That's big news, Trung. Vietnam!'

Now, with time to reflect, watching the deepening night from his balcony, Trung agreed. It was big news. Should he tell his mate, Duncan, who treated his cab like a royal carriage, polishing it every weekend, adding little knick knacks to the dashboard? No, Duncan wouldn't understand. But Trung would visit Lily tomorrow. He would tell her about his forthcoming trip. She would tease him and then ask him to bring back duty free perfume. No problem.

CHAPTER 21

A week later Renata was sitting under an umbrella outside Fair Dinkum when the maroon Rolls pulled up and Duffy's driver stepped out and walked around the car to open the back passenger door. Tricia, who was from Ireland, and Gerry, from Canada, were both agog. Renata, waved from the back seat, keeping her hand vertical and rotating it slightly the way Queen Elizabeth did.

At Duffy's she was shown to the conservatory again. This time it was set up for a full meal, the silverware gleaming, and crisp, white napkins standing up like sentries. She tried to forget the wire she was wearing. Duffy entered, dressed in a navy business suit, white shirt, and cravat.

Renata had a twinge of guilt knowing every word would be recorded.

'Renata,' he said. 'I'm so glad we could work this out. And I'm sorry I doubted you.'

'You are forgiven, *Opa*.'

Duffy recoiled, then recovered. 'That's German, is it? For grandfather?'

'*Ja*, it is a term of affection,' said Renata coldly. She hadn't forgiven and she hadn't forgotten.

'I suppose I'll get used to it,' was all Duffy managed to say. 'Shall we have some lunch? Just a simple meal. I always think breaking bread together is the best way to heal hurts and misunderstandings.'

Renata imagined posing for a photo of her and her newly discovered, opa. He would be smiling his Air Force smile and she would not smile at all. She would be serious, like the women in classical paintings. 'Ok,' she said.

They limped through the lunch. Duffy exhibited little curiosity for Renata or her German family or her travels. He talked about his return to Australia, his family business, and the lectures he gave to school children at the museum.

'Do you tell them about your lucky escape? About the *frau* who gave you shelter?'

Duffy gave her a look. 'More salad?' he asked.

After lunch Duffy insisted on giving Renata a tour. There was a library which reached up to a mezzanine level, with a tiny walkway to allow access to the rare volumes on the upper shelves. There was a spa bath on an upstairs deck with a view of the river. There was a billiard room. Back downstairs there was the yard with its pool full of carp, sculptures, a studio, and a garage containing a Morgan Plus 4 and a couple of vintage motorcycles.

'You must have made a lot of *geld* from the funeral business, *Opa*,' said Renata.

Duffy looked puzzled.

'*Geld*—money! You learned no German while you were our guest?'

'Oh! No. Or if I did, I've forgotten it. But perhaps if we keep meeting, I can pick some up.'

Duffy saw her off and once again she found herself luxuriating in the white leather upholstery at the back of the Rolls. The driver said nothing, other than his name was Hugo and if she wanted anything she just had to say. His car phone rang.

'Yep,' he said. 'It's Joey's job. No, not Northbridge. Northcliffe. We're keeping him out of the limelight, know what I mean? Yeah, miles away. It's way down south, through Pemberton. Yeah, that's right. The golf club. *Ciao.*'

Hugo hung up. 'You want some music?'

'Yes please,' said Renata. 'Something classical would be nice.'

For the rest of the trip, she enjoyed a Beethoven symphony. There was something to be said for luxury. When she reached Fair Dinkum, she went straight to the phone in reception and called Robin Edwards.

Later that day she met DS Edwards in the front bar of the Regent. He ordered white wine.

'That's from the Hunter Valley, over east,' he said. 'How do you like it?'

'It's ok,' said Renata. 'I prefer something a little sweeter, like *Liebfraumilch.*'

'Loved lady's milk?'

'You speak German!'

'*Ein bischen,*' Robin said in an exaggerated German accent.

'I think it refers to the Virgin Mary.'

Edwards lapsed into silence. The bar was busy, packed with businessmen and lawyers. 'So,' he said finally. 'You wanted to talk about Mr Duffy.'

'He is not a very nice man, my grandfather,' said Renata.

'I thought you said he'd disowned you. Why do you think he changed his mind?'

'Guilt?' said Renata. 'I commented that he must have made a lot of *geld,* meaning money. Maybe it triggered something.

The two words sound the same.

Edwards looked at her appraisingly.

She had finished her wine. With a slight movement of his head, he signalled his intention and walked towards the lifts. She watched his back, waited a few minutes, and followed. In the lift she turned to him and kissed him passionately on the mouth.

'You've booked a room?' she asked.

'Room 702,' Edwards said.

'I guess you've got it all worked out,' she said. 'We will be looking out towards Kings Park and the river, yes?'

Edwards held his breath.

'I will cross to the window and watch the peak hour traffic crawling across the Narrows Bridge. You will stand behind me, gently easing my blouse out of my skirt. Without touching me, you will undo the buttons and gently untape the wire. You will fold it away and lock it in your briefcase. How does it sound so far?'

'Amazing,' Edwards whispered.

'Then you imagine that I will turn around and face you, remove my hair clip and shake my hair loose from my ponytail. Slowly, you imagine, I will unclip my bra and drop my skirt. And that's when you will snuff the lights and move across the darkened room. Is that the narrative?'

The way she said it sounded like *narrativ*. 'Are you a poet?' he asked.

The lift stopped on level seven. Renata reached across to the buttons and pressed G. 'Not a poet. An avid reader,' she said.

'Fiction?' he asked. 'You prefer fiction?'

'I prefer tenderness,' she said. She kissed him on the cheek, made her way out to Adelaide Terrace and hailed a cab.

PART TWO

CHAPTER 1

Hanoi, Vietnam, November, 1998

'I'll be back before you know it.'

Gunther Baumann kissed his German wife of forty years goodbye. Bertha was tearful as always. She felt isolated when he wasn't around. He thought to himself, as he always did, *we've been here twenty years, and still she knows no Vietnamese.* It was some comfort that the November nights were cooling off and Bertha could sleep.

Gunther lowered himself arthritically into his Mercedes 500 SL coupe, grabbing the door handles as he squeezed into the driver's seat. At 77 years he knew he should be driving a sedate sedan that was easier for his aged bones to exit and enter. But painful or not, Gunther loved his car. Even in Hanoi, a city of some four million people, the car was a head-turner: as it should be. His export business had brought him great wealth and he enjoyed his reputation as the powerful businessman with the black Mercedes.

He sped into the suicidal mess that was the Hanoi Road system. He'd left his gated community—King Palace at *Thuong Dinh*—early, hoping to avoid the worst of the traffic and looking forward as always to the five-hour drive to Sapa, high in the mountains. Sapa, a village so high the clouds flowed through the streets like the tear gas Gunther remembered unleashing in Warsaw in 1939.

Officially, the *Wehrmacht* never used tear gas but Gunther new differently. Gunther hadn't enjoyed the war, but he'd survived it. He'd avoided the Russian front. Captured in Africa, he'd spent time in a British prison camp where he had learned to speak English.

Gunther's first stop was an orphanage in old Hanoi. The address was Train Street, a street where trains tore through at breakneck speed only inches away from the dwellings lining both sides of the track. The Baumanns were generous donors to a variety of good causes. Gunther felt obliged to visit the SOS Orphanage and make sure his donations were being correctly utilized, not disappearing into the coffers of one of the many triads. He enjoyed seeing the children. They were clean, bright, inquisitive, and utterly charming. The staff treated him like visiting royalty. Coffee and mung bean pastries were always on offer.

At the end of his inspection, Cam, the supervisor, walked Gunther to his car.

'Oh, Herr Baumann. Just look at Duc.'

Gunther had to smile at the sight of ten-year-old Duc wiping down the Mercedes with a chamois.

'What a good boy you are. Come here, Duc.'

Gunther removed a 500 dong note from his wallet.

'Excellent work, Duc. When you are a bit older, I may have a job for you.'

The boy bowed, running off with the money clutched firmly in his fist.

Inevitably, the Mercedes ran into the midmorning chaos of Hanoi traffic. Noisy two-stroke motorbikes carried families of up to five people. There were pigs on the road and some crowing roosters. Three-wheeler cyclos, Vietnam's answer to the rickshaw, weaved in and out of the chaos. If you were a pedestrian the best way to cross the road was to close your eyes and walk blindly out into the ocean of traffic. He had never tried it, but it seemed to work.

Sapa always had the same affect on Gunther. The beautiful apricot, cherry and plum flowers, the spectacular mountains, even the hilltribe people in their colourful costumes selling handicrafts and trinkets managed to lift his spirits. The Mercedes slid into a vacant space in Tran Quy Cap Street, in front of the Legend Hotel. A delightful hill tribe urchin immediately pounced, before he had the chance to open his door. The little girl thrust a silver bracelet at him.

'How much?' he enquired in Vietnamese.

After some haggling a 10,000 Dong note changed hands. He was sure Bertha would like it. Gunther locked the car before laboriously climbing the stairs to the apartment above.

Standing on the landing, he reached into his jacket, pulling the Russian 9mm Makarov pistol from its holster. He checked the load. Old habits died hard. Gunther preferred the German Luger but in Vietnam there wasn't a lot of choice.

He knocked on the rattan door. 'Open up, Dung, Hien.'

The door jerked open.

The room was spacious with polished parquetry flooring; a double bed, a tatty stained beige divan and an old black and white TV on a rickety card table. Dung and Hien had been watching a football match. Behind them, the view of the mountains from the picture window was truly magnificent.

Tied to a red plastic chair next to the divan sat a quivering

Vietnamese woman, gagged. Tears ran in rivulets down her face. Gunther screwed up his nose at the pungent ammonia smell of stale urine. The woman had wet herself.

'Well, Cai, you have been a naughty girl, haven't you?'

'Mr Baumann, she has assured me she will never do it again. And, well, we believe her.'

'Not your decision, Dung.'

Gunther Baumann screwed the silencer on to the Makarov.

CHAPTER 2

November 1998

When the Major Crime Squad met to confer on a case, they occupied an all-purpose briefing room on the top floor. This morning Robin Edwards was in charge, and he was nervous. Maybe it was inexperience—he was the youngest detective in the squad—or maybe it was the flimsiness of his evidence. Whatever it was, he brushed it off as he took the stairs to the meeting. He was convinced that business man, Alan Duffy, was at the centre of something very unwholesome and he intended to uncover it. Weeks had passed since Renata had agreed to wear a wire. He hadn't been lucky with that so far, or with Trung, and Robin was desperate for more information.

He had planned his arrival early, allowing time to prepare the white board. Armed with markers, magnets, and the evidence he'd assembled thus far, he let himself into the airless room, closed the door and began. In the centre of the board he put a recent picture of Duffy, Underneath he wrote the name of the company in capitals and a note, *Established 1921.*

From the centre he drew a line and placed a picture of Trung, taken from his Taxi Licence file. Next to the picture he wrote, *victim of unprovoked assault connected with Satinwood private transfer vehicle, later reported stolen.* At the end of another line he wrote, *fines accumulated by Satinwood vehicles over the past two years*. At the end of another line, he stuck the picture he had taken of Hugo's muscle car, landscaped so that it included a scowling Hugo in the background, and wrote his details next to the photo. Other items grouped around the centre included the disputed insurance claim for the missing vehicle, and also a list of other recent unsolved crimes cross referenced in date order with missing persons reports.

The first arrival was Jack Dutton, a long-serving member of the MCS and veteran of some memorable encounters with the criminal underworld. He had been wounded in a shootout five years ago and walked with a slight limp, which he regarded as a badge of honour. Next came Brendan O'Brien. Brendan, not much older than Robin, was an ex-football player. Tall and athletic, he was known for his aggressive approach to every aspect of police work. This sometimes got him into hot water with the Internal Affairs people, especially when the media splashed slogans such as, VIOLENT END TO ARMED ROBBERY all over the front page. Brendan had shot two bank robbers, killing one and maiming the other for life. Brendan would have been at home in the American wild west, Robin thought. Last to arrive was Gillian Mortlock, the first woman to be recruited by Major Crime. Gillian had a keen intellect and could be relied on to think of angles nobody else did.

'Thanks for coming,' Robin began. 'This won't be long meeting. I'm addressing several quite distinct events over the last six months and keeping one man, Alan Duffy, in focus at the same time. The context is the rise in high-grade heroin finding its way onto the streets. The connections between this and Duffy are tenuous, but I'm flagging them as significant and worth watching.'

Robin remembered that he was one of the new wave of graduate recruits to the force and as such must watch his language and phrasing. It was too easy for veterans like Jack Dutton to dismiss his concerns as 'academic' and therefore not able to be actioned. In any case, they were waiting for the arrival of the big chief, Vincent Lukashenko. Only he could decide how the unit's resources were to be deployed.

'So, while we're waiting for Vince—he said he'd be delayed— let me spell it out. Duffy is the head of Satinwood Funerals, a family company established in the 1920s. He piloted a Lancaster bomber in the Second World War, earned a DSO, and returned to civilian life to take over the business from his father. He became very rich. When I investigated further, I realised the businesses he was involved in were classic money laundering ventures. That doesn't mean they're not legit, but you can draw your own conclusions. My interest in him began when I met Trung Nguyen, a taxi driver of Vietnamese extraction.'

There was a murmur in the room. Concern about gangs of Vietnamese youths terrorising some newer suburbs in the east of the city had become an issue of late. Edwards ignored it and continued. He talked the group through the links he'd made on the whiteboard and then called for questions or comments.

'Niall Norman's a cheap hood who'll work for anyone,' Gillian Mortlock said. 'He used to work as a bouncer until he king hit a queue jumper one night. The poor kid was dead before he hit the footpath. He spent a little time inside for that but was out on parole in less than a year. Had a good lawyer.'

Jack Dutton chipped in. 'The Duffy guy was a bomber pilot. Bit of a test of character, wouldn't you say Robin, to make it through a world war in one of those things?'

Edwards took this as a generational challenge. He had nothing against war heroes but didn't believe they were all angels either.

'What's the fine print, the stuff you took from the wire?' asked Brendan O'Brien.

Edwards had written down the fragments Renata had picked up from Hugo's carphone conversation, essentially two words: 'Northcliffe' and 'golf club'. He was about to answer when Vincent Lukashenko entered the room. Lukashenko with his $1000 Italian suit and business-like manner immediately took control.

'Morning, chief,' said Edwards. 'We're almost there.'

'Forget all that,' said Lukashenko testily. 'I've been talking to the Commissioner, who's been talking to the Premier, who's been reading the *West Australian*. There's a gathering storm concerning the amount of child pornography that's coming in via the internet. More and more people have access to the world wide web through personal computers and it's getting out of control. I'm putting together a task force, headed by you, Gillian. You comfortable with that? Anything that's speculative will have to go on the back burner.' He pointed towards the white board, not exactly dismissing Robin's work but it was clear he wasn't encouraging it either.

Robin might normally have felt devastated at being minimised in this way but during his presentation he had become aware of the flimsiness of some of his evidence and the tenuous nature of the links he had drawn. In a way it was a relief. He rubbed the whiteboard clean. 'Over to you, chief,' he said red-faced, and sat down.

CHAPTER 3

Trung pulled up outside the cluster of factory units in Carbon Court, Osborne Park. He parked the decommissioned cab he had borrowed from Jack, found the numbered door he was looking for and rang the buzzer, unsure if the ancient apparatus worked.

He peered through the dirty, tinted glass door, etched with the words 'Allstar Entertainment', and saw an office with furniture scattered haphazardly about. There was no one in sight. A black Mercedes van rested against a shuttered roll-a-door. The van looked eerily familiar.

The door jerked open. 'Well, if it isn't my favourite slope,' said Hugo. 'Come in. The boss is here.'

There was no warmth in his greeting. Trung ignored the insult and stepped past him and a plywood room divider to find Duffy reclining on a staid but serviceable old swivel chair, his long legs stretched out in front of him and coffee in hand. The garage was dimly lit. Dirty skylights allowed the morning rays to claw their way in, illuminating a collection of cars and... Trung stared. Steel racks lining two walls were stacked with plain, serviceable steel coffins. One coffin, partially dismantled, rested on a low wooden work bench. Trung suppressed a shiver. What if they knew about him and the cop? Maybe one of the coffins was meant for him.

'Ah Trung. My little mate!' Duffy grimaced as he climbed to his feet. He was dressed in overalls and had skipped his morning shave. 'Thanks for coming. I want to show you the Satinwood special body transporter.'

'Body transporter?'

'Coffin, Trung. It's a bloody coffin. Now, look here. As you can see, these locks mean business. The Aussie government insists they be tamperproof. Anyway, I want you to accompany these little beauties to Vietnam where you will see a Mr Baumann. Baumann is going to be organizing the bodies for transport.'

'How many coffins, Alan?'

'I'm sending ten over with you.'

Trung was puzzled. 'Really? I wouldn't have thought there would be that many Australians dying in Vietnam, Alan.'

Duffy displayed a flash of annoyance. 'Trung, let me worry about that. As I said before it's not only Aussies, but Americans, British, whatever. Also, as it happens, Baumann has told me there are Vietnamese who live in Vietnam but have relatives here, in Australia. Wealthy relatives. And they want them to be buried here. Happy now?'

Trung was puzzled. Families in Vietnam wanted their deceased buried there. There were rituals to observe. The family would create an altar, filled with offerings and a portrait of the deceased. The loved ones might be kept at home for as long as a month. They sure as hell didn't want to send them to Australia.

'What I need from you, Trung, is to supervise the first shipments.'

'There are bodies now ... really?'

'Trung, for Christ's sake! Yes, there are bodies. I want you to make sure everything is right with the Vietnamese authorities. You must supervise the loading of the locked coffins onto the aircraft. Baumann knows his stuff, but I just need to make sure. I want someone there I can trust. I can trust you. Can't I Trung?'

'Of course, Alan.' Trung's mind was whirling.

'Good. Now the next thing you must do is find a metal fabricator in Hanoi to make these coffins strictly to my specifications. It's too damned expensive to make them here.'

'Sure thing. I can do that.'

'You have your passport?'

'You bet.'

'Good man. You leave in next week. Monday morning, Singapore Airlines. You'll be staying at the Sofitel Metropole in Hanoi. Nice hotel, sport.'

The Queens Tavern in Highgate was buzzing. Trung sat looking out on busy Beaufort Street. Although it was late November, Christmas had come early to the Queens. Silver tinsel glittered brightly from a plastic tree.

This wasn't the sort of place he was comfortable in. Too many beautiful people. Not an Asian in sight. He'd paid an eyewatering amount for his pint, and had to tell himself he could afford it. He had money from Duffy and money from Edwards. Lily had already been the recipient of some of his newfound wealth.

Robin Edwards' unmarked police Commodore glided into a spot at the front of Sienna's. Trung had to smile. Robin wore blue jeans and a T-shirt with a ridiculous Bugs Bunny emblem on it. Trying hard not to look like a cop, Trung thought.

'Good to see you,' Robin said, his hand out.

He climbed on to the bench seat and glanced at his watch. 'Hope you don't mind, but I've invited some company.'

Trung was surprised to see Renata waving as she crossed the road. She smiled warmly at Trung, gave Robin a kiss. The detective climbed to his feet.

'How about we go inside? Away from prying eyes.'

Trung and Renata pushed through the crowd at the bar and made their way to the dimly lit interior. The Queens was built in the 1880s and was one of the first pubs in Perth to be transformed into a hipster playground. Old jarrah floorboards, with even older marble bars, half-finished brickwork and partially rendered walls were considered the height of chic. Trung and Renata sat on bentwood chairs placed before a small oak table, while Robin grabbed some beers.

'Cheers.' They clinked their pint glasses.

'I hope you don't mind, Trung, but I've told Renata what's going on.' He smiled and reached for her hand. Renata took a pull of her beer. it made sense. Robin was a dynamo and handsome too. Renata was beautiful. He wished them luck, sort of.

'So,' said Renata. 'I have found out that my *opa* is not the wonderful hero-man my *oma* said he was. I have agreed to help Robin. Duffy seems to want to stay in touch. A part of me feels bad. But if he's really a crook then ... you know...?'

Trung told Robin about the coffins and his pending trip to Vietnam.

'Run it past me again Trung. You say there's no way Vietnamese people would agree for their loved ones to be buried in Perth?'

CHAPTER 3

Trung nodded.

'Well, girls and boys. The question is, just what is the old bastard up to? And Trung, watch yourself over there. I won't be able to help you... you're my sort of *unofficial informant*. I don't think you'll have a problem, but if you do need to talk, don't call me from your room. Phone from the hotel lobby.'

The detective seemed to be in his element. But his relationship with Renata troubled Trung. Were cops allowed to fuck their witnesses? What if they had a falling out? And how reliable was Renata, after all? If she changed her mind and decided that her grandfather was really a fine old gentleman, she might spill the mung beans. He needed to go home and prepare for his journey. He had said goodbye to Lily, to Jack Sprague and to his mate, Duncan. He had told his brother he was taking a holiday in Bali. No need to worry him with any more information. Trung shook hands formally with Edwards and Renata and left. The last he saw of them they had their heads together. He was pretty sure the subject wasn't police business

CHAPTER 4

Late November 1998

Sandy felt the hot wind as he emerged from the terminal building and into the Perth morning. The last remnants of his European holiday, soon evaporated in the rush and bustle of the place, passengers pushing their baggage trolleys, families reuniting, a billboard flogging American Express Cards. He'd extended his holiday with a scenic cruise down the Rhine. But he remained haunted by the memories. Sandy joined the taxi queue, remembering Trung and wondering what it would have taken to book his ride ahead of time. Instead, he scored a sullen Greek man who seemed to consider lifting Sandy's bag into the boot of his Holden the ultimate indignity.

'Maylands thanks, mate. Swan Bank Road.'

The brief respite in the back seat gave Sandy a chance to think ahead. First, he would have a nap. Then a bath. Then he would walk up to the golf club and order fish and chips, one of the positive things about returning home. The fish would be snapper—beautiful, marbled flesh, grilled the way he liked it— not something bred in a pond, tasting of mud and something indefinable. Maybe German sewage, he thought. This was unfair. He had eaten well while he was away, He smiled to himself. Duffy had been such an airman too. In his briefcase were the photocopies of the article that Horst had shown him of Duffy's old football scarf. It had been put to terrible use.

They reached his town house, and on an impulse, Sandy tipped the sullen Greek ten dollars. The driver smiled, which made Sandy smile back at him. He thanked him for carrying his bag to the front door and let himself in with a sigh. It was good to be home.

In the morning he woke late and thought about the day ahead. Choir practice was on today. Was he up for it? He pulled out the card Trung had given him, dialed the number, and reached Jack Sprague. Trung was in Vietnam for a few weeks. Maybe a month. Could he book Sandy a different cab? Sandy agreed.

Later that day he was driven out to Guildford by a perfect gentleman who wasn't Trung. Pity. He wanted to tell the little bugger about his travels. At choir he was welcomed warmly, but without curiosity. Taking time off to go caravanning or on holidays to Asia was the norm in a group made up of seniors.

After the rehearsal he invited Liv to join him in the corner tea shop, Liv was always good for a chat. After the usual preliminaries about his trip and the weather, she got right down to it.

'Did you get to see my friend in Baden-Baden?'

'I'm afraid not,' Sandy smiled. 'But I certainly managed to recover a few memories under my own steam. I am grateful, Liv, but can you imagine me unburdening myself to a stranger in a dark room in a foreign city?'

'What makes you think her room would be dark?' she asked.

'Ok,' said Sandy, 'my memories are dark.'

Liv laughed. He really liked the way this was going. Maybe he had recovered more than memories while he was away. He felt a stirring in his blood that he hadn't felt for a long time. Liv's laughter picked him up, the way Maisie's laughter once worked on him. He topped up Liv's tea and leant across the table.

'Liv, would you like to come out for a meal with me one night?' Sandy wondered if this could possibly be the start of a final fling. *Intimacy and old age? Could it work?*

The next night Sandy found himself at the golf club again, earnestly recommending the snapper to Liv. She was wearing large gold hoops in her ears and what Sandy would have described as a peasant blouse, which showed off her freckled cleavage to advantage. The looks he got from the other wives, who had known Maisie, were priceless. They walked up to the counter and made their choices.

'I'll have my fish grilled,' said Liv.

'Battered for me,' said Sandy. 'And extra chips.'

'You should watch your cholesterol, mate,' said Liv. She was smiling, but also serious. Sandy shrugged.

While they were waiting for their prawn cocktails, Liv filled Sandy in on what the choir had been up to and the news from the community garden she belonged to. 'But you're not interested in all that. Tell me what you discovered in the Black Forest!'

Sandy launched into the whole story: training in Canada and England, the posting to Lincolnshire, the raid on Stuttgart and the deadly strike by the night fighter. He described his blind instinct to survive, the miracle of escaping the burning plane, his parachute opening in a flak-filled sky, and the eerie quiet of the forest he'd landed in.

'There was a certain point beyond which everything was still a blank. But this archaeologist chap, Jules Whitechurch, was very helpful. Once he realised I wasn't interested in the wreck, he set me up so I could walk in the surrounding forest and try to join the dots, after all these years.'

'And did it all start coming back?' asked Liv.

'Not exactly. The first day I reached a point where I just felt like sitting down, and fell asleep. I woke up worried that I'd run out of light. It's a creepy place. But then the next day I had a car and a driver—a smart young woman—and we managed to pick up the trail and follow it all the way to the farmhouse where I remember trying to catch up with Duffy.

Sandy ordered some more wine. Liv seemed tuned to every word he said. He told her about his picnic in the woods, the farm gate with the name Freiderjes on it, the sudden flare of recognition, like a light in a darkened room. And even as he said it, in the comfortable dining room in Maylands' answer to a country club, the rest of the story began to unspool in his mind—a truck and a man called Otto. A hiding place made from a packing crate.

'It's coming to me as I talk, Liv!' said Sandy. 'It's like you've lifted the curtains for me.'

'So, it wasn't the therapist's curtains you imagined darkening the room!' said Liv. 'They were curtains of your own making. Isn't the human brain amazing.'

Sandy didn't stop talking until he'd spilled the whole story: the long wait at the Swiss border while the guards examined the load; his fear that he would sneeze or fart or worse. There were papers to stamp and a long wait until the border gate was finally raised and they were able to drive to Bern and freedom.

'That's amazing, Sandy.'

Sandy looked across the table at Liv. How old was she? Sixty, perhaps sixty-five Too young for him, that was for sure.

But there was no harm in looking, surely. Her breasts filled his eyes. He longed to reach out and fondle them, as he had once fondled Maisie's.

'Where was I?' Sandy realised that the wine, combined with jet lag, was catching up with him. He closed his eyes and tried to remember the next part; presenting himself to the Swiss authorities, and his fear that because they spoke German, they might turn him in. It didn't matter. He had it all in his file at home; the precious photo copies and newspaper clipping, and all his notes he'd painstakingly jotted as snatches of memory returned. He wanted to nail Duffy to the wall for his part in the whole thing. And he wanted to cherish his own memories, the wonderful moment when he set foot once more on Australian soil.

Liv put her hand gently on his arm. 'Sandy, you must be tired. How about I walk you home?'

'Thanks, Liv. I do so much enjoy your company. I don't know if it's the wine, or maybe I'm just a silly old man, but there is something else I want to talk about.

Somehow, he managed to pay the bill and walk unsteadily out the door, one hand on Liv's shoulder for balance. They strolled up the path past the brickworks. Across the road was the golf course and beyond that the river. And they talked.

'You live in a lovely part of the world,' said Liv. They had reached his front gate. 'Will you be ok from here? And yes, I enjoy your company. Let's just see where it all goes.' She smiled and grasped his hand. 'Goodnight, Sandy.'

***

CHAPTER 4

He slept for almost twelve hours, a dreamless dive into oblivion broken only by the need to empty his bladder sometime in the middle of the night. In the morning, he stepped outside to fetch the paper and noticed a handwritten note tucked under his mat. It was from Liv.

Dear Sandy,

Thank you for dinner at your golf club. I really enjoyed it. Even though you didn't follow up on my therapist friend in Baden-Baden, I still believe you should release that incredible story of yours. Set it free! And yourself, of course. Here is the number of a man who works as a ghost writer. You could produce a memoir under your own name and reach a wider audience than just me—much as I appreciate your confidences. His name is Robert Petale, and he is the real thing.

Love, Liv.

At the bottom of the page was a phone number. Sandy stuck the note on the fridge with a magnet and put on the kettle. Before anything he needed to have breakfast and read *The West*. It was a terrible rag, but it did have a TV guide.

CHAPTER 5

Friday the 4th of December 1998

'I think there must be a mistake?'

'No sir, I can assure you there is no mistake.'

Trung stared, mouth agape at the beautiful, sarong-clad Singapore Airlines service agent. She smiled, handing him back his passport and boarding pass.

'Well, fuck me,' he muttered on his way to the boarding lounge. 'I'm in the pointy end.'

Trung's mind was filled with a myriad of confused thoughts. How could a boy who arrived on a boat, hungry and thirsty, filth in every pore of his body, become an international businessman rubbing shoulders with the elite? He gazed down at his second-best pair of Kmart jeans and worn Adidas track shoes and wished now he'd spent some of his newfound wealth on better gear.

Trung took his seat and accepted the flute of French champagne, still coming to terms with his changed circumstances. He sipped on the chilled wine, half his attention on the safety drill, and the rest bound up in worry as his natural caution began to filter through. *Duffy puts me into an upmarket hotel in Hanoi, pays for business class and only wants me to perform a few simple transactions any dimwit could do. What does he really want?* At their last meeting even the thuggish Hugo and the monosyllabic

Grantley appeared to be showing some grudging respect. Trung felt he'd moved a little up the corporate ladder, but he remained suspicious. Duffy had handed him an American Express travel card and two thousand US dollars, smiling as he patted him on the back. 'Enjoy yourself, son,' were his parting words. 'Just make sure everything goes to plan.'

A two-hour stopover at Changi Airport offered Trung a window for guilt-free enjoyment. There he treated himself to a polo shirt, a pair of ridiculously priced Hugo Boss cargo pants and a pair of Florsheim casual shoes. Handing over his travel card with all the aplomb of a Saudi oil prince, he had a moment of panic as he worked out the conversion rate of Singapore dollars to Aussie currency. Changi Airport wasn't for bargain hunters. It was time to board.

Wearing his new clothes and dining on the best food he'd ever had in his life helped to dispel any lingering fears. Trung lazed back in the wide, soft seat watching *The Truman Show*. For most of the journey to Hanoi the story kept him diverted. It was funny, really. The guy's entire life was just a TV show, manufactured for entertainment. As the final credits rolled off the screen the parallels between Trung and Jim Carey's character hit home. Maybe what I'm doing isn't real, he thought. The Carey character decided to escape once he found out the truth. Was he, Trung, fooling himself? Reinforcing his doubt was the Vietnamese newspaper he picked up while the plane was docking. Two drug traffickers had been executed by firing squad in Hoa Lo Prison. Trung collected his solitary suitcase from the carousel.

'Business or pleasure?' The bored customs official repeated himself. 'Business or pleasure sir?'

'Oh! Ah, business, I guess.'

Trung followed the throng into the arrival's hall. Standing at the front of a group of mainly Vietnamese limo and taxi drivers was an older European man with a cardboard sign with Trung's name on it. Trung approached him. 'Hi, I'm Trung,' he said.

The man greeted him with a warm smile 'Trung eh? My name is Gunther. Gunther Baumann. I will drive you to your hotel.'

Trung was impressed. His fears subsided. Gunther prattled on in accented English, complaining about Hanoi traffic, pickpockets and how dangerous it was to cross the street.

'But I guess you know all about this Trung. You're from Hanoi, originally?'

Trung told Gunther a little of his history. He was glad he'd changed into his new clothes in Singapore. Gunther's next question confirmed that nice clobber created an impression.

'So, you and *Herr* Duffy, you are business partners. Yes?'

'No, Gunther, not really,' Trung admitted. 'I work for Mr Duffy.'

Trung's feeling of self-worth continued its upward spiral as he climbed into Gunther's Mercedes, and they honked their way to the Sofitel with the top down.

'I'll leave you to check in. How about we catch up tomorrow, yes? I can show you what's going on. I imagine you'll want an early night.'

It was a nice feeling to be treated so respectfully. The hotel looked vaguely Parisian with its wrap around awnings, cane tables, white tablecloths, and a blackboard menu. Trung knew about the French connection with Vietnam. His father could recite the country's colonial history on cue.

He threw himself onto the king size bed, grinning from ear to ear. The bedspread was pure white with a gold bolster. Not that Trung knew what a bolster was for. The view of old Hanoi from the picture window was exactly as he remembered from years gone by. Only the fashion and cars were different. Now there were less bicycles and more advertising. He checked out the bar fridge and helped himself to a can of 333 beer. Sometime later he was awakened by a gentle knock on the door. He padded to the door, his feet sinking into the plush carpet.

'Trung?'

She was Vietnamese and about eighteen. Black mini skirt, high heels and a fitted long sleeve white T shirt with a cartoon picture of a geisha splashed across the front.

'My name's Hue. May I come in?'

'I'm sorry. Who are you? I'm not sure...'

Hue giggled.

'Mr Baumann sent me. He wants you to have a nice time ... with me. Is that ok?'

'I see. Yes, that is very much ok.'

What the fuck, thought Trung. Hue means Lily in Vietnamese. She flung her arms around him. 'How about a beer?' he asked.

Trung grabbed two Heinekens from the bar fridge and popped the tops. Hue was truly beautiful. Slim, pert, and he suspected, good at what she did. He lay back on the dishevelled bed. The bathroom door was open. He could make out the steamy outline of Hue in the shower. She smiled as she strolled into the bedroom, drying her hair. He noticed the tell-tale sign of track marks on her arm. She sat on the bed. Trung held her hand and ran his finger along the row of tiny scars. She snatched her hand away.

CHAPTER 5

'I just use sometimes. It doesn't control me. I can stop anytime.'

'Hue, it's dangerous. You get caught with that stuff; it's you know...firing squad.'

She laughed.

'My supplier is a very important man. The police are his friends. Understand?'

Now Trung was worried.

'That would be Herr Baumann, right?'

'Let's not talk. What do you want now? Fuck or eat?'

'How much time do you have?'

Hue kissed him passionately.

'I'm yours anytime you want me.'

The kiss surprised Trung. Back home, Lily never kissed him.

CHAPTER 6

Robert Petale operated from a tiny office in the back garden of his house in Mount Lawley. He welcomed Sandy to his hideaway, cautioning him about the low-hanging grape vine over the doorway. Sandy had no idea what to expect from a ghost writer, or any writer for that matter. He shook hands carefully and took the seat Petale offered.

'Water?'

Sandy took the glass Petale offered him and looked around the office. There were pictures of Petale standing next to men and women Sandy didn't recognise but assumed were other writers. Another picture showed Western Australia's Premier, Richard Court, presenting Petale with some sort of award. Without preliminaries, Petale began to explain how he worked.

'I'm not sure how much Liv has told you, but let's get the money thing out of the way first. I charge a dollar a word. If your story comes out to fifty thousand words, say...'

Sandy took a gulp of his water.

'Does that include *ifs* and *buts*?' he asked.

'It does,' said Petale, chuckling. 'Everyone asks that. But I'm only talking about the finished result. Interviews, drafts and research are all included in the price.'

Sandy agreed. He would have to use the money he had been saving up for a cruise. Did it matter? The only woman he'd like to cruise with was Maisie, and she was dead. This would be something else; a permanent memorial to his life. He would donate some copies to the library, send one to the War Memorial in Canberra and another one to Bull Creek.

'Ok,' he said. 'Where do we start?'

'Let's start with that brief case full of papers you've got there.'

There wasn't a lot to tell about his early life. He'd grown up on a dairy farm in Mundijong, south of Perth. Once he realised that Sandy had no interest in farming, his father had sold his holding to his brother, Sandy's uncle. His parents had sent him to a Christian Brothers boarding school in the city from the age of 11. When he left school at 15, he managed to get a job as a copy boy at the *West Australian*. Then the war came. He had brought papers that he realised had no interest for anyone, not even for himself: his birth certificate, his exam results and his marriage certificate.

Petale put them to one side. 'Any images?' he asked.

'How do you mean?'

'Photographs.'

'Oh, sure,' said Sandy. 'I've got albums and a few shoeboxes full.'

'I guess it boils down to this, Sandy,' said Petale. 'Are you after a story that reflects the times you grew up in, or are you after something more personal, your own story, particularly any adventures, near death experiences, dramatic events of any kind? Of course, you can have both, but I'm wondering which way you'd like to go.'

Sandy nodded vigorously. 'This is what I'm interested in,' he said.

He handed over the photocopy of the news clipping Horst Weber had given him in Baden-Baden along with the typewritten translation which Jules Whitechurch had obligingly sent him. Petale grunted and read through it.

'Phew,' he said. 'Heavy stuff. You'd better tell me the background. The whole story. I'll turn on my tape recorder, if you don't mind.'

It was close to lunchtime when he'd finished. Petale muttered a few words into an intercom and soon after a young woman arrived with a tray of sandwiches and a pot of tea.

'This is my daughter, Rebecca, who is also my assistant. Rebecca, this is Mr Tuckwell.'

'Sandy, please.'

The two men sat outside in the garden to have lunch. Petale told Sandy that he too had lost his wife to cancer a few years ago. His consolation was in his work, he said, and the fact that his daughter had joined him in the business as soon as she graduated from uni.

'Another cup?' he asked, waggling the teapot at Sandy. He poured for both of them and then sat back.

'This is a sensational story, Sandy,' he said. 'It's dynamite. I get so many old diggers—no offence—who want to tell me war stories. Many of them are the same story. But what you've told me, the escape from the plane, the trek through the forest, the incredible heartlessness of your pilot ... it's a knockout. It will also be actionable; I hope you know that. Are you prepared for this Duffy fellow to sue you; to try and stop you publishing if he possibly can?'

'Let him do his worst,' said Sandy. 'I hate the bastard.'

CHAPTER 7

Hanoi

'This is our little mortuary,' Gunther said, waving his arm.

The warehouse was modern, with polished concrete floors. Apparently, it had been a supermarket. The windows were now boarded up. Stacked in a corner were the coffins, just arrived from the airport. Gunther strode over to one wall, comprised of six-foot-high stainless steel doors. He jerked a door open. A blast of freezing air greeted them. There were rows of small, rectangular compartments, just like in the movies. Gunther opened one and slid out a steel tray. Trung recoiled at the sight of a naked Vietnamese man, stone cold dead and gazing sightlessly at the ceiling.

'What did he die of, Gunther?'

'*Gott in Himmel*! How the hell would I know?'

'You're packing him up to send back to Duffy? This is the part I don't understand, Gunther. Why would his relatives want him sent to Perth, or anywhere? Vietnamese have traditions. You know, chopsticks across the face. Three coins in the mouth. All that.'

'Trung, I don't know. I don't care. They're dead. They're going to Perth. That's it.'

'Mr Duffy said most of the bodies would be Australian, or

American, or European even. Are any of the corpses here from Australia?'

'No, I don't think so. Not at the moment. I'm not sure why you're asking so many questions. We have enough bodies to fill the coffins you brought over with you. I believe you're going to organise more to be made here in Hanoi?'

'I have the address of a factory at Minh Khai,' said Trung.

The fabricator was the uncle of one of the cooks in Bao's place in Northbridge. Trung had sworn him to secrecy and slipped him a tip.

'Well Trung, you'd better get to it *schnell*, eh! Johnny Ho will take you there and then back to your hotel. How was Hue? *Schon*? A beautiful girl. Excuse me a moment, I am expecting a phone call.'

Trung was alone in the mortuary. How long did he have? Five minutes? He took out a penlight torch and approached the first compartment. Sliding out the drawer, he played the tiny light down one side of the body. Nothing. He lifted the body slightly and rolled it to one side. There was a small scar where an incision had been made just below the ribcage, to one side of the spine. He quickly closed the drawer and opened the next one. The body had the same scar. He rolled the body the other way. An identical scar. Rattled now, he closed the drawer and turned around. He could hear Baumann's footsteps getting closer.

'Let's go, Trung,' he barked.

They walked over to a corner office and found Johnny slouched behind a desk reading a newspaper. He climbed to his feet, gathering up his car keys and aviator shades. Clad in jeans and a tight T-shirt, his muscular body was covered in tattoos.

His head was shaved, apart from a ponytail at the back.

'Johnny, time to leave,' ordered Baumann. 'Take Trung to wherever he needs to go.'

Trung introduced himself in Vietnamese. Johnny just grunted. Triad, for sure, thought Trung.

'I've put a coffin into the Kombi, so they can copy it,' said Baumann. 'When they make new ones, they must be identical. *Verstehen sie?* Identical.'

The Kombi crawled through the traffic of old Hanoi at a snail's pace. Johnny Ho wasn't into conversation. He chain-smoked Marlboros and muttered in Vietnamese. Things weren't going as Trung had planned. For a start, he didn't like the way Baumann talked to him, as if he was both deaf and stupid. Then there was the matter of his own dead countrymen being shipped off from their native land to faraway Perth. It was all wrong.

At the metal workshop, with the prototype unloaded and Johnny waiting outside, he was able to settle down. Dien was a normal, hard-working man who reminded Trung of his brother. Speaking in Trung's native language, he greeted his visitor enthusiastically and offered him a cold beer. Trung watched while Dien moved his hands over the surface of the prototype, paying attention to the joins and the finish.

'What do you think?' asked Trung.

'Yes, no problems,' said Dien. 'The coffins will be ready in a week; all identical to the original. Twenty US dollars each. I will start immediately.'

Trung felt a little more relaxed as Johnny drove him back to his hotel. Hue was coming around at five for a drink and some dinner. He thought he'd ask her to stay the night. Back in his own room, Trung leaned against the balcony door, gazing down at old Hanoi. He was on his second Heineken from the restocked bar fridge when the phone rang.

'Trung, this is Dien.'

Trung laughed. 'Don't tell me they're ready?'

There was a moment's silence.

'Trung, I think you'd better come over to the factory. I must show you.'

'Show me what? I don't understand.'

'I'm not going to talk on the phone. I show you.'

Trung took a cyclo taxi back to the factory. Outside it was still hot and steamy, and Trung regretted having to leave his comfortable room to mix it on the street with the hordes of people shopping, working and moving from place to place. He caught his own haughty attitude and reminded himself that he had once been the lowest of the low: a boat person escaping from a ruined country. The workshop came into view. This time there were no beers offered. Dien looked angry.

'Look. Look here.'

Dien had the disassembled coffin on a cluttered metal workbench. Trung's stomach dropped as he stared at the false bottom. Only an inch of vacant space. One inch. An inch that could be packed with ... well, there was only one thing that made sense. Trung had visions of firing squads, or of spending endless years in the hellhole of a Vietnamese prison. He stood in stunned disbelief. Dien broke the silence.

'I will still make the coffins. $100 US. Each.'

Trung blundered out of the workshop, his mind in a whirl, and stumbled into the street. He waved down a cyclo. It sped through the traffic faster than any car could. Trung had no idea what to do about his dilemma. When they reached the hotel, he jumped out of the three-wheeler and handed the driver five 100 Dong notes. He checked his watch: a quarter to five. Perth time was an hour behind Hanoi, so there was a good chance Robin would still be at his desk. He walked into the lobby and looked around for a phone.

'How's it going over there, Trung?' Edwards asked.

'Shit creek,' said Trung, talking rapidly. 'The coffins...'

'Are you in trouble?' Edwards asked.

'Will be, I tell you,' said Trung, his voice high.

Edwards told him to get a grip. Trung took a few breaths and told him what he'd seen at Dien's workshop and before that in Bauman's mortuary. 'That's great, Trung. Great work. When the bodies come back, we'll nab Duffy. You should get out of there as soon as they're loaded on the plane. Any questions?'

Trung had plenty, but halfway through his first question he saw Hue stroll into the lobby. As she drew closer Trung noticed her bloodshot eyes and the dark circles. He hung up mid-sentence.   '... Gotta go. Got company.

Are you hungry?' he asked Hue.

Hue shrugged, managing a small smile.

They ate hamburgers and drank beer at La Terrasse. Trung was not in the mood for small talk. He was beginning to feel like a rat in a trap.

'Who were you talking to? I heard "Robin". Is that your Australian girlfriend?'

'No. Nothing like that. Business. Always business.'

'You want me to come to your room?' asked Hue. 'Maybe stay the night?'

Trung studied her for a moment. She seemed sad and out of sorts. 'Are you ok?'

She managed a wan smile. 'I'm good. Shall we go to your room?'

'Not tonight, Hue. How about tomorrow?'

'You still want me? Have you found another girl?'

'No other girl. It's just... I have things to do. You know ... business things.'

'I really like you, Trung. Please be careful.'

As he stood, she put her arms around him, kissing him. She turned on her heel and sauntered off. What the fuck was that about? What did Hue know? Trung signed for the meal and made his way back to his room, where he watched the news. His nice hotel and his full wallet had begun to lose their appeal. Maybe driving Don 82, picking up fares and getting tips wasn't so bad after all. But there was one thing that might lift his spirits: the Hang Da Market. Maybe it would take his mind off his predicament for a while. He needed to get the job done and get the hell out of Vietnam as quickly as possible.

The market was exactly what he expected, a seething hub of humanity situated in a sprawling 1950s concrete building which still carried a hint of French style. This was his Vietnam. Fresh produce, DVDs, clothes and cheap Chinese toys. Trung started to unwind. It was strangely comforting to be surrounded by his own people. He enjoyed haggling over his purchases, and Duffy's money went a long way in Hanoi. But he was still worried. Baumann was a very scary man.

Maybe he was worrying about nothing. So, the coffins had a false bottom. It wasn't really his business. Whatever Baumann was or wasn't transporting surely couldn't be traced back to him? Trung hailed a cyclo and made his way back to the hotel. He had heard nothing from Baumann.

Back in his room he slipped on a new pair of bathers and a T-shirt with a picture of Mickey Mouse beaming his confident grin. Trung remembered how he'd laughed when he'd met Robin Edwards at the Queens Tavern. Edwards had on a similar shirt and Trung thought Robin was trying too hard not to look like a cop. The thought was sobering. Was he now a cop? An undercover cop?

After a sauna and spa, Trung changed and wandered down to Le Club, the bar on the ground floor, where he flopped wearily on one of the high-backed teak chairs. He ordered a beer and turned his gaze on the other patrons. There was an interesting collection of European and Japanese visitors. He looked at the drinks menu and realised the locals probably couldn't afford the drinks; all listed in US dollars.

He glanced at his watch momentarily regretting Hue wasn't going to be there to comfort him tonight. A man with a blonde crew cut took the seat next to him and scanned the drinks list. He was dressed in the sort of smart, casual outfit that would pass anywhere. Trung guessed he was about 30.

'Holy shit!' said the stranger. 'Wadda they think we are? Millionaires!'

His accent was American, perhaps West Coast. He turned to Trung. 'Name's Mike Cornish.'

Trung offered his hand. 'Trung,' he said. 'Trung Nguyen.'

They exchanged the usual pleasantries. Trung enjoyed the fiction he managed to spin about himself: visiting businessman, making deals back in his native country, a resident of Perth where he enjoyed the coastal lifestyle, and the pleasure boat he kept moored in Fremantle. He had no doubt Mike's story was equally conflated: record producer, a studio in Burbank,

California, a bachelor pad at Huntington Beach. He was in Vietnam searching for original talent, he said. It was an unlikely story, but Trung was happy to suspend disbelief for a while. He liked the guy, he thought, and he liked himself a bit more for talking to him. Mike bought the first beer and Trung returned the shout.

'You know what?' asked Mike. 'I wasn't sure what sort of reception an American might get in Hanoi, but so far, it's been very positive. How long since the war ended? Almost twenty-five years. I guess that's long enough for a new generation to grow up free of hate.'

Trung wasn't so sure. His brother Bao still loathed Americans and so had his father, right up to the day he died.

'Could be different on the back streets,' said Trung.

'I would like to test that out,' said Mike. 'Let's go find a bar that's a bit more fun and hopefully a bit cheaper. You speak the language, right? What are we waiting for?'

CHAPTER 8

December

Robert Petale sat in his car outside Alan Duffy's place and reviewed the questions he'd prepared. Since turning to ghost-writing to revive his stalled writing career, he had sharpened his interviewing technique to a point where he was rarely caught unprepared. But he knew he needed to change tack at times. He didn't expect a man like Duffy to roll over and admit the sort of charges Sandy Tuckwell was bringing. To soften him up, he had faxed some questions about Duffy's version of the escape through enemy territory.

When he knocked on the front door, Alan Duffy opened it, introduced himself and invited him in. 'There's a study I use upstairs for the serious stuff,' he said. 'Like a drink? Grantley here will bring you a Scotch.'

To be sociable, Petale agreed to a half Scotch and soda. It was little early in the day, but why not? Duffy passed on the orders to a large man who was standing at the foot of the stairs. Ready for what, Petale wondered. Could Duffy not pour his own drinks? Upstairs he settled into a high-backed leather chair facing Duffy, who had situated himself behind a desk facing a window which looked out at the river and beyond that, the Darling Range.

'So, you're working for my old mate Sandy Tuckwell,' he began. 'Good chap. Excellent bomb aimer. It's a pity he's losing the plot.'

An aggressive beginning thought Petale. 'Mind if I record this?' he asked.

'Go ahead,' said Duffy. 'I've got nothing to hide. Where would you like me to start?'

'Thanks, Alan,' said Petale. 'Sandy has decided he would like to write a detailed account of the night the Lancaster came down, your escape through the forest and your lucky rescue, which I understand did not include Sandy.'

'Is that what he said?' Duffy sneered. 'Five times I called to him to get on board. This woman just happened to be driving the back road through the forest to her farm. When she offered, I jumped in, as any sane person would. Sandy didn't trust her. He thought it was a trap set by the Germans. I pleaded with him, but he wouldn't come at it.'

Duffy's man appeared with the drinks.

'Thank you, Grantley,' said Duffy.

What a great name for a butler, thought Petale. What a pity he looks like a heavyweight who has taken too many blows to the head. He took a sip of the whisky. Lots of peat, he thought. Must be the good stuff.

'So, what does the name 'Hogenkamp' mean to you?' asked Petale.

Duffy sat up, stroked his moustache, and shook his head.

'Nothing,' he said.

'What if I told you, it's the name of the farmhouse next door to where you stayed? And what if I told you the lady of the house was murdered at, just about the same time you were, making your escape?'

'What if you did tell me that, Mr. Petale?'

'You have no memory of that, Alan?' Petale could see he was getting nowhere and decided to change tack. 'Sandy tells me you were very attached to a scarf from your old football club. East Fremantle Sharks, was it? He said it was a sort of lucky talisman for you, you wore it on every mission.'

'Well, he got that right. It's true. My mother packed it for me when we took off for the training scheme, the Empire Air Training Scheme they called it. Shipped us off to the Canadian prairies where we learned to fly the big kites. It took us months, and a lot of study before they let us loose on the Hun. We couldn't wait of course. Eventually, we were shipped back to...'

Duffy droned on. Petale began to feel nauseous. When he tried to stand up, the floor spun and suddenly he was down.

***

He opened one eye, then the other. It was dusk, and he was slumped inside the front gate of his house in Mount Lawley. His daughter, Rebecca, was leaning over him and shaking him.

'Dad? Dad, are you alright?'

He sat up. How the hell had he got home? He patted his pockets and found his car keys and wallet. He looked for his briefcase. It was missing. He had a splitting headache and his limbs felt too weak to bear his weight. Rebecca helped him stand up and walked him inside, where she made him a cup of tea and talked to him until she was convinced, he was at least lucid. By seven he was in bed, still none the wiser about what had happened. It would have to wait till morning, he thought, and fell asleep.

The next day he woke early and asked Rebecca to drive him over to Duffy's place. His car was parked where he left it. Inside, his briefcase was sitting on the back seat, intact. Petale checked the contents. Sandy's photocopy of the German newspaper article and the translation were missing. 'Wait here,' he said to his daughter.

Petale pounded on the door of Number 56. Grantley answered.

'Come in,' he said.

Petale stepped inside and immediately regretted it. Grantley slammed the door behind him and picked up the writer by the collar while at the same time he backed him into the wood panelled wall.

'You listen to me, arsehole,' he said. 'Mr Duffy is not interested in your bullshit. Mr Duffy strongly suggests that you write about something else. He strongly suggests that you omit all references to him in Sandy fucking Tuckwell's life story. *Strongly suggests*—get it?' Grantley relaxed his grip on Petale's collar.

'And if I don't take up his suggestion?' asked Petale.

Grantley drew a pistol from his trouser belt and waved it in Petale's face. 'You know what this is, clever guy?'

'I think so, yes,' said Petale quietly.

'And you know what comes out of it, yes?' To demonstrate, Grantley removed the magazine and emptied the bullets into his hand. 'Lead,' he said. 'Fire these into the face of a girl like your daughter and she's not so pretty anymore. In fact, she's dead. Got it? Now fuck off and don't come back.'

Petale walked back to his car.

'Everything all right, Dad?'

'Yes darling,' he said. 'Apparently, I drank a little too much of Mr Duffy's fine malt whisky and passed out. They couldn't wake me, so they dropped me back home.'

'Are you sure?' asked Rebecca. 'It seems pretty odd to me, leaving you inside the gate like that.'

Petale just stared unseeing at the pewter-coloured river. *Christ, if I write this fucking bio, I'm dead.*

CHAPTER 9

Trung and Mike strolled past the showrooms and upmarket bars surrounding the Sofitel and found themselves skirting a lake before arriving in the Old Quarter. In Hang Gai Street they found stalls bursting with street food, richer and more complex than anything Trung's brother Bao served. After a liberal sampling of anything that looked familiar—lemongrass chicken and beef *pho*—they sampled some strange seafood. The taste was agreeable, but Mike decided the texture was too much 'like dogshit'.

'How you know what dogshit tastes like?' asked Trung.

Mike looked up, his face smeared in grease and some strands of seaweed. 'Let's go find a bar,' he said. Mike led the way, Trung noticed he had a limp.

'You ok to walk? That looks a bit sore.'

'Nah, buddy. Old football injury.'

Further into the Old Quarter, down tiny lanes and busy intersections, they found a karaoke bar and settled into a corner. A scrawny young woman in an oversized white blazer and short black shirt was singing 'Closing Time', which Mike recognised as a Semisonic's hit. Mike was singing along. The woman, not much older than a girl really, was doing a reasonable job of it, Trung thought.

'Pretty cute!'

Mike hailed a waiter and ordered two double vodkas. 'You wanted to drink, right?' he said. 'Whooo hoo. We're drinkin' and havin' fun. Lighten up, my friend, you look like you've just been to a funeral.'

Which was true in a way. Trung had been to a mortuary, where bodies were laid out waiting for shipment to Western Australia as cover for enough heroin or coke or whatever to keep all the Northbridge addicts going for a year. The smell of death and addiction seemed to hang on his skin like the watery boat sores he remembered from childhood. The drinks arrived and Trung downed his before the waiter had left the table. 'Two more!' he said to the waiter.

After four more doubles, Mike and Trung decided to sing.

'Do you know 'Piano Man'?' asked Mike. 'You know, Billy Joel.'

Trung liked the song, although he knew from feedback Lily had given him he was a lousy singer. 'I do instrumentals,' said Trung. 'You know—air piano.'

They booked a place in the line-up, Trung translating. Certainly, they had a video disc of piano man. But the words were in Vietnamese.

'No problem,' said Mike. 'I know it off by heart.'

When their turn came Mike, true to his word, knew the song backwards. Trung found himself to be very good at air piano, in fact he could have sworn he was playing the cascading chords himself. He even joined in the chorus. 'La la la, la la, la la la la. La la la, la la, la la la...' followed by the descending run on the bottom notes of the keyboard.

'And now for something completely different,' said Mike.

The American winked at Trung and made his way to the

stage. Trung immediately recognised the intro to the Olivia Newton John hit, 'Xanadu'. Mike pranced like a Las Vegas chorus girl as he belted out the hit song, in a perfect falsetto. Mike bowed to the thunderous applause from the audience.

'Wow, that was amazing. You sounded just like her,' said Trung.

'Thanks buddy. Part of my old drag act. Wish I had my costume!'

It was the most fun Trung could remember. They ordered two more double vodkas. There were more songs; songs he didn't even know that he knew. Soon he started singing, using the voice that Lily had said was shit and Mike praised. 'Authentic', was the word Mike used. After a while, his and Mike's performances, and the Karaoke machine, all blended into one glorious symphony of pop. And his fans loved it, at least the two girls who had appeared from nowhere to join them in a booth said they did. One sat on his lap; boobs in his face. Mike shoved some notes under the other girl's G-string, but left it at that.

Closing time arrived, actual closing time, not the song. Outside in the lane, the neon lights had been replaced by dull orange streetlights. A hooker asked them if they wanted a girl, and another if they wanted a boy. At the end of the lane two men, both dressed like Johnny Ho, bailed them up.

'Your money, Yankee,' said one.

The other raised a baseball bat and aimed it at Mike's head. Mike reacted immediately, kicking the bat wielder in the groin, and then spinning around to deliver a devastating karate chop into the other man's throat. He dropped like a stone. The first mugger fled, wailing. Later, Trung would remember the force of Mike's defence and wonder how he did it, despite the limp. With reflexes like that and high-level skills in unarmed combat, Mike was not likely to end up behind a desk running a recording studio.

Trung felt legless. What the hell was in that vodka? They walked back to the Sofitel. Mike, it turned out, was staying there too.

'Great night, buddy,' he said. 'See you in the morning.'

CHAPTER 10

December 1998

Trung awoke with the lyrics of 'Truly Madly Deeply', the poignant love song by Savage Garden, wafting gently through his subconscious. The aching in his skull ebbed and flowed like a cold tide. Bile rose as he peered at his reflection, his eyes a lattice of pink veins. He'd used the bedstead to pull himself to standing, before lurching to the bathroom. He threw down a handful of the hotel's complimentary paracetamol. Fucking vodka, he thought. Never again.

Memories of the previous night began to return: Mike singing an old Beach Boys tune at the karaoke bar, and reclining in a booth with two Vietnamese party girls on either side of him. Now mostly sober, he tried to remember the conversation with Mike. Christ, how much had he told him? Mike had been very interested. Had he told him about Duffy? About Baumann? Trung now remembered Mike quizzing him about his business in Vietnam.

And what about Mike? Why would a jet-setting Californian want to hang out with a Vietnamese taxi driver anyway? Maybe he was just lonely. A stranger in a strange land? What was it about the guy? Smooth, neat and orderly. The sort of guy who'd get out of the shower to take a piss.

Trung splashed water over his face, wondering what the day held. He could hear an insistent ringing. The phone. It was Baumann.

'Trung, *mein kleiner freund*. Johnny Ho is on his way. Should be just about there. We are having a meeting at the mortuary. He'll meet you in the lobby, *ja*?'

Trung inspected his recent purchases, selecting a pair of 501 jeans and a bold Guns N' Roses T-shirt. Grabbing his wallet, room key and passport he made his way to the elevator, his stomach curdling. The impenetrable Johnny Ho was already in the lobby, smoking a cigarette and glancing at his watch. The Kombi looked tired and out of place at the hotel entrance, squeezed between a gleaming Rolls Royce and a BMW. Johnny opened the passenger door for him. As Trung climbed in he noticed two coffins in the back.

'Don't tell me I'm riding with two stiffs?' Trung said.

Johnny lit another Marlboro, squinting as smoke leaked from his mouth. 'Nah, they're empty. At the moment.'

Trung closed his eyes and took a deep breath, telling himself there was nothing to worry about. He was going to do what he had to do, and get the fuck out of Vietnam. But it would help if the taciturn Johnny would just chat, like a normal guy— complain about the boss, or his wife and kids—anything. The heat and humidity weren't helping his hangover. Nor was the frenetic Hanoi traffic. But what was the rush? 'Say man, you got anything to drink? Water?'

'Motherfucker!' Johnny cursed as a Vespa weaved in front of the Kombi. 'No water. When we get there.'

They pulled into a spot in front of the mortuary. Johnny bounded out and slid open the side door.

'Give me a hand here,' he muttered.

They manhandled the coffins out of the van, stacking one on top of the other. Johnny went first, pushing open the glass doors of the entrance.

'Just here,' he said. They lowered the coffins to the floor. Johnny pointed towards the mortuary doors.

'After you,' he smiled.

The room was bright. Three people were present: Gunther Baumann reclining behind his teak desk, a broad smile pasted on his face, Hue was hunched and quivering on a steel dining room chair, and leaning over another steel chair, his arms curled around its back, was Mike.

'I don't understand,' Trung stammered. But he understood, all too well.

'Trung, my little buddy,' Mike boomed. 'What a night! I tell you, Gunther, the boy's a star. He could go on to have a professional singing career.'

'Enough.' Gunther said, his voice barely a whisper.

'Hue, what's happening? How come you are here?' Trung asked.

Hue glanced at Baumann before answering. 'I told you to be careful Trung. Didn't I?' She turned her gaze towards Gunther. 'Herr Baumann, I've done nothing wrong. You can let me go.'

Baumann ignored her. 'We are going to chat about many things,' he began. 'First up, I know you phoned a certain Detective Sergeant Edwards from the lobby of your hotel. Now that was silly. Thank you, Hue, for bringing that to my attention. Which raises the question, what does Edwards know? I really need all the details. I think, too, that Mr Duffy will be very interested.'

CHAPTER 10

Trung didn't fight when the needle slid into his upper arm. He knew there was no point. The last thing he remembered was Hue's tear-streaked face and Johnny Ho's malignant sneer as he withdrew the hypodermic.

CHAPTER 11

December 1998

Renata ran the rake over the lawn for the third time. She had agreed to meet Robin at his home address, but as yet he hadn't arrived. She didn't have a key, so to fill in time she had tried to clean up the front yard. As soon as it was properly raked, she would water it. She wasn't enjoying the December heat. Peninsular Road ran snake-like down to the Swan River and she was hoping there would be time in the evening to walk there. Robin was always so busy. She felt nervous about meeting him here at his little brick bungalow, far removed from the glamour of the Regent. But he had insisted that he wanted to entertain her; to show her how he lived.

Robin's Commodore pulled into the driveway and he emerged, smiling broadly.

'Sorry I'm late,' he said. 'Bloody traffic.'

'You should have put your siren on,' said Renata.

'I didn't expect you to be cleaning up my mess,' he said. 'Like you're my maid!'

From the trunk he removed some shopping bags. Inside, he set out the contents: steaks to cook on the barbeque, potatoes for the oven, greens to make a salad. Renata watched him with wry amusement. The men in her life had never shown any interest in the kitchen.

'A glass of wine?' he asked.

They sat on the back deck while the day cooled and drank chilled chardonnay.

'So, you came to Australia for the sole purpose of connecting with your grandfather?'

'Yes, I guess. Sort of. I tell you the story.'

Renata unfolded the potted version of her family history: the man she thought was her grandfather, his crimes, and the discovery that Alan Duffy was her grandfather.

'Wow, that's heavy stuff. So, your idea was to go see Duffy, say, "Hi Opa, I'm your granddaughter!" And then what? You all live happily ever after?'

Renata laughed and took a generous swig of her wine.

'Well, there is more. I have been doing a journalism and media degree course at Berlin University. I realised I had a sensational story at my fingertips. Everything about my family is melodrama! Action! War! Sex story! It has everything. This story will open doors to get me a position on *Der Spiegel*.'

'What's a spiegel when it's at home?'

'It means mirror. Guess you could say Germany's equivalent of the *Washington Post*. It's a left-leaning weekly that loves exposing conspiracies—Nazi secret stuff—all that sort of thing. My story reveals how, even now, war crimes are still hidden from view. And then this stuff with my grandfather adds an international slant on things. This will be my, in. My dream is to be an investigative journalist and I'm prepared to follow this story to the ends of the Earth if necessary.'

'Wow. I had no idea. No idea at all. I thought...'

'Ja, you thought German tourist girl, here to have a good time. Nice *titten* and all of that.'

Robin chuckled. 'You're right about the *titten*. Bloody gorgeous.' He reached out and tried to unbutton her shirt. She slapped his hand away.

'Later, we eat first.'

Robin lit the barbeque and checked the potatoes. Renata made the salad. They ate out on the deck with a bottle of Barossa cab sav to keep them company.

'Trung called,' said Robin, scraping the last of the salad onto his plate. 'From Vietnam. I think he'll be home sooner than expected.'

'I think of him,' said Renata. 'Is he in danger?'

'Bloody hell, I sure hope not. But he is a tough little guy. And smart,' said Robin. 'I have every confidence in him. Anyway, there's simply no reason whatsoever for them to suspect him of anything'.

They cleared the plates and Robin agreed that walking along the river would be excellent. He locked up, and they set out down East Street to the jetty, where they paused to admire the panorama of the city office blocks. After that, Robin suggested a walk to the old brickworks, from where they could take a shortcut back to his place. 'How nice that you've come for a sleepover,' he said. 'Did you remember your pyjamas?'

Renata smiled. 'I don't own any pyjamas.'

***

At the brickworks, Sandy Tuckwell walked fiercely in the opposite direction to the young couple. They were so wrapped up in each other they barely acknowledged his muttered, 'Good evening.'

CHAPTER 11

Sandy had just attended a very confusing meeting with his ghost writer, Robert Petale. For some reason Petale had backed away from including any but the most glancing reference to Alan Duffy in Sandy's book. After initially encouraging Sandy to focus on the drama of his trek across Germany and Duffy's treatment of him, he now considered that the story ended with the plane's demise and 'Sandy's lucky escape' as Petale put it. For legal reasons, he said, he could not make any reference to Duffy's part, nor to the unsolved murder of the German woman and the photograph of Duffy's football scarf.

'Duffy has got to you, hasn't he, eh? I may be old, but I'm not stupid. At least you could tell me the truth.'

Sandy asked for his photocopy back. Petale told him it had been mislaid. Petale would get it back to him as soon as his daughter found where it had been filed.

Sandy left the meeting boiling with rage. Tomorrow he would cancel the contract! Petale had reminded him there were penalties. Sandy had signed a complicated agreement which included steps to be taken in the event of conflict between the ghost writer and the subject. Well, this was a bloody conflict all right, thought Sandy. The bastard won't write what I want him to write. Am I not the boss, and he just my 'ghost'? Maybe he should calm down. He could feel his blood pressure rising. It would be better to turn for home, and once there, have a Scotch and maybe call Liv.

He made it to the front door, fumbled for his key and staggered inside. Maybe I should call Liv and *then* have a Scotch, he thought. It seemed important. Liv picked up.

'Liv, I have to tell you something about that ghost writer of yours,' said Sandy.

CHAPTER 11

'Sandy, you sound puffed out. Have you been exercising?'

'No,' gasped Sandy. 'Listen, if anything happens to me, I want to tell you how to get into my place and what you need to find.'

'I can come now, if you like,' she said.

'Not necessary. I'm tired and my chest hurts. I'm going to have a Scotch and go to bed. Now listen. Petale is backing away from that story I told you. I think Duffy's got to him.'

'Who was Duffy again?' she asked.

'Doesn't matter. Listen up.' He told her where to find the spare key and once inside, the key to the safe. 'There's a file in there with his name on it, Alan Duffy. In it is a spare photocopy of a newspaper article and a translation from the original German. I want you to give it to the West Australian, and keep a copy for yourself in case you need it. Can you do that?'

'Are you sure you're alright, Sandy?'

'I'm fine Liv.' He hung up the phone. The pain in his chest seemed to expand and run down his left arm. He levered himself out of the chair, walked two steps and crashed to the floor.

CHAPTER 12

Edwards woke up early, enlivened by his night with Renata but keen to get to work. He showered, dressed and grabbed a piece of toast to eat in the car. On his way out he kissed Renata tenderly on the forehead. In sleep, she looked just as beautiful as she did in the rest of life.

At work, he took out the file on Duffy. Were there any loose ends? As soon as Trung tipped him off about the coffins, the net around Duffy would tighten considerably. In the meantime, all he had outstanding was the enigmatic few words Renata had recorded when Hugo returned her to the backpackers after her last meeting in Jutland Parade. Edwards called information and got a phone number for the Northcliffe Golf Club. He was about to hang up when someone picked up.

'Hello?'

The voice was shaky, Edwards thought, yet not from age. A hangover perhaps? He introduced himself. 'Who am I speaking to?' he asked.

'Northcliffe Golf Club,' said the voice.

'And you are?'

'Peter Duffy.'

CHAPTER 13

The garden gnome by the front door grinned its perennial smile. Underneath it Liv found the key, just where Sandy had told her it would be. She cleared the mailbox and picked up a bundle of newspapers yellowing on the lawn. Liv had castigated herself for not guessing that Sandy hadn't been well when he'd hung up the phone so abruptly. It had taken a week for the news to get through to her, breathlessly announced by the choir master, a young composer who always dressed in black and slicked his hair over his shapely scalp with too much gel. They talked about Sandy in the tea break; his rich voice, his kindly manner. Sandy's body had been found by a nurse from Silver Chain. What a way to go! After tea they moved onto a new piece, a Balkan folk song.

The house was untouched, filled with the musty odour that seemed to invade the homes of the elderly. Yet he hadn't seemed all that old. She remembered the twinkle in his eyes, and the way he'd ogled her breasts the night they'd had dinner at the golf club. Men were all the same, she thought, young or old. You wear your favourite blouse and that's what you get.

Liv prised open the ancient cream venetians in the kitchen. Tiny particles of dust danced in the rays of light invading the room. She lowered herself onto a Laminex dining chair that must have been forty years old and tossed the contents of the letter box onto the table. Rifling through the mail, Liv threw power bills and a rate notice to one side. A letter caught her eye, stamped Deutsche Post. Without hesitating, she tore it open and pulled out the typewritten letter.

10/11/1998

Dear Mr Tuckwell,

Please forgive me if my writing is not good. My name is Bruno Ruevoldt. I live in Freiburg in Germany. My family has lived here for many generations. I read a story in the Badische Zeitung, our local newspaper, about an Australian World War airman named Sandy Tuckwell who was helping find wreckage from his crash plane. I could not believe my eyes. My late grandfather Otto Ruevoldt told me many years ago how he helped an airman escape to Bern in Switzerland. Clearly, I remember he said the name Tuckwell. My grandfather owned a trucking business and regularly crossed over the Swiss border. He hated the Nazis.

He told me how you were afraid for your life and how the two of you found a hiding place for him in an old wooden crate, even though you spoke no German and he had only a word or two in English. I'm not sure of the right words but I think he said you were out of your head. It was of great concern for my grandfather that you might cry out at the wrong moment.

I hope you are well Mr Tuckwell. I would like very much to go on holiday to Perth in Australia and make your acquaintance. I am enclosing a photo of my grandfather and his truck.

Your friend

Ernst.

Liv peered at the grainy black and white photo of a smiling, pleasant-faced man wearing a dark leather trench coat. His hand rested on the driver's door of a large, black truck emblazoned with the name *Ruevoldt*.

As Liv gazed at the image, a tear splashed onto the picture. She quickly brushed it away. At dinner that night after Sandy after had returned from Germany, he'd begun to tell her how he'd become disoriented after the Lancaster crashed, the gap in his memory and his incredulity at finding himself safe in Switzerland. Even as he drank too much wine, the memories were tumbling out like water from a busted dam.

Liv knew Sandy would have been overjoyed to have this confirmation of his shaky recollections. She knew he would have been thrilled to meet Ernst, if he ever made it to Perth. She folded the letter carefully and put it away in her handbag. Liv knew Sandy had no living relatives, and she accepted, willingly, it would be her sad duty to write to this kind man and tell him about Sandy's death.

As instructed, she checked the safe and removed the newspaper clipping Sandy had been so anxious about, placing them in the envelope ready to send to *The West Australian*. He'd wanted to settle things with the pilot. It was some sort of feud; the kind of thing old men could spend their lives settling. No wonder we have wars, she thought. If only Sandy could have basked in the memories of his lucky escape rather than trying to settle old scores.

CHAPTER 14

Peter Duffy scuffed his way down Salmon Beach to check his fishing rod, which he had planted in a plastic tube after casting it far out into the boiling surf. Between visits to renew his bait he like to fossick in the sand dunes, collecting shells and flotsam. Anything attractive he would take back to his shack at Windy Harbour. It was still early. There was plenty of time to brew a nice coffee, cook the fish he was almost certain to catch, drive into Northcliffe to pick up his mail and get to the golf club by 11 am.

The mail would reliably include a cheque from his father. The cheque was Alan Duffy's way of keeping his son at bay. Duffy senior didn't want questions about the death of his late wife Annette from head injuries suffered in a fall from the balcony of 56 Jutland Parade some thirteen years earlier. Peter had been 25 at the time, a greenkeeper at the local golf course. He had never understood how his mother, herself a golfer and very fit, could have lost her balance at the end of the regular sundowner she enjoyed with her husband, Peter's father. Neither did the police, until mysteriously they stopped asking questions. Duffy senior offered Peter a lifetime income in return for his silence, and since Peter was the opposite of his father, a bit shy and introverted, it seemed acceptable. It wasn't as if Peter had any evidence of his suspicions. It just hadn't seemed right, especially when he went to view his mother's body and saw the odd angle of her head where she had hit the driveway three floors below. He had no intention of setting foot in the Dalkeith mansion ever again, nor of seeing his father.

At Northcliffe, he filled up his old Suzuki soft top at the Post Office, collected his mail and then picked up the day's *West Australian* at the General Store. He had time for a coffee at the Hollow Butt Café before driving down to the golf club, where Ladies Day would be in full progress. Sipping his cappuccino, he thumbed the paper without much interest. There'd been a bikie rally in Perth, bushfires near Esperance. An Eagles midfielder had been involved in a brawl in Leederville. He was about to fold up the paper for later when he spotted the following on page ten:

HISTORICAL WAR CRIMES CHARGE FOR WWII BOMBER PILOT

Alan Duffy DSO, who piloted a Lancaster bomber during the Second World War, has come under scrutiny by the RAAF for his alleged part in the murder of a German female on a farm near Freiburg in 1942. The bomber crashed near Freiburg following an attack by a German night fighter. The charges arise from historic photographs of the murder scene together with testimony gathered from the late Sandy Tuckwell, who was the bomb aimer in the ill-fated Lancaster.

Duffy and Tuckwell, the only members of the seven-man crew to survive the crash, made their way separately to the Swiss border, where they were given asylum and repatriated to Australia.

Although historical war crimes are not subject to the criminal justice system, the RAAF is expected to withdraw Duffy's privileges and all his service awards if the charges are substantiated.

That would be worth clipping and putting on the fridge, thought Peter. I always knew my father was rotten, and this proves it. With a smile on his face, he drove down to the golf club. His duties as groundsman were not onerous. Since the 'greens' were made of sand, there was no trimming needed. The fairways were rough to begin with, and nothing Peter did made them smoother. Compared with the Nedlands course, it was a breeze. On a day like today, when the ladies invaded the course, he minded the office and answered phone calls.

He parked the Suzuki in its usual place at the back of the equipment shed. A shiny black Holden muscle car was there too, along with two men who looked like bouncers. Peter's instinct was to ignore them, the way he ignored all but the most obvious threats. The larger of the two men approached him and loomed over the driver's side of the Suzuki.

'Nice little heap you're drivin'. Vintage, is it?'

Peter sat looking straight ahead. He remembered the man. *Shit, it's my father's goons again. What in hell are they doing here?* They all looked the same. When they reached 30, they would be put out to grass. This one was particularly threatening, with his muscles bulging out of his T-shirt and his neck as thick as tree trunk.

'So, me and Joey here just want to have a look around, alright?'

'It's Ladies Day,' said Peter.

Hugo guffawed. 'Glad you warned us about that, Peter mate. Very glad. Come on, Joey. Let's take a squiz.'

Peter Duffy said nothing. Did his father's reach extend to every place on the planet? Was there nowhere a man could go to escape? It was only a month ago they were last here. What the hell is my father up too? Or was this just a reminder that his father was always in control, and not to rock the boat. He waited for the two men to leave, climbed out of the Suzuki and walked up to the clubhouse. From the shop window he watched the black saloon perform a burnout on the eighteenth green, tearing the compressed sand into deep ruts before revving its way back onto the fairway and disappearing in the direction of the front gate.

CHAPTER 15

Trung moved his arm, banging it on metal, then the other arm. Bang. That hurt! He opened his eyes, turning his head. Grey steel. He turned the other way, saw the same grey steel. He cautiously stuck his hand in the air. Nothing. He sat up. He was in one of the coffins. There was an awful smell. What was that? Vinegar—a strong vinegar—with a whiff of rotten eggs.

A woman's voice, nearby. 'This is where they make the heroin.'

'Hue? What's going on?' Trung peered into the semi-gloom. Hue sat against a rough plaster wall; her hands clutched around her knees.

'We're in Sapa,' she said. 'This is where Baumann makes the heroin.'

Trung let this sink in.

'He's going to kill us,' she added.

Trung climbed out of the coffin. They were in a large room with two thin mattresses, pillows and rough blankets in one corner, and a small pile of magazines scattered over the floor. The sight of an old-fashioned chamber pot with a roll of toilet paper resting next to it caused Trung to shudder. He glanced at the high ceilings. A row of small, barred windows allowed a little light to filter through. If he could get to the windows maybe the bars could be forced. But there was nothing to climb on. There were stout teak double doors. Did they lead to the outside? Striding to it, he shook the steel handles and yelled. 'Anyone there? Mr Bauman, can we talk? Please?' His voice echoed through the room; a forlorn lonely sound. There was another door on what looked like an internal wall. 'I suppose that door is locked also?'

Hue retched and began to weep. 'I'm sick. I just want to die,' she wailed.

She looked much older than her eighteen years. Trung suspected she was in withdrawal. She struggled to her feet, shuffling towards him. Hue put out her arms. The smell of shit along with her putrid breath made him step back.

'I'm sorry Trung,' she whimpered.

'What for?'

'I told the German pig I saw you on the phone. Otherwise, no score.'

'I don't get it. I was on the phone. So what?'

'Trung, I have no idea how he knew. But he knows everything.'

'Ah shit. It doesn't matter now. I'm going to check this place out.'

Trung moved noiselessly across the wooden floor. Were the brownish stains blood, he wondered? He pushed open the door. Inside the pristine, compact space the room had sheet rubber floors, white tiled walls and strong overhead lights. Just like a hospital. Against the wall he recognised a row of stainless steel anaesthesia carts.

From outside a gruff male voice barked, 'Get back from the door!'

Trung rejoined Hue.

'We have to answer,' she whispered.

'What do you mean?'

'Tell him you're standing back.'

Trung shrugged. 'We're standing away!'

The double doors swung open, revealing a Vietnamese man clad in jeans and T-shirt and a red bandana that gave him a vaguely piratical air. He held an AK47 which he waved menacingly around. Satisfied Hue and Trung were nowhere near the door he turned and grabbed a four wheeled metal trolley laden with a neat stack of patterned porcelain food containers. Two identically patterned eating bowls with chopsticks and serviettes completed the set. It reminded Trung of room service at the Sofitel. Maybe Baumann wasn't going to kill them after all?

The guard slung his weapon over one shoulder and with a grunt pushed the wheeled trolley into the room with his foot. The doors slammed, and they heard the dull thunk of a key turning.

Trung realised he was hungry. He lifted the porcelain lids. The tantalizing whiff of Pork noodle dishes, spring rolls, and a fish curry with a touch of coriander made his mouth water. 'I'm eating,' he said. 'You?'

'I should eat,' said Hue, and began to spoon pork noodles into her bowl.

'You seem to know about what goes on here. I don't understand.'

'You've been asleep for at least eight hours. And this place ... Trung, people die here.'

CHAPTER 16

The bed clothes were a mess. Renata's fingers brushed Robin's stomach and the trail of fine hair drifting up from his navel, spreading like threads of gold on his chest. She'd decided that she enjoyed his body. It was lean and hard with old battle scars. Just twenty-four hours ago she had left Fair Dinkum, and without a lot of discussion, moved her meagre possessions into Robin's Maylands house.

'I'm going to Vietnam.'

Renata's eyes raised. 'I don't understand. What about me? Us?'

'Ok, here's the story. Trung has disappeared.'

Renata's hand went to her mouth. 'What do you mean? He's in Vietnam, you said.'

'I told you how he's gone there working for your grandfather?'

'Yes.'

'Well, he was escorting some coffins to a local heavy, Gunther Baumann, who works for Duffy. He was also organising to have similar coffins manufactured in Hanoi.'

'So? I'm not sure I understand. What do you hope to do? Is it a work thing? What?'

'I'm taking some leave I'm owed. I don't know, but I think the little bastard may be in trouble. I've phoned the Sofitel in Hanoi. I've left messages for Trung to call. Nothing. I'm afraid

Trung was onto something and now ... I have a bad feeling.'

'I'm coming too. Two heads are better than one. When are we leaving?'

'Not this time. I'm flying tomorrow to Singapore, then Hanoi. I want you to stay here. It means a lot to me. You mean a lot to me.'

'I'll stay. But I'm not happy. We have lots to talk about.'

Hanoi was wrapped in a pall of grey when the jumbo lurched to a stop at Noi Bai airport. For some reason Robin had expected humidity and balmy skies, not rain that felt like gravity had been turned up a notch. As he waited in a long line of travellers the feeling of confidence and resolve that he'd displayed to Renata deserted him. He was an alien, without status. He'd forgotten how a new arrival had 'sucker' stamped across his forehead. It seemed everybody was out to clip you. 'How much to the Sofitel?'

The taxi, a battle-scarred Datsun 180 B, inspired zero confidence. The matching driver was no help. Robin did a quick mental calculation of the amount he'd been quoted, something like his monthly mortgage payment. Eventually, an amount equal to US ten dollars was agreed upon. The wheezing Datsun hurtled straight into the traffic, oblivious to the lumbering trucks which bore down on all sides. The cacophony of sound and the layers of diesel fumes and other lethal gasses made Robin's eyes water. In his misery he was nowhere near alert enough to notice the battered Volkswagen Kombi tailing them. The chain-smoking Vietnamese man with the aviator shades stayed right behind, inconspicuous in the rain and smog.

The Parisienne styled awnings of the Sofitel somehow restored him. This was a world he understood: smiling uniformed staff who spoke English; a welcoming fruit cocktail, with a dinky little umbrella perched on the top of the glass; lovely women in sarongs, smiling and serving drinks.

Now sprawled on his king size bed, Robin's mind was in a whirl. He stumbled to his feet, liberated an ice-cold Heineken from the bar fridge and consulted his notes. One name on the list stood out: Gunther Baumann. Surely all that could wait until tomorrow. Robin dialled the hotel operator requesting a call to Australia. The phone rang and switched to the message machine. He listened to his own voice politely asking the caller to leave a message.

By now it was 8 pm Vietnam time and he was hungry. He glanced out of his hotel window. The rain had ceased. Steam was rising from the streets, which now resounded with the frenetic sounds of commerce, Hanoi style. He dressed and headed for the restaurant with the most European-sounding name. Food always helped.

To his relief, the menu featured everything Robin was familiar with. The chargrilled burger with Roquefort cheese, French fries and an icy San Miguel restored his equilibrium. He was ready to deal with Herr Baumann and anything the Vietnamese underworld might dish up. After the meal he strolled downstairs and into Le Club Bar, where he slid onto one of the high-backed bar stools. Next to him, a blonde-haired man with a crew cut scowled as he scanned the drinks menu.

'Holy shit! Wadda they think we are? Millionaires?'

CHAPTER 17

'Back from the door!'

Hue threw her arms around Trung. They were united in misery, sitting side by side on their mattresses. Trung had flicked through a German motorcycle magazine for the hundredth time. On the wall, he had marked off each day with his belt buckle.

'It's not mealtime. This is it Trung, they're coming to kill us.'

Hue had recovered from withdrawal and now looked like the pretty 18-year-old she was. So far, Trung hadn't told Hue of the significance of the operating theatre. Perhaps she knew anyway. He stood, bracing himself. It would be suicidal, but he could try throwing himself at the AK 47-wielding guard.

The doors were flung open. Not one guard, but two guards appeared. Suspended between them, held by his upper arms, was an unconscious Caucasian man. Like a sack of potatoes, they threw him roughly onto the floor before closing the doors. Trung raced to the man's aid. He felt for a pulse. The beat was strong. He turned the man over and gasped. Robin Edwards.

'Fucking hell, Robin. What brings you...?'

'You know him?' Hue was beside him.

'I guess you would say he's a friend. A cop. From Perth. I have no fucking idea what he's doing here.'

'Get back from the door.'

Trung and Hue gazed fearfully at the doors again. Leaving

Robin unconscious, they scurried backwards. One guard this time. He threw in another dirty mattress, slamming the doors shut again.

'Give me a hand please, Hue,' said Trung.

Together they dragged the unconscious Robin across the floor and gently rolled him onto the dirty fabric.

'Trung! What's he doing here?'

'As I said, he's a cop. His name is Robin Edwards. I reckon he must have been worried when I didn't call, and he's come looking for me. Somehow, Baumann has found out who he is and they've grabbed him. I'm surprised. Robin is a smart guy.'

Time passed. Trung waited impatiently for Robin to awake, who twitched occasionally and uttered an occasional low groan but otherwise remained unconscious. Trung and Hue lay facing each other.

'I don't think they're about to kill us any time soon.' Trung said quietly.

'Oh yeah?'

'We have been here more than a week. They could have killed us before now if they'd wanted. They could have killed Robin ... but ... So ... who the fuck knows?' Trung rolled on his back, then turned back to face her. 'Hue?'

'Yes, Trung.'

'You really are very beautiful.'

Robin was out to it for several hours. He began to moan, curling himself into a ball. Finally, he sat up, 'Trung,' he said hoarsely. 'What's going on? How the hell did you get here? How the hell did I get here? Who's this?'

'This is Hue.' He told Robin the whole story, omitting to mention Hue's involvement.

CHAPTER 17

'So, Robin, how in hell did they snatch you?'

'I don't know how it happened. I was in one of the bars at the hotel. I was having a drink with this rather annoying Yank—'

'His name was Mike?'

'You too, eh? Let me guess. One of Baumann's goons?' Robin held his head in his hands.

'You got it. He's a smooth operator. So, what happened?'

'We had a few drinks. I remember a karaoke bar. Jesus, how embarrassing. I remember singing that stupid version of 'Living next door to Alice'. You know the one? Alice, Who the fuck is Alice?'

Trung didn't have a clue, but he smiled politely. 'And then?'

'And then? And then nothing. A complete blank till I woke up here. So, we both fell for the smooth Yank bastard. I don't know if that makes me feel better, or worse. Anyway, where are we? And what about you?' Robin waved a hand at Hue.

'I am sorry Mr Robin; I did some work for *Herr* Baumann but I had no idea this was going to happen.'

'Forget the mister. Tell me what you can. Like where are we?'

'We're in the mountains outside of Sapa. It's about five hours from Hanoi. This is where Baumann processes the opium into heroin.'

'So, the heroin gets packed into the coffins, and Duffy goes through this bullshit in Australia about a decent burial for expats?'

'Not just expats. It's anyone. And I don't think they necessarily died of natural causes. And there's more. Can you walk? I need to show you something. This is where they perform some of their surgery. I reckon they do some of the bodies in Hanoi and some right here.'

Robin hauled himself to his feet, steadying himself against the wall. They made their way into the adjoining room. Robin was puzzled until Trung explained how he'd seen the corpses with neat surgical incisions. Robin's face paled. 'It's a bloody hospital. Harvesting body... Christ, that's value adding.'

CHAPTER 18

Renata's spirits lifted when she heard Robin's message. She was already missing him. There had been lovers in the past, but no one like Robin. He instinctively knew what she wanted and in return she felt the urge to go beyond limits she'd set with previous lovers. But the warm fuzzy feeling was not to last.

Renata phoned the Sofitel in Hanoi.

'I'm sorry ma'am but there is no answer. Do you wish to leave a message?'

'Yes please, could you say that… No, sorry it's not that important.' Panic immediately started to gnaw. *He'll phone tomorrow.*

Renata tossed and turned, plagued by nightmares. She awoke in the morning feeling ill. She knew he was in trouble. She tried the Sofitel again, this time asking after both Trung Nguyen and Robin Edwards. Mr Nguyen, she was told, had checked out days ago. The smooth voice of the concierge now sounded evil and malevolent. Renata new she was being paranoid, but… She paced the loungeroom, disturbed by how spartan it looked. Two framed photos of his parents and a banner of the Collingwood Football Club decorated one wall. The other walls were bare.

She consulted the Teledex and phoned CIB headquarters, but immediately hung up. She knew nothing about Australian police. The thought crossed her mind that corruption might be an issue. Maybe someone in the force had told someone in Vietnam about Trung. Her stomach lurched again. Maybe Robin had been set up.

Renata had taken notes from what Robin had told her. The journalist course at the Berlin University had drummed it into her, time and time again: take notes. Don't trust anything to memory. She read through everything. One name shone through, again and again, Herr Gunther Baumann. It took no time to book tickets, but an annoyingly long time to board the plane and get airborne.

Renata gazed at the disreputable taxis waiting impatiently on the rank at the Hanoi International Airport. Parked in an adjoining bay she spotted an immaculate white Chevrolet Nova with a uniformed driver leaning against it, cigarette in hand. Grabbing her rucksack, she stepped past the expectant cabs. 'Excuse me? Could you take me to the Sofitel?'

The driver threw his butt onto the street and checked his watch. 'Ok. Fifty US.'

'I'm sorry,' Renata smiled her best smile. 'I'm a poor student. I only have twenty Aussie.' Her worn jeans and faded shirt must have helped.

'Sure. Get in.'

She had decided on a plan of sorts: to remain anonymous and not ask any of the staff about the whereabouts of Robin and Trung. After a quick shower and a change of clothes she made her way to the lobby. She strolled nonchalantly to the row of telephones. Pressing the button for the concierge, she asked after Robin Edwards and Trung Nguyen. No joy.

Time to put plan B into action. Three Mercedes sedans with the Sofitel logo discreetly emblazoned on the front doors waited at the front of the hotel. The first driver leant against his vehicle, reading a newspaper.

'Excuse me,' said Renata. 'Do you happen to know of a *Herr* Gunther Baumann?'

The driver put down his newspaper, quickly appraising the shabbily dressed tourist. Anything to do with *Herr* Baumann could mean money. 'I may do.'

'*Ach gut.*' Renata smiled, holding the backpack so the driver could see the German flag on it. 'You see, I'm his niece from Germany. I am going to make a surprise visit.' She now had the driver's attention.

'Well, I can take you. Of course, I know where he lives. But I should warn you, it's a … protected address … they have a gate … a guard. You really should phone first.'

'It'll be ok. Once he knows who I am he will let me in. Can you take me there?'

Baumann's neighbourhood was far from the Hanoi of mean streets and meandering lanes. This was high rise and smart shops. Designer labels, classy restaurants and upmarket jewellery shops lined the street. Renata stared at the gated community at the other side of the wide boulevard. An armed guard glanced in her direction and continued reading his magazine.

'Well, nothing ventured,' she thought.

The plan hit a brick wall higher than the one containing the enclave. No, she couldn't go in. He wasn't prepared to say if a *Herr* Baumann lived there. In other words, *piss off*.

Renata wandered past the high fashion shop fronts. She paused in front of the German Backhaus. The tempting fragrance of espresso coffee and the sweet yeasty aroma of *Mohnkuchen*, German poppy seed cake and fresh bagels made her mouth water. She ordered a Berliner—the German answer to a doughnut—and an espresso coffee from the traditionally dressed German assistant. As an afterthought she enquired, did she know a Frau Baumann?

'Oh yes. She comes here every Tuesday at ten, before her bridge club meeting.'

So Tomorrow, Frau Baumann, you will tell me what I need to know.

CHAPTER 19

Renata munched on her smoked salmon bagel, sipping her second espresso. She glanced at her watch; 10:10. Where was Frau Baumann? Outside the shop window, a chauffeured Mercedes slid to a halt. The driver dashed to open the rear passenger door. This had to be her.

Renata observed what might charitably be described as an abundant lady. Everything about her suggested money: the carefully permed hair, the casually elegant Louis Vuitton bag, its monogrammed canvas announcing to the world who the designer was. She wore a figure flattering black shantung silk pantsuit—in the case of her figure, a big ask—with fine silver threads woven into the design. Renata waited until she sat down and placed her order for a cappuccino and a strawberry torte. She approached the table, clutching a copy of the *Der Spiegel*.

'Frau Baumann?' she said in German. 'Please forgive the interruption. My name is Greta Schultz. I'm a journalist.' She held the paper up like a badge of office.

Frau Baumann ran a disparaging eye over the apparition before her. 'Yes. What can I do for you?'

'I'm doing an article about important Germans in Asia. Your name and of course your husband's name came up as being influential in Hanoi. We would like to do a story on your life.

We want to do a feature article with you both at home. With colour photos. Also, a story about your husband's business.'

At the mention of photos, Frau Baumann was interested. 'Please sit down, my dear. Would you care for some torte, and a coffee? I would have to talk to my husband. He's such a busy man you know.'

'What does your husband do exactly?'

'Oh, ah,' Frau Baumann said vaguely. 'He's an exporter. I'm afraid I'm not very interested in business things.'

'And what does he export?''

'Oh, um, you know, rice, fruit, that sort of thing.'

'So, he has, what, plantations, I guess?'

'I think so. The business is run from the mountains. Have you heard of a place called Sapa?'

Renata jotted furiously in a small notebook as she spoke, every bit the journalist. But it was Sapa she was focusing on. By lunchtime she had checked out of the hotel.

Renata edged her Hertz Toyota Corolla into the Hanoi traffic. She had studied the complimentary map at length and concluded that if she headed northwest, she would eventually stumble across the right road. Frau Baumann wasn't terribly helpful as to the exact address of Gunther Baumann's business in Sapa, but Renata was trusting in luck that someone would give her directions. There was no plan. She had no idea apart from a gut feeling that Sapa held the answers to her questions.

***

Robin paced angrily around the room. 'I'm going to fix this *kraut* bastard. What time does the food come?'

'Are you hungry?' Hue asked.

'No. I can't really think about food now. I just need to know the timing. There's no doubt in my mind we're dead meat if we don't get out of here. So, let's all put our heads together, ok? The only way we're going to break out is through that bloody door.'

Trung looked worried. 'Hey Robin, you forget. The AK 47?'

'Sure, I get it. An AK 47. Forget that for a minute. Did either of you see anything when the door was opened? Any idea of what's around this building?'

Hue held up her hand like a schoolgirl. 'I came up here a few times with Herr Baumann.'

'Great. Tell me.'

'Next to this building is another big, factory type place. It's where they make the heroin. That's the funny smell.'

'How close?'

'Fifty meters.'

'So, if we get out ... I should say when we get out... What else?'

'There's a big car park where the workers park their motor scooters. There's a gravel track leading out. At the top there's a house where Herr Baumann lives when he is here. He sometimes entertains there. I had to go there sometimes. Me and other girls. You understand?'

'Sure,' said Edwards. 'So, we get out of here. Where to from there? I assume you know the road that leads out of here, Hue?'

'Yes of course. There is only one road. But it's impossible. We are right up in the mountains. It's too far to walk. It's freezing cold at night.'

'Mmm, yeah. Let me think. Trung, when the door was opened did you notice a car outside? Or any sort of vehicles?'

'I did. Once I saw Baumann's Mercedes. But every time I see also a Jeep.'

'What sort of Jeep?'

'You know Robin, like you see in the movies. One of those green army Jeeps. The old ones.'

'And it's been there every time?'

'I think so.'

'Bingo.'

Trung stared hard at Robin. 'What the fuck is bingo?'

'I'll tell you why bingo, my little mate. Those old Jeeps don't have a key. They have a starter button. If we get out, we should be able to start the bastard and fuck off out of here.'

'Great, but how do we get out? AK 47. Guard. Bang bang, you're dead.'

'We have to use the assets we have,' Robin said slowly.

'I don't follow.'

'I don't understand,' Hue echoed.

'What time's breakfast?'

'Usually about eight, give or take.'

'Lunch?'

'One-ish. Dinner is usually about six.'

'More like six-thirty,' Hue threw in.

'You have some sort of plan, Robin?' Trung asked.

'Yeah, you bet. And it involves a pretty girl.'

'What do I have to do?'

Robin noticed the steely glint in Hue's eyes. 'It's not perfect but ... here it is. When the guard comes, his only concern is that we are not too close to the doors. Right?'

'Yes, of course'

'You and I go into their little hospital room. I'm going to lie flat on one of those steel gurneys. When the guard comes in, he's going to be distracted.'

'How?'

'I'll get to that. Trung, you're going to push that bloody stainless steel missile with all your strength, me on the top. I'm going to run right into the prick and flatten him.'

'I still don't get...'

'Hue, this is where you come in. Ok?'

Hue smiled hesitantly.

'I notice you're wearing jeans and a long shirt. When he opens the door, you stand as close as he will allow. I want you to take off your jeans and stand there wearing your knickers and your shirt. Unbutton your shirt—you need to look cute— sexy. You understand?'

Hue nodded vigorously. Trung threw his hands in the air. 'Shit Robin! You reckon that'll work?'

'Trung. Listen to me. Most men think with their dicks. He won't see us, so there's no threat there. He sees Hue, and he's sure as hell going to be distracted.'

'When do you want to do this?' Hue asked quietly.

'I think breakfast time. That gives us the whole day to get to Hanoi.'

Sleep was fitful. Each was lost in his or her private thoughts. There was so much that could go wrong.

'Away from the door.'

A Jeep was clearly visible in the car park. Hue leant provocatively against the wall, her shirt unbuttoned and the zip of her jeans, partially open.

The guard licked his lips. Hue was very familiar with men and their thoughts.

'Where are the others?' he said in a hoarse voice. Hue smiled.

'They're asleep in the other room. They like being alone. Together.'

The guard grinned as he kicked the food trolley forward. He'd just started to unbutton his trousers when the swing doors to the surgery opened with a bang. The steel trolley flew across the floor like a rocket sled, the top of Trung's head just visible as he pushed Robin with all his might. The guard stared wide-eyed, grabbing his trousers which had fallen to his knees. With a curse he tried to unsling the machine gun. Too little, too late. The gurney hit him in the midriff. He flew backwards half in and half out of the teak doors. The gun clattered onto the verandah. Robin tried to grab him. With another curse the guard retrieved the gun, and before Robin could stop him, a spray of bullets erupted above his head. Hue screamed. Robin now had the man's head in his hand, bashing it repeatedly against the floor. Trung appeared, kicked the guard's head and scooped up the AK 47. The back of the man's skull was a bloody mess. Robin felt for a pulse and grinned.

'The prick's finished.'

'Robin we gotta go,' yelled Trung. 'Everyone would have heard the noise.'

Screams and yells erupted from the heroin factory. A collection of mainly white-suited women stood pointing and arguing, with no idea what to do.

'Hue, come on. We're going.'

The Jeep was exactly where it always was.

'Hue, Hue,' Trung yelled. 'Shit, Robin, she's been hit.'

A pool of blood leaked out of a wound in her chest. Robin grabbed her and walked her to the Jeep. 'We'll get you out of here. To a hospital.'

Hue smiled. 'How did I do. Mr. Robin?'

'You did just great.' Robin placed her as gently as possible into the Jeep. As he'd anticipated, there was no ignition. But how to start it?

Striding across the car park were two male workers, one with a machete. Robin grabbed the assault rifle, firing a spray into the air. The two workers fled back to the safety of their hut. 'Jesus, I simply have no idea how to start this fucking thing. There's no key. But no fucking starter. Shit, shit, shit.'

Hue coughed up some blood. 'On the floor. Starter button is on the floor.'

Robin glanced down. There it was. He jammed his foot against it and the ancient Jeep rumbled into life. The relic was slow and noisy. The motor rattled and a plume of smoke gushed from the exhaust, but the engine didn't miss a beat. The way out was easy, one road in and out. They passed a bungalow. A maid paused as she swept the porch, open-mouthed. Robin checked the rear vision mirror just in time to see her scuttling inside, no doubt to call her boss.

***

The rental Toyota had no air-conditioning. Renata alternately shivered or was boiling hot. In the dips, the temperature rose, at the peak the temperature plummeted as clouds swirled across the busy road. It was like being on fairground roller coaster.

There seemed to be endless steep hills and plunging valleys. As she drew closer to Sapa she tried to come up with a plan. All she could think of was to go to the town itself and simply ask directions to Gunther Baumann's residence. A flimsy plan at best, she realised.

The Toyota had just groaned up another hill and was hurtling down the other side. Renata noticed the temperature gauge had moved marginally towards the red zone. Traffic was slow, mainly heavily laden trucks, and the occasional yellow Daimler bus, always packed to the gunwales. Then she noticed a vehicle heading towards her—an open topped American Jeep. She stared.

'My God. Robin, Trung.'

She stood on the brakes. The car slid to a stop. Taking a quick glance, she executed a three-point turn, anxiously aware of the steep drop on the unprotected road shoulder. The little motor screamed as she pushed the pedal to the metal. The temperature gauge was closer to the red. She quickly caught up to the slower Jeep and honked her horn.

She saw Trung turn, stare at her raise a gun and point it towards her, then he lowered it.

'Shit, Robin,' said Trung. 'It's Renata.'

'What? You're kidding.' Robin turned his head. 'I don't believe it.'

Robin eased the Jeep onto a narrow lay-by. 'Trung, check on Hue.'

The Toyota had managed to squeeze in behind the Jeep. Robin ran over, jerking open the door. 'How in hell?'

Renata threw her arms around him. 'What's going on? Just how much trouble are we in?'

Robin quickly told her the basics. Trung yelled out from the back of the Jeep.

'Robin. Hue's dead.'

'Who's dead?' Renata's face paled.

'Hue. It's a long story. Shit, let me think.'

Renata ran to the Jeep and checked Hue's pulse. She was indeed dead. 'They're after you, right?' she asked.

'Damn right.'

'You know what you need to do?'

Robin, blinked. His eyes were on Hue, her young life extinguished.

'She's dead,' said Renata. 'I know this sounds cruel, but I reckon, leave her in the Jeep. Send it over the side of the mountain. Baumann will figure that you and Trung were in the Jeep and are in one of the ravines or washed down the river. What else could he think? It will buy us some time.'

There were tears in Robin's eyes. 'Yeah, you're right. I'll tell Trung.'

The three of them pushed the Jeep to the edge and gave it a final shove. They watched horrified while it bounced and turned end over end. Hue's limp body shot out, to lie spreadeagled on a rock. The Jeep burst into flames.

PART THREE

CHAPTER 1

January 1999

On his first day back from leave, Robin Edwards decided to act like anyone else who had just enjoyed a holiday. Yes, it was a good break, thanks. Two weeks hadn't been enough. To explain his pallid complexion, he just had to mention Bali. Of course. In Bali it rains every day. Next time, it would be Surfers Paradise he assured his workmates.

Since his failed attempt to convene a brainstorm about Duffy a lot of water had passed under the bridge. The head of Major Crime, Vincent Lukashenko, had shifted his focus away from child porn to bikies. Heroin related crime was on the increase and deaths by overdose climbing. Edwards now had the opportunity to form a small team and assign investigative tasks without rocking the broader boat of the squad. Lukashenko had given him the task, with one piece of advice: focus on the crime, not the man.

'Just one man, you run the risk of a backlash,' he told Edwards. 'Track down the source of the stuff, who is distributing it; then you're halfway there. The kingpin, whoever he is, is not going anywhere. We can nobble his business first and pick him off later.'

I've done more than track down the source of the stuff, thought Edwards. He'd almost been picked off and put on a slab himself. He knew quite a lot about the factory in Sapa, had seen the workers and smelt the noxious product they were turning out. But how to nab Baumann? And how to prove the link with Duffy, since Trung's coffins had never been dispatched? Trung was in hiding.

He tried to focus on the big picture, as Lukashenko had suggested, but his mind kept returning to Duffy. In his conversation with Duffy's son Peter, he had learned something else about the heroic airman with the stiff upper lip and the RAAF moustache. Alan Duffy's wife Annette had died in a fall from the top balcony of the Duffy mansion in 1985. The post-mortem led to an investigation by homicide detectives. Duffy told them he had gone inside to top up their drinks. When he returned, she was missing, having thrown herself over the rail and onto the driveway three floors below. Given that Annette had no history of depression, the squad interrogated Duffy several times but got nowhere. And then the case was dropped.

Were historical homicides the way to go? Edwards felt sure Duffy had at least two to his credit, but historical murder investigations were expensive and low yield. He made room in the corner office, arranged the chairs in a semicircle and waited for his hand-picked team to arrive. When the seats were filled, he began.

'The focus of our efforts for the next little while is heroin: where it comes from, who distributes it, who controls it. We have information pointing to a big operation in a neighbouring Asian country. Sorry to be vague at this stage. The crime we are focusing on was reported by Trung Nguyen, a taxi driver and police informant, now in hiding. He reports two men in butcher's uniforms unloading a van from Satinwood Funerals in Northbridge on September 18th last year. The van was later reported stolen. Our witness, Trung, identified the driver of the van as one of Duffy's men. He helped unload a body-sized bundle wrapped in a stitched canvas bag. Trung's curiosity cost him a severe beating. This was in broad daylight. I doubt whether he'd have come out alive otherwise. Brendan, I'd like you to front two gorillas in the employ of Satinwood, Grantley and Hugo, real names Rodney Chamberlain and Niall Norman. Gillian has had a brush with Norman, talk to her.

'Next up, Jack. You made a comment at the first meeting about the character of the director of Satinwood, Alan Duffy, DSO, a bomber pilot in the Second World War. And you may be right, he served his country heroically. It's possible that he is blind to crimes being committed on the lower deck. Would you please follow up the insurance claims lodged for the Satinwood van, who signed them, and if the claims have been rejected, why?

'Gillian, you can work with me on what's left, in particular, any missing person's reports around that time. Also, we will need to analyse trends in morphine supply around that time and take another look at deaths by heroin overdose.'

'What exactly am I looking for in the missing person angle, Robin?'

'Frankly, Gillian, I'm not exactly sure. But see if there is anyone who could possibly have any connection with the two lowlifes, Grantley and Hugo. I know that's a wide net. But if you shake a few trees, you never know what might fall out. Also, I'm going to speak to Duffy's son Peter, he might reveal some family secrets.' Edwards looked around the circle. 'Any more questions?'

There were none. Nobody expected big things from such a modest effort, but nor had Edwards ruffled any feathers. None that were visible, anyhow.

'I understand that the links between the crime in Northbridge and the heroin issue is at this stage tenuous. I'm sorry I can't give you more background that leads me to make the connection, but I believe it's real, and it is serious. Please keep me in touch with your findings. We will convene again in a week's time unless something urgent comes up.'

He picked up his papers and arranged his first get-together with Gillian for the following day. Back in his office he called Renata. Since returning from Vietnam, she had spent days on her journal article, double checking every word and apparently revelling in the feeling that she was doing something important.

'How's it going?' asked Edwards when she picked up. She giggled.

'This is very strange, living in your house, picking up your phone,' she said.

'Not as strange as tearing down mountain roads in Sapa,' he said.

'I am trying so hard to put all of that behind me. But I'm still having nightmares. That poor girl' Her voice quavered.

'I don't mind admitting I'm having some bad bloody dreams as well. You'd never guess what haunts me the most?'

'Tell me? The escape when the guard was killed?'

'No, surprisingly, the sheer terror when you drove Trung and I back to our hotel to retrieve our luggage and those bloody passports. Jesus, I was sure Baumann's goons or the cops would've grabbed us. And then...?'

'And then? 'Renata asked.

'When we waited at the airport to fly out. Jesus, I nearly threw up. For the very first time I had an idea of what drug smugglers must go through.'

CHAPTER 1

'Oh, Robin, it's been one long horrible nightmare. I still don't feel safe.'

'Don't be afraid Renata, please don't. It's over.' They had trod a dangerous path together and it had brought them closer. Edwards admired the way she had handled herself, in fact saved his and Trung's skin.

'Is it over, Robin. Is it really?'

CHAPTER 2

January 1999

Grantley sprang to his feet, his VB frothing. In the driveway below he could see the sparkling Rolls Royce he had just polished and beyond that the blue-grey expanse of the Swan River.

'Jesus, sounds like it's all turned to shit. What the fuck do we do now? Cops on our doorstep next, wouldn't you say?'

The subject was the shambles in Vietnam. Present at the meeting were Grantley and Hugo, with Duffy holding court from the comfortable cream leather kid chair he prized.

'Sit down, Grantley. And watch your beer.'

Hugo was sprawled across one of the divans, nursing a Scotch and soda.

'Sounds like you have things sorted. Right, boss?'

'Right. Now to get down to business. I've been speaking to Gunther Baumann.'

'Who?' Grantley interjected.

'Grantley, you need to follow things. Sometimes I doubt you made it all the way to the end of the assembly line. Baumann! Our man in Vietnam. Remember? He is more than happy to send the smack, using the coffin trick. He's sweet.'

'I remember him now,' said Grantley. 'What about the cop? He's going to be a problem, surely?'

Duffy stroked his moustache. 'No, he won't be a problem. Trust me. I have friends in high places. The investigation is going nowhere. Now, listen up. This is important. I have decided to cancel any body retrieval operations from other countries and just focus on Vietnam. Baumann is a very switched-on operator and it's going to be plain sailing.'

'Why don't we just whack the cop?' asked Grantley.

'Been watching *The Godfather* again?' said Hugo.

'Both of you,' said Duffy. 'The last thing we want to do is kill a serving police officer. For God's sake you two morons, pay attention. Forget the cop. Now just listen. Please. From now on and for the foreseeable future we will only be receiving bodies from Vietnam. And if the ice business is as successful as I believe, we will stop this import aspect to our business model. It means you two won't be travelling to Godforsaken countries, bribing officials and all of that nonsense. It'll be streamlined, efficient and a walk in the park. Any questions?'

Hugo sipped his drink, then put his hand up like a schoolkid. 'Look, Boss, that's all good, but going to other countries to source the stiffs was a big part of mine and Grantley's job. We'll still have a job, won't we?'

'Yeah, Boss, Hugo has a point.' Grantley's eyes narrowed.

'Hey you two, be happy for Christ's sake. There's always something in Perth that needs attending to. Your ... umm special skills are always going to be needed.'

'On that very subject. The taxi driver? The slope,' said Hugo. 'He's a loose end we don't need.'

'He's under the radar at present,' said Duffy. 'Don't you love that expression? You know, to beat the radar in the war we used to use this metal stuff—'

'We know that, Boss,' said Grantley. 'You told us before.'

'Yeah,' sighed Duffy. 'I guess I did. Anyhow we have other fish to fry. Anyway, as far as that idiot Trung is concerned, he's not going to say anything, I'll guarantee that. He'd have too much explaining to do. But like I said we have a very exciting development. We're all going to make money.'

The two men waited expectantly.

'Methamphetamine.'

'Hey! I know about that.' Hugo beamed. 'I did Chemistry at school.'

'I didn't,' Grantley muttered.

'Not saying I was top of the class or...' Hugo mumbled.

'Listen, methamphetamine is going to be the next big thing. Bigger than smack. And we don't have to import it. All I have to do is find someone with a bit of chemistry know-how and we can make this stuff ourselves. We're not going to let the grass grow beneath out feet. What we need is a house, a shed, a hall—any bloody thing will do. I've been talking to guys in the know in the States and they say they're cleaning up with ice.'

'Ice?' Grantley queried.

'Ice. Apparently the finished product looks just like ice. Like I said, we need a place away from prying eyes, somewhere in the bush. Down south I reckon.'

'Your son Peter lives down south,' said Hugo. 'Me and Joey paid him a visit. Remember?

'I don't,' said Duffy. 'Remind me.'

'You said we should head down there and see if he was behaving himself. Seriously, I can't see him being a problem, and also you said to introduce ourselves to this Dougal McBain, the developer you know. We gave you a report about it.'

'I know him well. Dougal and I go back a long way,' said Duffy. 'He's got way too much money, pays too much tax. He needs to smoke some of it, and I said I'd help him. Now, as it happens, he's a developer. That means he works with builders.

'Yeah, he does. He's a big wheel in Windy Harbour and he's building a sea rescue clubhouse or some shit,' said Hugo. 'Joey knows more, he talked to him.'

'Really?' said Duffy, smiling broadly. 'Ok, here's what I'm thinking. Hugo, if you seriously think you can cook this stuff, I'm prepared to let you have a go. I've got my hands on the recipe. It doesn't look that hard. There'll be extra bucks in it for you. The first thing is to buy the ingredients, they're all readily available; lithium, ammonia, something called ephedrine. Your job is to go and source all this stuff. The next thing I was going to say was to find a secure joint where you can churn it out. And this McBain and his clubhouse sounds like the answer. I'm going to be having a pow wow with my old friend, Mr McBain. We're going to be nicely sorted with our own little *private* clubhouse.'

'Just tell me what I gotta do,' said Grantley. 'Does McBain need working over?'

'Leave it out, Grantley,' said Hugo. 'This operation requires subtlety. But what gives with McBain?'

'Just leave it to me. I know how to handle Dougal McBain. The only other potential fly in the ointment is my son Peter, he may just stick his nose in, he's a bloody lefty who wants to save the planet. He could be a damn nuisance, particularly if he enlists the help of some of those misguided tree huggers.'

'You want us to give him a bit of a smack?' Grantley said hopefully.

'For Christ's sake Grantley, just a bit of intimidation. He's a cowardly little shit. I tell you when we climbed into a Lancaster, we...'

Hugo cut him short. 'Yeah, boss we know, you're a hero.'

'All right, all right, you both know what to do. Grantley, no rough stuff, ok'

Grantley scowled. Duffy laughed. It seemed the meeting was over.

'One more thing,' said Grantley. 'That Renata. Your granddaughter. You seen her? I could stake her out, if you know what I mean.' Grantley was leering.

Duffy levered himself out of his recliner, and grabbed a walking stick with a brass horse's head for a handle. Taking it by the tip, he smashed it into Grantley's face and then brought it down hard on the top of his knee cap. 'Get my granddaughter's name out of your mouth, ape!' he yelled. As he left the room he saw Hugo mopping his mate's face with a hand towel from the bar. A satisfying amount of blood was pouring from Grantley's nose.

CHAPTER 3

Peter Duffy was standing under the peppermint trees in his yard cleaning the morning's fish when the second truck rumbled past, leaving a cloud of dust and the heavy stink of diesel fumes behind it. He shrugged and turned back to his task. He was proud of the table he'd built from driftwood and an old benchtop his mate Ronnie had found at the Northcliffe tip. A stainless steel sink from the same source had been added at the last minute, along with a tap and a length of hose to feed it. That was the thing about Windy Harbour. You could build anything from anything down here, and most of the residents did just that. It was very rare for a new building to rise here in the land of second-hand, but that was what was happening down at the harbour where the new Marine Rescue clubhouse was taking shape.

Peter had first heard about it from his neighbour, Lester Dann. Lester was a retired farmer, never happier than when he was towing his runabout down to the sea behind his old Massey Ferguson, also retired. Most days Peter would hear Lester firing up the tractor and peek out the window to see him sitting majestically at the wheel, off for a day of fishing.

'I dunno,' he'd said when Peter ran into him at the kiosk. 'The bloody thing is bigger than the Taj Mahal. Did I miss something? There are about fifty active fishermen down here, not counting the professionals. When was the last time one of them got lost at sea? It's the Shire. They want more shack owners so they can get rich on the rates. Bloody fat cats.'

Ernie Briggs, the caretaker, agreed. The new clubhouse was over the top and unnecessary. There were too many weekend fisherman out there anyway, all of them armed with fancy boats and fancy gear, crowding out the locals. Whose fault was it? Dougal McBain, that's who. A Mandurah developer, he already had the biggest house in Windy Harbour.

'Now he wants to build the biggest fucking shed!' said Ernie.

Peter hadn't lost any sleep over any of it. He tried to steer clear of local politics, which was mainly centred on leaseholds and fire prevention. He listened to Ernie and Lester out of politeness, rarely offering his own opinion. He wanted a quiet life, an ambition rarely threatened down here on the heel of the continent. But ever since his father's goons had torn up the 18th green he had felt on edge. One night he even packed his bags, then next morning told himself he was being irrational and unpacked them.

He ate his breakfast on the tiny balcony overlooking the road. For once, Windy Harbour was still. Up on the top of the dune an old man kangaroo stood and sniffed the air, scratching his belly at the same time. Peter loved this place— loved the wild bush and the thunderous surf out on the point beyond Cathedral Rock—loved the remoteness. Growing up in Dalkeith he had suffered from bullies at school, the sons of tycoons and lawyers, and suffered again at home, where his father ruled the place with an iron fist. His mother had told him about his father's war record and had even taken him along to one of his father's public addresses once. The man who stood on the podium and addressed the audience with his plummy voice and smug countenance was far removed from the tyrant Peter lived with; a man who berated his wife constantly and occasionally, behind closed doors, beat her.

He dumped his plate in the sink and put on his walking boots. He would walk through the swale and up to the lookout, watch the majesty of the Southern Ocean as it smashed against the cliffs, retreated, and then returned like a vengeful warrior. Is that what his father had once been; a warrior pitting himself and his crew against the enemy? Peter wanted to think the best of his father and wished he could admire him as others did. It wasn't easy.

On the way back he walked along the beach to the harbour. Beside the launching ramp the foundations of the new Marine Rescue clubhouse were in place. Steel girders had been neatly stacked to one side, ready for the frame to be bolted into place. An electrician Peter knew from the golf club was standing by his ute, scratching his head. Spread across the bonnet was a detailed plan of the whole structure.

'G'day, Alf,' Peter greeted him.

Alf grunted, deep in thought.

'Big job?' said Peter.

'It doesn't make sense,' said Alf. 'There's a room upstairs labelled club room. They want it double insulated with safety trips on every switch and a dedicated backup generator. You'd think it was a hospital or something. McBain seems to be able to whatever he bloody well wants. I tell you; it's got me fucked.'

'Tricky,' said Peter, and kept walking. He passed the kids' playground and came to the community notice board. There were second-hand fridges for sale, a generator, and this notice under a green banner:

CHAPTER 3

GREEN ACTIVISTS! MAINTAIN THE RAGE!

Come to Denmark, WA, for the annual rally of green groups from around the state. Sponsored by the Conservation Council, this is the opportunity to gain important updates from local activist groups making gains in Ningaloo Reef, the Bungle Bungles, Esperance, and other frontiers of direct action.

Not connected? Learn how to seed a local action group and rally others to your cause. Keynote address by Senator Bob Brown, followed by special interest workshops.

Peter took a tag from the bottom of the notice. Although the rally was months away, it was enormously exciting, to think that he could do something about the monstrosity that threatened to degrade the precious environment of the D'Entrecasteaux. His father had always accused him of laziness. He would show him. He would write to him, proudly proclaiming his commitment to something, something he really cared about.

Back in his shack there was a note from his neighbour Lester Dann, who sometimes took phone messages for him since Peter had never bothered to pay for a connection. *Please call Detective Sergeant Robin Edwards when you can.*

First, he would write his letter while it was still alive in his mind. He sat down at the kitchen table, took out a writing pad, sharpened his pencil and began.

Dear Father,

Not that you are all that dear to me. I think you know that

CHAPTER 3

I am unlikely to get close to you after all that's happened. You came to fatherhood late, was that the trouble?

Two of your lieutenants paid me a visit, leaving a trail of destruction on the 18th green. It was not appreciated. But that's not why I am writing.

I thought you would want to know that I have developed an interest in preserving the wonderful environment I am so lucky to enjoy down here in the D'Entrecasteaux. There is one big project that threatens to upend the quiet community we enjoy and that is a marine rescue clubhouse being built by your old friend Dougal McBain. I can't figure out why your men seem to be taking such an interest in its construction. But I know if McBain's involved it's probably shonky.

Anyway, I think we can stop it. And I can just imagine you and McBain taking delight in the puny efforts of our little community. Don't be too cocky. We are coming for you: the Green Army.

Peter.

He folded the sheet carefully and propped it on the mantelpiece ready to post the next time he drove into Northcliffe, wondering if he had crossed a dangerous line with his father.

CHAPTER 4

January 1999

'I don't suppose you wanna ... like, talk about it. You know like why you're gonna be in a safe house?' The young constable asked.

Trung glared at the cop in his freshly pressed uniform. *The kid's about sixteen, I reckon.*

'Nah, it's... Look, it's no big deal. It's some triad stuff.'

'Triad? What's a triad?'

Trung rolled his eyes. *You gotta be kidding me.* 'Triads are Asian crime gangs. That sort of thing.'

'Oh, I see. Nasty buggers some of these Asians. Oh, I'm sorry mate, I don't mean, like all Asians are bad like, in fact...'

'Let me guess, some of your best friends are Asian?'

'No, not really, but me and Roxy, that's my girlfriend, we often have ... like, Chinese takeaway on a Friday night. Anyway, this is it. This'll be the place, alright.' The constable turned the unmarked Falcon into the driveway of a nondescript California Bungalow.

The old house had discovered the company of nature, with a forest of unkempt weeds and an antagonistic bougainvillea that climbed up the front porch in a riot of purple.

'Give us a hand here with all the food, mate? Grab one of

those cartons and we'll go inside. Jeez, I hope they have TV here. The Eagles are playing the Dockers tonight. You follow the footy, mate? By the way, I'm Constable King. You can call me Trevor.'

'Trung.' Trung cast a suspicious eye over the provisions. *Dammit, no bloody beer.*

'Hey, Tring, check this out?' The constable held up a matt black electronic console.

Trung glanced around the lounge room with its faded pattern wallpaper, and stained velvet sofa. A solid scratched timber coffee table rested on a rug that was in an incongruous Aztec design. In the corner sat a late model Sony TV in dull grey plastic. Placed on the coffee table a pile of Women's Weeklys, a chess set and of course the Nintendo Trevor was lovingly caressing.

'Actually, Trev, the name's Trung. Are you sure you're supposed to be playing games?'

'Yeah, of course. Trung ... gotcha. There's nothing to worry about. Anyway, it's my job to protect you. She'll be apples.'

Trung noticed a telephone on a small table in the entry hall. 'Do you know if the phone works?'

'What...? Oh, the phone? Yeah, I guess. Hey this Nintendo is bloody great.'

Trung padded into the hallway. He picked up the phone and dialled.

At his desk, Robin Edwards pondered the big picture. Trung had been in the safe house for a week and had phoned several times.

'Robin, you gotta get me out of here. All this young copper does is sleep, watch TV, play Nintendo and talk to his bloody girlfriend on the phone.'

The pair had already debriefed on the way back from Vietnam, but they were all so rattled by events there, they couldn't get a handle on what the bad guys were up to.

Robin tossed thoughts around until his head spun. *Would Duffy send his thugs to sort out Trung and Robin? An old-fashioned hit perhaps? Surely not? He wouldn't be fool enough to murder a serving police officer. But what about Baumann? If he found only Hue's body, would he put two and two together? Baumann was quite capable of despatching the lethal Mike Cornish. And Lukashenko? What is it with him?* 'Shit, this is a bloody mess.'

'You ok Robin? Swearing in the office?' Gillian said with a grin as her head popped up over the partition.

'Nothing that a beer after work won't fix,' Robin forced a smile.

Calling Trung that morning, Edwards had confirmed that the fabricator in Hanoi had indeed agreed to make the special coffins and that as far as he knew they would have been picked up and paid for by one of Baumann's men. So, all they were waiting for now was a shipment of bodies to Satinwood from Vietnam, and then they could pounce. But he was well aware that Duffy would be covering his tracks, and even if Customs exposed the scam, there would still be nothing to incriminate the old airman.

Jack Dutton poked his head above the partition that marked off Edwards' world.

'Hi Robin,' he grinned.

'Jack, how did it go with the insurance people?'

'Hmm, bit of a story there, mate. As soon as the van turned up their investigators combed it. No result. They refused the claim, which I understand is pretty standard in these sorts of cases, and waited for the claimants to scream. No screams. Unusual, you might say, but perhaps Satinwood is so cashed up they don't care. Now, what was interesting was the blood stains they found under the carpet in the back of the van. Our forensics are onto it, also collecting hair samples and other matter from the carpet itself. The trouble is we don't have a body, do we? We have missing persons, but so far there doesn't appear to be any possible connection, but in any event it's hard to match hair samples and blood with a photograph. I'd say it's an ellipsis situation, son. Dot, dot, dot.'

Robin hated it when Jack called him 'son', or explained words he thought might be missing from the younger man's vocabulary. But he thanked Jack for his work and returned to the paper trail.

After lunch he took the lift to the top floor, where he had an appointment with Superintendent Lukashenko.

'Come in, Sergeant Edwards,' said Lukashenko. 'How was your holiday?'

Something about the way he asked the question put Robin on alert. He ignored the feeling and sat down.

'Any progress on your enquiry?' asked the chief.

Robin summarised the story so far. There were still an annoying number of loose ends and the whole Satinwood thing kept on leading to blank walls and dead ends.

'Maybe you should forget the Satinwood connection,' said Lukashenko. 'It was only ever a theory, and sounds like you've got nothing to back it up. I don't want to say too much but we're about to raid a big-time dealer, and he's certainly not connected to Satinwood.'

Robin's ears pricked.' And who might that be, sir?'

Lukashenko chuckled 'Does the name 'Greasy' mean anything to you?'

'Wow. Greasy Mal Farrand. No kidding. I mean everyone suspects but...'

'Yeah. Got it in one. Well, I reckon we've got the goods on the slimy bastard. But for Christ sakes keep it under your hat for now. In the meantime, what about rounding up a few dealers off the street and giving them a going over?'

This was certainly exciting news, but Greasy Mal Farrand aside, Robin knew Duffy was certainly not kosher. But maybe this was simply political. Urbane Duffy—war hero—probably very well connected politically. Robin really was not that surprised Lukashenko didn't want to go after him. The chief had always been political and was averse to rocking any boat that might bring disapproval down on his head from the powerbrokers, be they Liberal or Labor. WA Inc, which had blown up in the 1980s under Premier Brian Burke, had not yet, in Robin's opinion, left the building. After making suitable sounds of agreement, he headed straight back to his cubicle and called Peter Duffy.

He wasn't surprised to learn that an oversized Marine Rescue facility was in the early stages of construction under the leadership of one Dougal McBain, a developer who had made his fortune building canal-style developments in the southwest. McBain had survived several scandals in Perth that Robin could remember, usually over kickbacks to local councils. Perhaps he'd moved permanently down South to avoid scrutiny. He turned over a new page in his notebook and scribbled furiously. Robin's thoughts were in a whirl. All of a sudden everything sounded like conspiracy, murder and fraud. Peter Duffy had previously stated categorically he believed his father had murdered his mother. Dougal McBain was very suss. He tried to crystalise his thoughts. Duffy equalled murder and conspiracy. Powerful and very probably corrupt developer. And what the hell was Duffy up to? Robin shivered, he realised he was in very dangerous territory.

When it came time to knock off, he found himself dawdling. Renata had told him she wanted to have a serious talk. In his experience, a 'serious talk' with your girlfriend could only mean trouble. As a precaution, he'd buy a top bottle of German wine on his way home, good enough to work as a sweetener at least. He resigned himself to whatever the evening held in store. How about that, he thought. I'm growing up.

'I'm home,' Robin yelled as he walked through the door. The smoky tang of steaks on the barbeque hit him, along with a warm feeling of welcome.

'Out the back,' called Renata.

Dropping his briefcase on the floor, he placed his revolver and holster on the kitchen bench and strolled through to the rear patio, clasping two bottles of wine; a German moselle for Renata and a cab sav for himself.

The table was set, wine glasses at the ready. Robin nuzzled her neck as she turned the steaks. Renata laughed, pulling his head down into her shoulder. Not-quite-married life has a lot going for it, he thought. 'How did you go today?' he asked. When he'd left for work that morning, she was already deep into her feature article, as she had been all week. He was impressed. Her seriousness of purpose was obvious. He sat down and waited until Renata plated up the steaks before digging into the Caesar salad.

'We've said little about Vietnam since we've returned,' said Renata. 'I'm sure it's not over. I don't feel safe. Trung's in hiding. I think we need to keep talking. What you know: I want to know.'

Their exit from Vietnam had been painless. Although on high alert, it appeared as if leaving Hue's body in plain sight had thrown Baumann off the scent. They hoped Baumann had initially concluded that Robin and Trung's bodies were carried away by the river. They flew out of Hanoi that same night without a hitch.

'I'll admit it's messy. Nobody knows I went to Vietnam; they think I went to Bali! But there's a bit of an issue with my boss.'

'That's Lukashenko? Renata asked.

'Correct. He's been briefed, but he still he seems reluctant to go after Duffy. War hero, pillar of society, all that bullshit.'

'He couldn't be on the take? Could it be? I mean does this sort of stuff go on here, in beautiful Perth?'

'Jesus, I hope not, but anything's possible. See, here's the problem. If I tell him I went to Vietnam under my own steam and got involved in uncovering this massive scam, he'd throw the book at me. I wouldn't have a leg to stand on. Police officers can't just go off the radar, waltz into another country and carry out clandestine drug investigations. It's become a real can of worms.'

'What have worms got to do with it?'

'Sorry, it's just an expression. Let's say we don't know which way they're going to slither.'

The front door screen rattled, followed by what sounded like a fist pounding the front door. Renata held a hand to her mouth. Robin leapt to his feet, ran back into the kitchen and grabbed his .38 from its holster.

'Robin, it's me, Trung. Let me in.'

Robin tore down the hallway and wrenched open the front doors, grabbed Trung by the shirt front and dragged him inside. 'Mate! You're meant to be in the safe house. What the fuck are you doing here?'

Trung was breathing hard. 'I've been running. Unsafe house is what it is.' He paused for breath, leaning, hands on his knees.

Renata appeared. 'Trung, are you ok?'

Robin pulled the blind back, peering outside. 'Were you followed?'

'Nah.'

'Talk to me. What happened?'

'You got a beer?'

Renata ran to the fridge, grabbed a can of lager and thrust it into Trung's hand. Robin pointed to the lounge chairs. 'Sit, talk, drink. In that order.'

Trung grinned. 'Yes, boss. Two things. I rang my cousin who's just come back from Vietnam. This has been in the news in Hanoi. You're not gonna believe this.'

'Try me,' said Robin.

'Baumann has gone to the Hanoi police. He's paying them off, right? Now we, that is you and me, are the prime suspects in the murder of two people—Hue Bui, and get this—Thuc.

'That was the guard in Sapa. Right?'

'Yep. The very same.'

'Ok, let me think about that for a minute.'

Renata threw her hands in the air. '*Wunderbar*. That means you can both be extradited to Vietnam.'

'No, it doesn't,' said Robin. 'Australia won't allow extradition to any country with the death penalty. There's more to this than meets the eye. Anyway Trung, what's the issue with the safe house? What happened to that young constable I placed there?'

'He was asleep, great help he'd be. But guess who I saw patrolling the street in their muscle car? Grantley and fucking Hugo. Bloody hell Robin, who else knew I was in the safe house?'

'My boss, Lukashenko. And would you believe he said we'd have to keep it quiet. No one else was to know.'

'Why would you tell him, Robin?' asked Renata.

'Because I had no choice. We can't just stick people in a safe house for no reason. As it happens, I made up a cock and bull story about Trung hiding from one of the triads.'

Renata stared hard at Robin. 'You know what this means?'

'Like you said. Lukashenko's on the take.'

CHAPTER 5

Robin read the nameplate on the half-open door. *Vincent Lukashenko.* There should be a tag on the end, he thought. *Crooked cop.* At Lukashenko's bidding he walked in, sat down. Lukashenko closed the door.

'I forgot to ask you at our last meeting. How was Bali?'

Robin shifted in his seat, like a naughty schoolboy in the principal's office. 'Yeah, nice,' he said.

Lukashenko leaned back in his chair, a half-smile on his face. 'So,' he said slowly. 'Bali was good huh? Where did you stay? Seminyak? Kuta? Hey, I reckon you'd be a Kuta kind of guy. Fast paced. Music. Lots of bars. Pretty girls.'

Robin had never been to Bali and he probably never would. 'Kuta, yeah.'

'Just what I thought. And I bet you went to La Lucciola. Right on the beach, great Italian food. Yes?'

'Yep, sure did. Every night. Terrific place.'

The glass pane door rattled. 'Come in Margaret. Coffee time already, eh?'

Birdlike Margaret served the men Nescafe in brown stoneware mugs, then she and her trolley trundled out of the room. The door closed. Lukashenko grinned, chuckling softly.

'Oh dear, Robin, La Lucciola isn't in Kuta. It's in Seminyak, a few miles down the track. You weren't in Bali. You were in Vietnam. And you're in big trouble, son'.

Robin's face paled. He stared sullenly at Lukashenko, who took an exploratory sip of his coffee.

'Jesus, I hate this shit. What we need in this place is a decent fucking espresso machine, right? Now, how about we talk about Alan Duffy? Here's the thing. I've had a good look at Satinwood and frankly they've come up clean as a whistle.'

Robin knew if he said what was on his mind he'd be sunk.

'But you? That's a different matter. It seems you and some Vietnamese guy, let me look in this folder, yeah here it is, Trung. This all sounds like an airport novel. A girl found shot at the bottom of a mountain and an innocent young man also shot and killed at the business premises of one Gunther Baumann, a respectable importer/exporter. And you and this fella Trung, are prime suspects. How about that now?' Lukashenko beamed as if he'd just handed Robin a golden egg.

'It's not what it seems,' said Robin and immediately realised what a pathetic defense that line was.

Lukashenko rose to his feet, gazing through the glass panes of his office at the detectives in the other room. 'To tell you the truth, son, I don't give a flying fuck about a couple of gooks who've come to a sticky end. Like I said, you and this idiot Trung, are prime suspects. But we don't have any extradition deals with Vietnam, and I guess you're not planning to go back there for a holiday, now are you?'

Robin said nothing.

'I have all the correspondence here from the cops in Hanoi.' Lukashenko waved a manila folder with 'Vietnam' splashed across the front in bold black. 'So ... it doesn't need to go any further.'

CHAPTER 5

Every word he said was loaded with threat. Lukashenko's voice changed to an oily baritone. 'I have to tell you Robin; I've been very impressed with you. Your clean up rate is second to none. However, you do tend to occasionally bark up the wrong tree. That aside, I think I can guarantee a great career path. Promotion even.'

'Thank you, sir.' Robin almost choked on the words.

'Now, I have a surprise for you.' Lukashenko slid open the drawer of his desk, pulling out a square canary yellow Bakelite box. Robin's eyes widened as he recognised the ship's anchor, the stylized 'B' and the winged emblem. He opened the box.

'Like it?'

The Breitling Navitimer gleamed in the strip lighting of the office. 'Hell, I can't accept this. Where the fuck did it come from? Is it hot?'

'Hot? Of course, it's not hot! We confiscated a few of them from a drug dealer. He's not going to miss them. He's been extradited to the States and won't be out of the slammer till January 2099.'

'I don't understand. Why me?' Robin knew the answer before it came out of Lukashenko's mouth.

'Let's just say it's a welcome to my own special little team. You will accept it.' No more oozing baritone. Lukashenko's voice was stone.

CHAPTER 6

'Something's up. Lukashenko's champing at the bit,' said Detective Sergeant Ron Costello, a beefy ex rugby player turned cop. The eight-person lift was packed solid with ten detectives as it wheezed its way to the top floor. Robin looked down at his new Breitling watch—the price of loyalty. Robin felt as if he'd been checkmated. Every time he glanced at his watch he was filled with self-loathing.

In the briefing room he focussed on Lukashenko, now deep in conversation with a uniform guy. Lukashenko as always appeared suave, in control and unstoppable. With his swept-back silver hair and tailored charcoal suit, Robin thought he looked like a taller, ageing Michael Douglas. The suit alone must have been worth a grand. When he moved to the lectern it looked even better.

'Listen up, men. We've got a raid on this morning. I'll hand you over to Sergeant Bixby here. Sergeant, take it away.'

'Good morning, guys. We have a tip off. You've probably heard of a thug named Mal Farrand.'

The detectives grinned at each other. Greasy Mal Farrand always seemed to get away with it. He'd been charged several times with drug possession, but somehow the evidence was always tainted. The jury never convicted. He always left the court smiling for the cameras.

'His estate in Swan View is the target,' Bixby continued. 'We believe he has a stash of stolen firearms and a few kilos of coke and heroin tucked away. And where there's drugs, there's money. We have a carload of uniforms waiting to rock and roll.'

The procession of police Commodores and Falcons sped up Morrison Road on the way to Greasy Mal's. The property on James Street was impressive; a fake Tudor two storey home set back from the road with glorious city views. A constable with bolt cutters cut the chain on the wrought iron gates as if it were candy floss. They roared up the long winding driveway, Bixby and Lukashenko in the lead. At the top of the drive a dozen uniformed and plain clothes police swarmed over the house and grounds like a colony of angry ants. It was the part of a raid Robin loved, designed to put the wind up the most hardened criminal.

Lukashenko strolled into the living room where a furious Mal Farrand sat perched on an emerald green leather club chair.

'What the fuck's going on Vincent?'

'It's a raid, Mal, old chap. I would have thought that was obvious.'

'You fucking...'

Lukashenko held up a warning finger. 'Save it, Mal. Not the time or the place.'

Robin glanced at the two men. Bile rose in his throat. *What the fuck was that all about?*

One of the uniforms burst into the room, holding up two plastic bags filled with white powder.

'Dear oh dear, Mal,' said Lukashenko. 'A trio of tuts in fact. Malcolm Farrand, I'm arresting you for being in possession of an illegal substance. Anything you say, etcetera. You know the rest.'

CHAPTER 6

'Shut the fuck up, Vincent. I want to speak to my lawyer.'

That evening the beer flowed freely at the Brisbane Hotel. The notorious Mal Farrand had been nabbed. It was a good enough excuse. Robin had temporarily forgotten about expensive timepieces and chic charcoal suits. He was caught up in the moment. Two kilos of smack, a kilo of blow, two sawn off shotguns and four handguns. Farrand was going to pull a fifteen at least. The team was on a high, the atmosphere infectious.

'What car are you driving Robin?'

It was Lukashenko, a glass of riesling in hand. It was a strange question at this stage of the proceedings. 'The green VL Commodore. Why do you ask?'

Lukashenko handed Robin some keys. 'Take the white ED Falcon. Ok?'

Robin's stomach lurched. 'Why is that, sir?'

'Just do as you're fucking told, DS Edwards.' Lukashenko sounded menacing. Then abruptly he smiled. 'Take the ED, son. And check it thoroughly before you lock it up for the night. We don't want any weapons going missing, do we?'

Robin felt a little unsteady on his feet. He had drunk two pints of lager, but he knew cops were pretty much untouchable. He spotted the white Falcon in the carpark. What the fuck was Lukashenko on about? Robin never left weapons in the car. He pressed the remote and folded himself into the driver's seat. Reaching over, he opened the glove compartment to find the usual logbook—and a white envelope. He ripped open the envelope. Lukashenko's tactics were on full display, about as subtle as a kick in the balls.

***

Renata paused and read over her day's work on the tiny screen of her Amstrad. She had acquired the laptop from Herman, a German backpacker she had met at Fair Dinkum. It was cumbersome, another possession she would have to deal with when it came time to fly home. But for now, it was adequate and despite the long-winded process of booting it up, using two diskettes, it gave her the feeling that her work was important and would be valued. The features editor at *Der Spiegel* had assured her they would take her work seriously. Young Germans were busy reconciling the nightmare of the Reich with the present peace and prosperity that pervaded German life. She read over the last page or two as a way of encouraging herself to persevere.

My grandfather was the kindest of men—or so I thought until he was arrested for a horrendous war crime, the burning of a barn full of innocent civilians in the town of Lidice, Moravia, in 1942.

Quite conveniently, I have been able to disown the shadow of that crime, if genes can be said to cast a shadow. Here in Perth, Western Australia, one of the most remote cities in the world, I have discovered my genetic grandfather, a man called Alan Duffy, an airman decorated for his service with the Allied Bomber Command during the Second World War.

What does that mean when applied to one's own father, or to one's grandfather(s)? In this essay I want to explore guilt—how collective guilt for what our grandfathers did in wartime gets mixed up with our own personal guilt which has grown inside us without out knowing.

She had found a lengthy quote—perhaps too lengthy for journalism—in a textbook in the State Library. The author was John Power, a young philosopher from Melbourne. At first, the language had tested her English comprehension, but as she worked through it, she found the thesis more and more persuasive. With each paragraph a new layer of meaning emerged, meaning which made her trip to Australia, her meeting with Duffy, and her adventures in Vietnam more valuable.

She sighed, saved her work and shut down the screen. Although Robin was generally encouraging of her writing life, he had laughed when she first showed him her computer.

'It's like something from *Doctor Who*,' he said. 'Pure science fiction. Does it work?'

When she pointed out how he relied on outmoded systems of data storage and retrieval in his workplace—something he often complained about—he had stopped laughing.

Robin! What was she going to do about Robin? Was he just one more *thing* she would have to dispose of when she returned? She smiled. He was so sweet. And soon he would be home. When he did finally arrive, the sweet man she'd been thinking about seemed somehow different. He smelled strongly of perspiration, as if he'd been working out in his suit. And his breath smelled of beer.

'I'll take a shower,' he said. He unbuckled his holster and placed it on the counter along with his watch and a dress ring his parents had given him when he graduated. Then he peeled off his clothes and disappeared.

Renata folded his trousers, hung his jacket on the back of a chair and went back to the counter. The watch was new and looked expensive. A Breitling. Made in Switzerland. A famous brand, originally made for aviators. Very expensive. She waited for him to emerge and offered him a drink. 'You want some olives with that, or will you wait for dinner?'

'I'm fine thanks.'

'Is something wrong?'

'I'm fine. What about you?'

'Everything is good. My work is going well. I received a very strange letter today. I will show you.'

The letter was from a solicitor acting on behalf of Alan Duffy. Its tone was stern. Mr Alan Duffy DSO repudiated any claim by Ms Renata Schmidt of a paternal link between Duffy and Renata's mother Marion Schmidt, nee Wagner. His only son, Peter Andrew Duffy, would be the sole beneficiary of his will. In repudiating all claims Mr Duffy wished to caution Renata Schmidt about her fanciful notion that Mr Duffy had somehow fathered Marion while on the run, in wartime Germany. He would be pleased if Ms Schmidt would refrain from contacting him in the future.

Robin glanced at it and handed it back. 'He's protecting his arse. He'll keep.'

'So, you are not so interested in my affairs, my birthright, said Renata.

'Of course, I am, it's just...'

'It's just?'

'I got a pretty strange letter myself. Not really a letter. More of a note. A very big note!' He opened the white envelope he'd been clutching and pulled out ten green polymer $100 notes, which he placed in front of him on the coffee table.

'Was zum teufel?'

It was clear an explanation was required. A red stain on Renata's throat was spreading up to her cheeks. 'Is this connected with your fancy new watch?'

'I know it looks bad, sweetheart,' said Robin. 'Lukashenko is just as crooked as we thought. Maybe more.'

'So now you are crooked too? Do you see where this leaves me? If I am living with a crooked cop, my future in journalism may be threatened. So too my chances of renewing my visa. I didn't think you were such a *dummkopf!*'

Robin took in the flush in her face and the angry words, and walked out of the room.

CHAPTER 7

'Gunther, thanks for returning my call.'

'My pleasure, Alan. What's on your mind?'

'In part just to have a brief chat. How's Bertha?'

Gunther Baumann sighed. '*Ach*, women, eh? Bridge.'

'Come again?'

'Bridge, my friend, bridge. The woman is obsessed. Her life is bridge, fashion and interior decorating. But I shouldn't complain, she has been a good and faithful wife for many years.'

Alan Duffy laughed. 'As I've told you, sadly I'm a widower. My wife died tragically in an accident some years ago. I must admit at times it's lonely, but on the other hand, I'm foot loose and fancy free. Given our business arrangements are now firmly in place, you and Bertha should consider coming to Perth on holiday. I have a large house with excellent guest accommodation.'

'Coffee please, Mai. I'll take it on the terrace. Sorry, Alan. I'm at my villa in Sapa and I've just finished lunch. Perth, eh? That's so kind of you. I will broach the subject with Bertha. It would do us both good to get away. But meanwhile, back to business. It has been a prosperous quarter. Things continue to go smoothly?'

'Indeed. Just to let you know, the first shipment has arrived punctually. No hiccups.'

'So, there will be many funerals, *ja*?'

'Well, we don't actually bother going through the rigmarole of a funeral.

There was a moment's silence. 'Surely, getting rid of bodies isn't that easy,' said Baumann. 'They have a habit of turning up, and then awkward questions are asked, *ja*? But I'm sure you know what you're doing. And it's none of my business.'

'Gunther, I can guarantee they won't be turning up any time soon. Let's just say, nothing gets wasted.'

'Man after my own heart.' Baumann chuckled. 'Goes to show there is money in death. Now what about our troublesome friends, are they ... how shall I say, still with us?'

Duffy laughed. 'All of that has worked out just fine.'

'The *polizei*?'

'You mean Robin Edwards?' Duffy asked.

'*Ja.*'

Duffy laughed again, 'Sweet as a nut. You might say he's on the payroll. It's always good to have another cop eating out of your hand. It's been a few weeks since that nonsense in Vietnam, everything should run smoothly from here.'

'Your man Lukashenko is very efficient.'

'Efficient, but expensive.' Duffy growled.

'What about that annoying fellow, Trung?'

'Well, initially I thought he might be a problem. I thought he might have to join the rest of his relatives. If you know what I mean?'

'And now?'

'Well now that the cop's been neutralised, the fellow is of no consequence. I'm not losing any sleep over him. What has me baffled is how they made their escape. From what you said they were securely locked away. One of your staff perhaps, Gunther?'

'That really is a mystery. As far as I know they didn't have any help from anyone here. My employees wouldn't dare. They know what would happen to them. There's just no way they could have made their way to Hanoi without help. One of my guys went to meet his ancestors. Oh, and there was another casualty, a girl. But, no, it was very mysterious.'

'As you say, odd, quite odd. I have another thing to discuss.'

'*Ja?*'

'I'm going into another line of business. Like what you and I are already involved in. I don't want to discuss too much on the phone, but it could involve some reciprocal trade.'

'Interesting. You have my attention, Alan.'

'As I get closer to the production stage, I'll get the information to you via our other channel.'

'Excellent. Anything else?'

'I may have another small problem.'

'And you think I may be able to help?'

'This is delicate. I may need a removalist.'

'One of your boys can't do it?'

'Of course. But as I said, it's delicate. Possibly a double removal. You have a man?'

'I do. He's American. Very smooth. A true professional. But Alan, I must warn you, he doesn't come cheap. His name is Mike.'

'Very interesting, Gunther. Maybe when the time comes Mike might enjoy an all-expenses-paid trip to Australia, as well as a tidy pay packet?'

'I'll tell him to make contact. *Wiedersehen*, Alan.'

CHAPTER 7

Duffy had made a decision. The war had taught him one very important thing. Destroy the enemy, before he destroys you. He slid open his desk drawer and withdrew an old black and white photo of his late wife Annette her arm around a gap-toothed and smiling Peter Duffy. From his pen collection he selected a black Texta and scrawled a cross over the image of his son, matching the existing black lines over Annette.

CHAPTER 8

Brendan O'Brien threw the can across the squad room. 'Hey Robin, catch.'

'Jesus, Brendan, you're not on the football field now,' said Robin, deftly catching it in mid-flight. He turned it over in his hands. 'Yeah, dog food ... so?'

'Read the label, dummy.' Brendan grinned and waited for a round of applause from the other detectives, Jack Dutton and Gillian Mortlock.

'You're an idiot, Brendan, you could have hurt someone with that,' said Gillian.

Robin examined the label, a stylized picture of a man leaning against a Spitfire. The man was sporting a bushy moustache, an RAAF icon. A happy Golden Labrador sat by his side. 'Hero dog food: The best food for Man's best friend. And you reckon our Mr Duffy is behind this? Really?'

'Really' smirked Brendon. 'Just look at the small print. Alan Duffy enterprises.'

'Interesting, but I think Lukashenko wants us to take the heat off Alan Duffy.' Robin wished everything about Duffy would simply disappear; yet Gillian especially was like a dog with a bone. He winced at the obvious simile.

'I hope you don't mind, Jack, but I've been researching this prick on my own time,' she said. 'I can I tell you, he's off.

Distinctly off.'

Gillian leant back in her chair. Clad in tight blue jeans and a black leather jacket, she could have walked straight out of *NYPD Blue*.

'Gillian, I know you,' said O'Brien. 'You see villains everywhere. So, what is it about Alan Duffy?'

'I'm so glad you asked, Brendan. For a start, he has crims working for him. As I've mentioned before, Niall Norman aka Hugo, and that other thug Grantley, are both career criminals.'

'Just for the record,' Jack Dutton chipped in, 'I gave my mutt Hero dog food and he's still alive. I also researched it and *Choice* gave it a top rating.'

Gillian started a slow hand clap. 'How's that for irrelevance?' asked Gillian. 'For Christ's sake, Jack, who cares how good the dog food is? Give me a break.'

Robin looked around the team. He liked working with them, and even better, none of them wore Breitling watches. 'Well look,' he said. 'There's no law against hiring ex-crims and that aside, I don't think we have much to go on. Do we?'

Gillian jumped to her feet and started writing on the white board. Smash repair. Alan's Tow Trucks. Gambling. Pornography. Funeral Parlor. *And drugs. Lots of drugs*. Robin remembered Trung's coffins with their false compartments. He really wanted to move on, but Gillian wasn't about to this let go. 'Can you explain a bit more, Gillian?'

'Ok, research. This is what vertical integration looks like.'

'Is that from the *Kama Sutra*?' asked O'Brien.

'Are you a bit excited by the mention of pornography, Brendan?'

O'Brien reddened a little but said nothing.

'The porn is legal,' continued Gillian That sex shop in Northbridge, Pussy Hut, belongs to Duffy. Also, he owns a smash repair place in Rivervale and the tow trucks associated with it. All of the towies have criminal records of course.'

'I've never come across a tow truck driver who didn't have a record,' said Jack.

Robin's interest was pricked even though Lukashenko had warned him off. 'So, what's with the gambling?'

'You may well ask, Robin. Gingers in Northbridge is an illegal gambling joint that's been operating for years.'

'And Duffy owns it?'

'You betcha,' said Gillian.

'Hang on, they got raided just last week and they were fined,' said O'Brien. 'What's the issue, Gillian?'

'I'll tell you what the issue is. Some fall guy sticks his hand up. He's charged, convicted, and fined. The club opens the next night with another fall guy to take his place. It's been going on for years.'

'I'm not convinced,' said Robin.

Gillian stood, her leather jacket open, exposing the 0.38 in her shoulder holster. She smiled. she's saving the best for last, Robin thought.

'And then we have the funeral business.'

'Gillian, we all know about the funeral side of things.'

'You think? Duffy's funeral business was started in 1921 by his grandfather.'

'And?'

'Not the biggest funeral parlor in Perth. Not the oldest.' Gillian paused.

'Yeah, we all know that.' Robin was drumming his fingers on the table.

CHAPTER 8

'I have a question,' said Gillian. 'How many funerals would you reckon Duffy's funeral business conducted in the last twelve months. What do you think? Anyone?'

'Five per week,' said Robin. 'Say two hundred and fifty.'

'I'll see that and raise,' said O'Brien. 'Three hundred.'

'Who cares?' said Dutton. 'Twenty, fifty, two hundred and fifty? What does it matter?'

'Three.' Gillian smiled a victorious grin. 'Just three.'

CHAPTER 9

Peter Duffy collected his mail from the Northcliffe Post Office and walked up to the Hollow Butt Café to read it. Still nothing from his father. But what did he expect? His father had never been interested in discourse of any kind, particularly if it contained an emotional dimension. It was obvious his father was behind the thugs paying a visit. But no explanation. It was meant as a warning obviously. How pathetic. But what on Earth could his father possibly be up to? He felt sad remembering the efforts his mother had made to work things out with her husband, all to no avail. His father would never reply. He must accept that and move on. He shuffled through the rest of his mail: a rate notice from the shire; the local rag, recently revived by a farmer's wife and filled with local gossip and bad jokes; some junk mail, mainly flyers from tradies looking for more work; and finally, an exciting note from the organisers of the rally in Denmark, set for the first weekend in spring. The note was handwritten in green ink on chunky, handmade paper.

Dear Peter,

We look forward to meeting you in September for our Big United Green Activist Rally (BUGAR). You are in the data base, and we will contact you as things develop. In the meantime, let us know of any local initiatives you are taking to stop the rot of big development.

Warm regards,

Eversley.

He read it over twice, each time registering a tingling feeling in his stomach. Eversley? He wanted to meet this woman with the soulful name, whoever she was.

He ordered a second coffee and pondered the note again. *Local initiatives*, Eversley had said. What could that mean? Did he have an initiative? It was a slack day at the golf course: no buses, no groups. One or two locals might want to play, but they could do it without him. He was going to pay Terry Tyack a visit.

Along the road to Pemberton, next to the old farm recently sold to developers, sat Terry's kingdom, the Northcliffe tip. The Suzuki eased up the gravel road and pulled up outside the open-sided shed which Terry used to sit in judgement over what came in, what went out, what went in the pit, and what was unclassifiable.

'Hi, mate,' he called, as he stepped out of his car.

'Peter,' said Terry. He was a man of few words. As Peter approached, he indicated a worn armchair that must once have graced the parlour of a farmhouse. Peter sat and the two men regarded the morning sky and the tip that was spread out beneath it. 'Got some nice lino in yesterday,' said Terry finally. 'Interested?'

'No, well off for lino thanks mate.'

'Wallpaper?'

'Who has wallpaper?

'Yeah, right.'

Another long silence, during which Peter considered whether to share his challenge. He had known Terry from the time he'd moved down to Windy Harbour, his Suzuki packed up with personals and a small trailer behind for the rest of his stuff. The old fisherman's shack he took over was supposed to be 'walk-in, walk-out' according to the estate agent. That meant that everything you might need would be there: utensils, beds, table and chairs, a stove, a gas tank. But the previous owner had stripped it, and so Peter had fallen into the habit of browsing the tip. He soon realised that Terry knew everyone and was a mine of information, a walking Yellow Pages. Not only that, he had an anarchistic view of the world, not so distant from Peter's own. Why not open up?

Terry listened in silence as Peter recounted the saga of the sea rescue project, his interest in it, and the very clever idea he had to smear old paint all over the building materials being assembled on the site. After what seemed like a full minute, Terry spoke.

'Why don't you talk to Alf?' he asked. 'Alf Longmuir. You know him? Sparkie. Good guy.'

'Yeah, I know him. Last time I talked to him he was scratching his head over the backup generator for a room upstairs. He couldn't understand why they needed it.'

'So, talk to him,' said Terry.

'And what?' asked Peter.

'Get him to wire in an extra switch that only you know about. Put it somewhere secret. If you want to disrupt things, you hit the switch. But seriously Peter, it's a bit bloody juvenile, isn't it?'

Peter grinned. 'Yeah, I know. A bit silly. But I just like the idea. Disrupt the pricks. I mean it's just a bit of a joke no real harm would be done. But you reckon he'd do it?'

'Just mention the name, Dougal McBain,' said Terry. 'Alf hates his guts. I'm surprised he'd even work on one of his projects. It goes way back. A blood feud. Don't ask, it's ancient Windy Harbour history.'

Peter drove back to his office at the golf club and turned to the most useful part of the *Northcliffe Bugle*—the trade directory. Finding Alf Longmuir's number was as easy as that. Now all he had to do was work up the courage to call him.

Peter held the handset of the fawn plastic touchphone in his right hand. Terry Tyack's words lingered: 'It's a bit bloody Juvenile'. He paused. 'Why on Earth would I do this...?' He grinned and dialled Alf Longmuir. 'Because I fucking well can.'

CHAPTER 10

April 1999

The Pioneer Women's Memorial Garden in Kings Park was bathed in warm sunshine this late afternoon at the beginning of April. The temperature had dropped to a mild twenty-six degrees and the easterly wind, which had earlier put an edge on the morning, had abated. Robin had claimed a grassy spot near the barbeque, spread out the rug and got the sausages cooking while Renata buttered the rolls. Now they were sitting on the rug and enjoying the view of the fountain.

'So, this is it, darling. A real Aussie picnic, complete with snags from the barbie.'

Renata looked cross. Perhaps her mood would improve after eating. He watched her load the roll with salad and reach for a sausage from the greasy tray Robin had placed between them. Tempted by the smell of the roasted meat, she lifted the first sausage to her mouth. The kookaburra came in low on silent wings, its angle perfect, its eyes fixed on its prey. In a snap of perfect precision, the bird grabbed the sausage from Renata's hand and continued on to its perch high above in an old paper bark.

'Fuck!' cried Renata. 'What was that?'

Robin was laughing, despite himself. 'That my dear was

a creature just down the food chain from us, but with better reflexes. A kookaburra. Here, have another one. Plenty for all.'

He passed her the tray. She grabbed another sausage, stuffed it in her bun, and ate it with one hand guarding her meal.

'If you laugh at me like that, then you are the cuckoo burra!' she said. It sounded spiteful, but he let it pass.

'So glad I finally got to show you just how beautiful Perth is,' said Robin after a beat. 'I've always felt a certain sense of serenity whenever I'm here. The manicured lawns, magnificent old trees, stunning views of the Swan ... how good is that, eh? Would you like some moselle? I brought your favourite.' Robin hoped he was playing the cheerful host with conviction.

'I'll have a beer, thanks,' said Renata. 'And what is this thing... Snags?'

'Yeah, snags. It's an Australianism. Means sausages.'

'Well, why not say sausages?'

'It's just ... slang. You must have slang words in German, surely?'

'In Germany, we have sausages,' she said. 'Proper sausages. *Bratwurst*, *weisswurst*, and a hundred others. And we serve them with sauerkraut. And good German mustard. So don't lecture me about sausages!'

'Would the kookaburras know the difference?'

Renata grabbed the can of Swan Draught from Robin's hand, ripping the top off and taking a generous swig. 'You know, sometimes I feel as if I'm in kinder school...'

'You mean kindy?'

'This is like talking to a five-year-old. Why is it you Australians love to shorten things?'

'What are you talking about?'

CHAPTER 10

'For Christ's sake! Snags on the barbie? It sounds like a child's doll. What's wrong with, *sausages on the barbeque*? And while we're at it, you always say, what's for brekkie? How about calling it *breakfast*? And you suggested later in the "arvo" we should go to "Freo" for a coffee. Really?'

Robin reached for a beer. 'Australianisms aren't the major issue, are they?' His hand slid over hers.

'No, I guess not.'

'You want to talk about it?'

'Well, I don't suppose your silly slang is that important. Part of the problem is me.'

'I don't follow...'

'When I decided to come to Australia, I had this stupid, romantic idea that Australia wasn't like Europe. I thought it was a young country—fresh, clean. I thought, God knows why, it was different. No corruption, a land of golden beaches, endless summers and everything was just about perfect. But what do I find? Through no fault of mine I'm caught up in something criminal, and you are as well. Turns out my grandfather is a gangster, along with your boss Lukashenko. Where in hell does it all end, Robin? And what about poor Trung?' He's in a safe house that isn't safe. I'm starting to think I'd be better off going back to Germany and turning my back on all of it.'

'Don't worry about Trung. I've had the word Duffy is no longer interested in him. He's out of the safe house, back home and driving a taxi. Trung's ok, he's a survivor. Now they believe I'm on the payroll, the Vietnam business is of no further concern to Duffy or Baumann.'

'Great. But that still leaves us. Doesn't it?'

'I'll sort it out. I promise.'

Robin didn't know what else to say. They finished the salad without enthusiasm. Renata nibbled guardedly at another sausage. Robin felt ill; the thought of losing Renata was like a solid blow to the stomach. 'It's going to be a nice evening. How about we pack everything into the Subaru. We'll take the freeway to Fremantle and have that coffee.'

'Or do you mean, we'll pack things into the "Suboo", and go to "Freo" for some "coff"?'

That got them chuckling again. They packed up the things and left two sausages for the wildlife. By the time they reached the car Renata was smiling, much to Robin's relief. They drove in silence along Mounts Bay Road towards the Kwinana Freeway. The Swan River at dusk was glorious. Robin thought the barbeque had been a mixed success. Renata sighed as she looked out her window at the old Swan Brewery and Mount Eliza nestled behind it.

They took the ramp onto the Kwinana Freeway, George Harrison crooning on the radio.

'Penny for them?' asked Robin.

'I don't understand … penny? What costs a penny nowadays?'

'What's on your mind?'

'You know what's on my mind. I thought I'd made that clear. I'll give you a more pointed version. I loved the man I thought was my grandfather and he turned out to be a war criminal. I come to Australia to find my real grandfather and I discover he's just as bad, maybe worse. And now I'm in love with a crooked cop.'

Now Renata was crying. 'Is this what I deserve, Robin? Is this my birthright? Am I being punished for what my German grandfather did? If I have children, will they be criminals?'

The tears slid down her face. Robin noticed she had said, 'if *I* have children' not 'if *we* have children'. 'I'm not a crook,' Robin said.

'Really?' And that money? A thousand dollars, wasn't it? What would you call that, eh?'

'I haven't touched it. I've put it aside.'

'*Wunderbar*. Then everything is ok?' Renata sneered.

'What I mean is ... look I'm not sure what I mean. Lukashenko has me, us, where he wants us. I'm going to figure a way out of it. Truly you must...'

'Robin,' Renata screamed. 'Watch out. Up ahead!'

'Shit,' Robin swerved into the emergency lane. A Chrysler Valiant station wagon had hit another vehicle and was on its side. Flames raced along the bonnet as steam erupted from the smashed radiator. They looked in horror at the wide, terrified eyes of a little blonde girl peering out of the rear window. Robin slammed the Subaru to a halt.

Renata grabbed the picnic blanket. Robin jumped onto the upturned side of the wagon and tried to wrench open the door. Angry flames exploded from the engine compartment. He recoiled and screamed as his hand touched the scalding metal. He banged futilely on the window. Rising to his feet, he kicked in the window and reached through the shattered safety glass, jerking open the door. The smell of burning flesh—his own— mixed with the stink of burning plastic. Renata climbed onto the wreck, grasping her beret to protect her hand as she prised the front door open. A hysterical woman clambered out.

'Luisa, Luisa,' she yelled.

'I've got her,' Robin cried as he wrapped the rug around the terrified child, dragging her to safety.

The mother sat on the verge; arms clasped around her daughter. 'Thank God, thank God. You've saved our lives.'

Suddenly cameras were flashing, and a reporter thrust a microphone into Robin's white face. He looked up, his burnt hands in his armpits for comfort. 'Where the fuck did you guys come from?' he croaked.

'How about that? We just happened to be passing by. You're a cop, aren't you? I've seen you in court.'

Robin said nothing.

'Well, you're both heroes,' said the newsman. 'It'll be on the six o'clock news.'

CHAPTER 11

June 1999

By early June the new Marine Rescue clubhouse had quickly taken shape as prefabricated wall sections were raised, trusses fitted for the roof and the first window frames slotted into place. Plumbing and electrical work sprouted from the concrete floor like so many weeds. A metal staircase was in place, giving access to the first floor.

Peter surveyed the work with a critical eye. The building was turning out larger than he had imagined, blocking out views of the harbour and the tiny green islands he had once enjoyed. Birds and tiny mammals which had made this corner of the bush their home had long since fled. From the top of a dune above the swale he could see who was working today from the vehicles parked on the site—some tabletop trucks bearing cladding, a few utes for the plumbing contractors and at the end of the line, the same ugly muscle car that had ploughed up the green at the golf course.

He moved closer. Next to the muscle car was a commercial van branded: *Henderson Wholesale Kitchen Supplies*. The driver of the van, a short man in overalls, was unloading cartons onto a trolley and carefully wheeling them across the lot to the receiving bay. From a half-open roller door, one of the men was lifting the crates and stacking them against a wall. The other one was directing operations. Peter watched the stack of cartons reach ceiling height. They looked heavy and clanked metallically when moved. A second stack was begun, this one made up of smaller wooden crates marked, *Fragile: Glassware*.

Peter found a sheltered spot on the dune and tried to make sense of what he'd witnessed. Why would a sea rescue clubhouse need to stock up on kitchen supplies this early in the game, with the building not yet completed? And what possible connection was there between his father's thugs and the operation he had just witnessed? What were they doing here in his backyard?

He waited for the sun to dip below Point D'Entrecasteaux, enjoying the chatter of the honeyeaters and the bark of a roo from deep in the swale. He heard the roller shutter rattle to a close and the car doors of the three men slam shut. Soon they were gone. He walked down to the loading bay and tested the shutter. Locked. Around the front of the building a large picture window was waiting its turn to be fitted to its frame. Above it, and to one side, the frame sat staring out to sea, empty save a cobweb that an opportunistic spider had begun. He levered himself up and through the open frame, taking care not to kick the heavy glass. Inside, he found his way around the sprouting cables and pipes to the far corner of the building, the inside door to the loading bay. A newly fitted lock secured it to the door frame. A shiny key had been left in the lock ready to be claimed by the new tenants.

A week later, sitting comfortably in his top floor room, Alan Duffy thought about life, the universe and almost everything. Had he been able to encompass everything in his thinking, he might have foreseen the way it would all end, how close his empire was to crashing down around his ears. But it is not often in the repertoire of petty dictators—or even major ones—to see everything. They see what they want to see, are flattered and cushioned from reality. They are surrounded by toadies and yes-men. In Duffy's case, his number one yes-man was this minute making his way up the stairs.

Before his reverie was interrupted, Duffy had time to congratulate himself on a number of fronts: his pet food business was booming, likewise his smash repairs, his tow trucks and his gambling interests. The pornography business was a little flaccid, he thought, and laughed at his own joke. As for the fledgling meth lab down south—well he was about to find out.

As expected, McBain had been a pushover, particularly with a bit of monetary encouragement, 'So here's the thing, Dougal. I need the exclusive use of the clubhouse for a few months, no busybodies no interference. No ... no I promise I will leave it in pristine condition. All I want is for you to stall the council. The permits, the final ... whatever. Just make sure that I have it for at least two months. Three would be better. How much? 'Duffy laughed. 'You Irish crook. Hey, never you mind what I want it for. Ok, done. When are you coming? Day after tomorrow. I'll have the folding stuff and a nice drop of Irish Whisky. You know my address? Yeah. The house. Dalkeith. The front door will be open.' Duffy smiled at the memory of the phone call.

Hugo looked distracted. He took his usual seat on a spindly chair opposite Duffy's.

'Where are the others?' Duffy asked.

'Sorry, boss. Grantley and Joey got busted for dealing.

They're inside.'

'Inside where?' asked Duffy.

'The slammer, boss. They might be there for a while.'

'For Christs sake Hugo, when did this happen? Why wasn't I told?'

'Boss, it just happened. Anyway, Grantley was pretty confident they'd make bail.'

Duffy stood up and grabbed his walking stick. For a while it looked like he might take it out on Hugo. Instead, he walked over to the French doors and gazed out at the river.

'We got most of the stuff together,' said Hugo. 'For the meth lab. It's all there, ready to go. There's only one problem.'

'What would that be?' asked Duffy, still staring at a distant sailboat.

'I can't do it alone. Which is why I've taken the liberty of inviting a real chemist, a guy called Doc, to join us. If that's alright...'

Duffy sighed deeply. He hated incompetence. Incompetence was what killed men in the last little skirmish, he thought. That and the fact the German night fighters outgunned us. 'Is he coming soon? Let's have a drink while we wait.' He moved over to the bar and pulled out his best Scotch. 'Join me?' he asked.

Hugo shook his head. He'd made the mistake of agreeing once and been castigated for drinking on the job. Duffy liked to set traps and Hugo worked hard to avoid them. There was a buzz from the door phone.

'Yes?' said Duffy. 'Push the gate. The front door is open.' He waited until he heard the gate latch, hung up and turned to Hugo. 'This'll be your friend. He'd better be good. And more to the point, we have to know he's kosher.'

'Kosher? Sorry, um, what do you mean like Jewish food?'

'Christ, you sure don't bring a lot of brains to the party. Is he, ok? Do I have to spell it out?'

'No, no, I know he's ok. He's done time. He's hungry for a dollar. He's gonna work out. I guarantee it.'

A man of average height wearing an open neck shirt entered. His hair grew wild on the pale expanse of his skull, which seemed overly large. He pushed his glasses, which were clouded with dirt, up the bridge of his nose and held out his hand to Duffy.

'Sir,' he said. 'I'm Drake Merriman. My friends call me Doc.'

'Right you are,' said Duffy. 'How do you know this clown?'

Doc looked at Hugo and then back to Duffy. 'We met at Atlas Studios downtown. I make and sell diet supplements to body builders.'

'I'm afraid Hugo's been overdoing it,' said Duffy, a malicious sneer emerging beneath his moustache. 'His brain has been crowded out by muscle, what was left of it. How do I know I can trust you?'

Merriman patted the pockets of his lab coat and presented a creased letter to Duffy.

'My CV,' he said. 'As you can see, I have worked in a range of scientific environments. Mind if I smoke?'

Duffy frowned, 'If you must.' He scanned the document and handed it back. Merriman had produced a chunky Zippo lighter and was taking pleasure in its operation.

'I assume Hugo has told you about our little project?'

Merriman pushed his glasses up to the level of his eyes again, not answering.

'How much do you want for setting up a meth lab and supervising the first batch?'

Merriman looked at Hugo and then back to Duffy. 'Five thousand dollars plus a travel allowance. You buy the chemicals.'

'Are you clean? Do you have a record?'

Merriman smiled broadly. The ash on his cigarette was growing longer. 'Of course, I do. But which bent chemist doesn't have a record?'

'When can you start?'

'Immediately.'

Duffy paced his Persian rug a few times, looked at Hugo, then back to Merriman. 'Start tomorrow. Hugo, go with him now and grab the chemicals. Then pick up Doctor Merriman at 6 am tomorrow. No time like the present, eh, Doc?' He moved over to his roll-top desk, removed a large chocolate box from the drawer and counted out fifty green notes.

Merriman sat down, his cigarette drooping from his mouth, and counted them carefully. They shook hands. 'Pleasure,' he said.

Duffy said nothing. When they had gone, Merriman in a trail of ash, he wiped his hand carefully on a towel behind the bar and poured himself another Scotch. Resuming his armchair, he raised a toast to the universe which, he hoped, would continue to be bountiful.

CHAPTER 12

A uniformed secretary ushered a sullen Renata and a nervous Robin into the inner sanctum of the halls of power, the office of the Police Commissioner of Western Australia. Len Bruce and Police Union man, Walter Jessup, rose to their feet.

'Please, Miss Schmidt and DS Edwards, have a seat.' The commissioner motioned to two tan leather chairs.

'Very nice,' Robin whispered to Renata, who grunted in reply.

On the drive into the city, they had managed to have yet another argument. It was becoming a habit with them, almost a daily necessity. Occasionally the passions they aroused in each other transformed into a fierce bout of lovemaking, but Robin was pretty sure that was a less than ideal preparation for a life together. He was more inclined to think it was a ticket to separation and sadness. This latest argument had begun in silence, malignant and hostile, until Renata finally spoke.

'I don't see why I need to be doing this,' Renata said. 'I'm going back to Germany; I've had enough of the police in Australia.'

Robin squirmed at the thought of the official ceremony to come. He didn't feel like a hero, just a citizen who happened to come across someone in trouble. The media had blown it up out of all proportion, shining the spotlight on Robin and

Renata when it seemed all the fissures in their relationship must surely be visible to anyone with eyes to see. They were both to be presented with the Star of Courage for their dramatic rescue of the mother and daughter from the burning car. The very thought of the Governor General and other dignitaries, gushing and gladhanding them, made him feel ill. On top of his natural reserve, he wasn't even sure that Commissioner Bruce wasn't himself corrupt. Surely it didn't just stop at Lukashenko.

The office, with its sweeping views of the Swan River, sent a clear message of power and influence, an office befitting a police chief. The customary photo of the Queen adorned one wall, along with solemn portraits of former commanders. But the cheerful little circle of chairs indicated that the meeting was meant to be informal, and that helped Robin to relax a little.

'Coffee, tea?' the commissioner asked.

Robin had Len Bruce figured as a political animal, a media darling who could work a crowd like a Southern evangelist preaching about Jesus.

'First, you should know the date! The ceremony will be in a week's time. The press will be there. TV, newspapers. It's a big event. And I will say how pleased I am that a serving police officer is receiving an award. What about you, Walter?'

The union guy rubbed his hands together, echoing the chief's words. A nervous Robin looked sideways at Renata, just as she glanced at her watch.

'As I said, the ceremony will be in a week's time. Naturally your boss Vincent Lukashenko will be there. He speaks very highly of you, Robin.'

Renata glared at the police chief. 'Lukashenko, you say?'

Len Bruce understood the power of publicity. Polished,

smooth and urbane, his square-jawed face radiated strength and professionalism. And he was nobody's fool. He read people like a book. 'Is there a problem, Miss Schmidt?'

Robin's stomach dropped. He knew what was about to be unleashed.

'I'll tell you what's wrong. I won't be sticking around for your silly ceremony. I am not a complete *dumbkopf*. I'm heading back to Germany. Your police force stinks. Your hypocrisy is sickening. Robin is an honest cop and even he has been sucked into the disgusting web of corruption you command, I don't want your medal. It's a damned insult.'

The silence was palpable. The causeway traffic seemed amplified. Robin tensed, waiting for the axe to fall. Commissioner Bruce's jaw went slack. He turned his gaze on Walter Jessup. Decorum had gone out the window.

'Wally, what the fuck's going on?'

'Jesus, Len, I've got no bloody idea.'

The commissioner sprang to his feet, open mouthed and red faced. 'Listen to me, young lady!' he stammered.

Walter Jessup felt the need to interrupt.

'Excuse me, Len, before we go any further, we need to lay down some ground rules. Robin is a serving police officer, and he needs to be aware of his rights. It sounds like we are going to need a signed statement. DS Edwards, are you happy with this? Do you want a solicitor? Miss Schmidt, I feel that I must warn you, silly vacuous, tales of police corruption are common place and are almost always without foundation. Now, for the moment you have the Commissioner's and my ear, but if what you have to report is simply hearsay you will be shown the door, and remember we do have laws of slander in this country.

And, DS Edwards take it on notice that as this lady is a friend and obviously a confidant of yours, this could well be a make-or-break career moment. Do you follow?' There was a fierce glint in Jessup's eye.

For Robin, it felt like an invisible load had been lifted. He grabbed Renata's hand. 'Gentlemen, this woman is the most important person in my life. As things stand, she would rather be in Germany than stand around and witness this disease grow and consume me and my team. If you guys are serious about corruption and are willing to take the appropriate steps, I'm prepared to tell you everything. I warn you, it's some story. The press will have to know. It's too big to sweep under the rug. Are you sure you want this?'

Commissioner Bruce sat back on his chair. He knew that such exposure would bring his career to an ignominious end. He padded silently to his desk and flicked the switch on his intercom. 'Carol, come in and bring your notepad and pen. If you have any lunch engagements, you'd better cancel them.'

The atmosphere back home in Robin's place was thick with unspoken resentment. They had driven home from the Commissioner's office in silence, each processing the long afternoon and what it had uncovered. The Commissioner had demanded every minute detail of what Robin knew, and what he suspected. Renata had been somewhat mollified by Robin's declaration of how important she was in his life, but the sleazy side of police life, the self-serving behaviour of its leaders, and Robin's weakness in accepting the bribes in the first place had left her with a bitter taste in her mouth. An episode of *Seinfeld*, a show which they had often enjoyed together, failed to repair the rift. For the first time since Renata had moved in, they slept apart, Robin on the couch and Renata in the double bed.

The next morning, Renata was up early cooking bacon and eggs. They ate together as normal and discussed safe subjects like the weather and the upcoming soccer World Cup. Renata cleared the table while Robin packed his bag for work.

'You know that letter from my grandfather,' said Renata. 'The one where he disowned me? He mentioned his son, Peter. Do you know him?'

'Yes, I do,' said Robin. 'I called him when we were tracking some intel we thought we had on the old man.'

'We are related. I guess he is my uncle, my mother's half-brother.'

'Wow! I never gave it a thought.'

'Do you know where he lives?'

'Sure. He lives in a place called Windy Harbour. Way down south in tall-tree country.'

Renata looked thoughtful. Robin went to work, determined to get on with the important task of nailing Renata's grandfather to the wall. Commissioner Bruce had wanted to stand Robin down until the dust had settled but at Robin's insistence and surprisingly also Walter Jessup, who had spoken up in his defence. 'For God's sake, Len, the boy's a star. You need him to be in the thick of it.' Jessup had turned and winked at Robin.

Len Bruce had initially glared at Jessup, but then threw back his head, laughing. 'Bloody hell, Wally, in for a penny in for a pound, eh. You're right. Ok Edwards, show us what you're made of.'

It was a strange thing to be doing, he mused, given how he and Renata had been thrown together in the beginning. He spent most of the day at his desk, drawing together elements of the Duffy case. When he reached home, the house was in darkness. Inside, the dishes were soaking in cold soapy water. Renata's backpack and sleeping bag were gone, along with her computer and some clothes. There was no note.

CHAPTER 13

Peter Duffy was sweeping his deck after lunch when he looked up and saw a young woman with a large backpack heading his way. Backpackers were commonplace at Windy Harbour. They came to walk the Bibbulman Track, to see the scenery and to experience difference. He stopped sweeping and watched her approach. She would likely ask him the way to the camping area. She reached the edge of his yard, took off her pack and regarded him.

'Peter Duffy?' she asked.

'Yes.'

'I am your niece! Renata Wagner, from Germany.'

She held out her hand, smiling broadly. He was immediately impressed with the confidence she projected, her stonewash jeans and crop top a badge of modern youth. Niece? How could that be?

'I would kill for a coffee!' she said. 'Do you have any coffee?'

He picked up her rucksack and invited her inside. *A niece? He asked himself again.* Strangely, he immediately took the visitor at her word. It felt as if he'd netted an exotic butterfly. Renata found a seat on the battered lounge he'd scavenged from the tip and watched while he fussed with the stove and loaded his Alessi induction pot, a treasure he'd discovered at a garage sale in Northcliffe.

'It's a fuck of a long way down here,' said Renata.

Peter smiled. He wasn't used to women who cursed but decided he liked it. 'How did you get here?' he asked.

'I caught a bus from Perth to Manjimup and then hitched the rest of the way. When I got to Northcliffe, a workman called Alf gave me a lift. A good man. He dropped me off up the road and told me where I could find you.'

Peter served the coffee and dragged a chair from the kitchen table across to face his visitor. 'You say you are my niece?'

'Yes,' said Renata. 'Your father Alan Duffy is my grandfather—although he won't admit it. I came to Australia to find him, all this way, and he's disowned me.'

Peter gazed at Renata, nodding his head. 'So where did you grow up?' he asked.

'On a beautiful farm outside of Freiburg, near the Black Forest.'

'And what made you come to Australia?'

'I was looking for this airman my mother told me about. She had heard the story from her mother, how his plane crashed, how my grandmother picked him up and took him back to the farmhouse. My grandfather was away at war, murdering people—that all came out later. Anyway, the airman and the farmer's wife became intimate, as people do in wartime. And it seems maybe your father, my real grandfather, was no angel. He is perhaps implicated—do you say that, implicated?—in the death of a woman on a neighbouring farm. My mother's father, the SS man, was blamed for it. But in my grandmother's version, she believed the airman was simply trying to escape on a motorcycle he found next door. She also believed the neighbour, who was a German patriot, would have tried to stop him and she paid the price. But according to my grandmother, it was no big deal. It was obvious my grandmother disliked the neighbours and well … that's what people did in that war. The airman was simply doing what he had to do. Seems like you could do anything in wartime!'

'Wow,' said Peter. 'That's quite a story. Another coffee?' This is a hell of a lot to take in. It's, it's gob smacking. It's like some sort of movie. My God, I really don't know what to say.'

'Do you not believe me? Do you think your father…?'

'Oh yes, I believe you. Don't get me started. My father is capable of just about anything. Oh yeah! I believe you all right.'

Over the next hour, and with the help of more pots of coffee, they talked. Renata said that she had never expected to get involved in all this intrigue when she first decided to fly to Australia. Young Europeans loved Australia—it was wild and surprising. And now here she was in this wild and surprising place, talking to her uncle.

'So, my father told you where to find me?'

'No. Robin Edwards, is my boyfriend. He knew where you were living. You know him?'

'I know him,' said Peter. 'I had reason to call him when I saw a news item about my father. Wait, I'll go and find it. Now, where, where? Here it is. I stuck it on the fridge, just cast your peepers on this.'

He passed it over to Renata, who scanned it quickly.

'Do you mind if I photograph this?' She pulled out her Minolta, so far only used to take mementoes of the places she'd seen. In Vietnam, things had moved so fast she'd forgotten all about it. Come to think of it, things were moving fast in Perth. She thought about Robin, how angry she was with him, how she had decided to walk out on him for a while and let him worry about her for a change.

They talked about nature, about the bush and the environment. Peter promised to show her some of his favourite places if she had time.

'I have time,' she said. 'Do you have a bed?'

She seemed straightforward to Peter, uncomplicated. He told her he had a spare mattress and that she could sleep in his loft, if she wanted. For now, the shadows were lengthening, and it was time to collect some wood and think about dinner. Did she like fish? He had caught some whiting that morning, he said, and she was welcome to share it, just a simple meal.

That night, Renata found herself in Peter's loft by 9 pm. Already she was missing Robin. The wind for which this strange place was named was buffeting the vertical surfaces of the little shack. Earlier, helping Peter with firewood, she had glimpsed a sky full of stars. This was the Antipodes, she thought, the end of the world. It could have been Patagonia it was so strange to her. Yet in the warmth of the fire and the reassurance of the solid timber beams she felt at home, as she had once felt on the farm, before things went awry.

CHAPTER 14

Hugo and Doc made strange travelling companions. Doc talked too fast and Hugo was left to fuss about the ash Doc was dropping on the leather seats and carpet of his Holden HSV.

'So how far is this place? Do they have snakes down there? Snakes are fascinating, you know. People are talking about using very small quantities of venom to get high, did you know that? Hey, how about my CV? Duffy was a pushover, wasn't he? It's amazing what you can find online.'

Hugo grunted, dropped the muscle car down a cog and passed a semi. He had to watch his speed. Traffic infringements had been Grantley and Joey's downfall and the beginning of their troubles. Best to keep a clean record so you could do really bad shit and not get caught, he thought. They were almost at Bunbury. In the boot were the bags of lithium, sachets of ephedrine and bottles of ammonia they required for the trial batch they were hoping to cook later that day. 'Piece of piss', Doc had said when asked how hard it was to produce ice. Hugo hoped so.

'What does online mean?' he asked.

'It means the internet,' said Doc. 'The world wide web. The most amazing bit of technology. Soon everyone will have it on their desk. Or maybe even carry it around with them.'

Hugo grunted again. He was more comfortable in Grantley's

company. Grantley mainly talked about his conquests, or his most recent challenge at the Leederville Hotel. Bouncers were out front and on display, thought Hugo. They were like the travelling boxers his father had told him about, standing up on a platform at a country fair or even the Royal Show, daring anyone to have a go. He had given up being a bouncer years ago, but Grantley kept it up. Or he did, until he got nabbed in a drugs sting on the streets of Northbridge. There'd be no Grantley for a while, no Joey.

They pulled in at Donnybrook for a burger. With luck, they'd be cooking by mid-afternoon. For the rest of the journey, they were silent; Hugo focusing on the road and Doc playing with his Zippo lighter. At Pemberton, Hugo cracked. 'Will you stop playing with that fucking thing?'

Doc clicked the lighter shut and stuffed it deep into the pocket of his jeans. Renata was reading, waiting for her uncle to wake up. My uncle, she thought! Her family connections were widening. Soon she'd have gathered a whole clan around her. She had slept like a baby, the soft light of the lamp moving on the ceiling whenever a gust of wind struck. Now she was luxuriating in her own company, a simple backpacker. again. Had she ever been a simple backpacker? Maybe not. She had set out with an agenda; but the way it had played out was totally unanticipated.

'Coffee, niece?' called Peter. He seemed to have gathered some confidence since the night before, when he had become tongue-tied whenever she asked him about himself.

She pulled on track pants, parka and beanie and climbed down the ladder.

'What's the *zeitplan* for today, Uncle?'

'The what?'

'The timetable.'

'I usually don't have one,' he said. 'But special occasion, I guess. How about this? After breakfast we drive around to Salmon Beach and catch some fish. We'll cook them for lunch and then go for a stroll through the swale...'

'What's a swale?' Renata asked.

'It's the passage behind the dunes. On the other side of the dunes is the beach. With luck we'll meet kangaroos and other critters.' Peter rubbed his hands together and grinned.

It was getting better and better, thought Renata. *He is such a nice man. Must be at least fifty, I guess.*

Salmon Beach was breathtaking: three kilometres of white sand, dunes at the back of it and behind the dunes rocky peaks and valleys; at either end, a headland; and to the west, the wild ocean. The best thing was, there wasn't another soul on the beach. While Peter set up his rods, baited his hooks and sank tubes in the sand, Renata wandered barefoot along the pristine shoreline, the surf a constant roar at her side. She came to the southern end, and on an impulse ripped off her clothes and dived in. She could feel the strong pull of the rip and was careful not to venture past knee deep. Even so, she could sense the danger— and the thrill of that wild beast—the ocean. When she quickly dropped below the surface the cold tore at her heart, causing her to gasp and run dripping from the water and back to her clothes. Without even bothering to dry off she dressed again, wrapped herself in her parka and returned to Peter's temporary camp.

'Like to try a cast?' he asked.

He handed her a rod, showed her how the reel worked and how to angle the whole thing back over one shoulder, and then cast before gently tautening the line. Her first two attempts were dismal failures. Her third launched the baited hook and sinkers well over the first line of breakers and into the sea.

'Perfect,' said Peter.

The morning yielded but one fish, an Australian salmon which gave Peter a good fight before surrendering. It seemed huge to Renata, who was amazed that such a creature might be lurking out beyond the breakers looking for a feed.

'They're not exactly the top delicacy to be had,' said Peter. 'But the way I cook it, I think you'll like it.'

He was right. Back home he bled it, cleaned it, and instead of filleting it cut it across the backbone into steaks, then cooked them on high heat on the barbeque. It was delicious and Renata was left to admire her uncle's skills, both on the beach and in the kitchen.

'Ready for a walk?' he asked after they'd washed the plates.

He led her on the road past shacks with quaint names and then to a track which led to the swale. True to his promise, an old boss kangaroo was there. It stood tall when it saw them, then decided to retreat. For the rest of the trail Renata scanned the bush for signs of its kin. At Cathedral Rock they sat together on a bench and watched the bay for signs of life. As if on cue, three dolphins appeared, trawling around the rock and then joining in a frolic in the surf. By the time they turned for home several hours later the sky was pink a sign of good weather to come. At the end of the swale Peter took the ridge trail back, aiming to show Renata the fishing boat harbour.

They came to the new sea rescue building and crossed the expanse of bitumen serving the boat ramp. Utes and trailers dominated the car park, except for a black muscle car which

Peter immediately identified. Perhaps this was the time to try the new circuit breaker Alf had installed for him. Whatever they were up to they'd be very pissed off when the lights went out. 'Back in a minute,' he said.

He and Alf had puzzled over where to put it. It had to be somewhere easy to access but not obvious. In the end they had put it in the old toilet, which was open to the public 24 hours. It was a primitive structure made of weathered jarrah beams with a rusty iron roof. Alf had placed it above the old concrete cistern, inside an innocuous wooden compartment painted the same colour as the walls. To reach it, Peter had to stand on the toilet seat and stretch. He climbed up, reached as far as he could with his head pressed flat against the cistern. The little door opened easily enough. With a quick prayer and a deep breath, he broke the circuit to the upstairs club room. There was no sound of a generator or anything else; just the rhythmic crash and swish of waves in the harbour. He imagined that whatever they were doing with their beakers and flasks, they were now doing it in the dark.

He walked outside. Renata was waiting for him, staring at a tiny bird that had landed on a shrub by the path.

'What happened to you?' she asked.

'Toilet,' he said.

Suddenly there was loud bang, a great whoosh and the smash of breaking glass. Red and green flames shot out of a hole in the wall panelling. Peter thought he heard a strangled cry before the flames took hold and the wooden floor went up in smoke.

Peter gasped and grabbed his chest. 'Jesus! Bloody hell. What have I done?' he mumbled. A clammy sweat seemed to seep from his pores. Sinking to his knees, tears were now running down his face. He kept mumbling, 'No, no.'

Renata had her Nokia out, desperately jabbing at the keyboard. Nobody had told her there was no reception at Windy Harbour. She turned her gaze to her distraught uncle.

'Peter, it's not your fault. Whatever happened ... *Mein Gott!* It's an accident, surely?'

They heard the siren before they saw any sign of a reaction. The caretaker's ute came barrelling up the boat ramp, still shedding sand and seaweed from its sprint across the beach. Ernie Briggs, the caretaker, aimed his fire hose at the inferno. It had little effect. In less than twenty minutes the blaze had reduced the new facility to ashes and mangled roof iron.

'There's nothing we can do,' said Peter. He tried to imagine what possible connection there could be between the circuit breaker he had activated and the conflagration that followed. It didn't make sense.

Equally uncomprehending, but totally unaware of her uncle's part in it, Renata was silent as she followed him back up through the bush to his cabin.

PART FOUR

CHAPTER 1

August 1999

Robin sat listening attentively as Gillian presented her findings. On a hunch, she had organised a visit to Duffy's pet food company, Hero dog food, first getting a warrant from a surprised and sceptical Justice of the Peace. Nothing to see, she said, just a lot of bored workers in white overalls monitoring vats of meat, which were then pumped into a dispenser which squirted the right amount of product into cans on a conveyer belt.

'Nothing to see,' she repeated, 'until this refrigerator van arrived and a couple of Asian guys in shorts and singlets climbed out, fired up a forklift and unloaded some barrels. Here, I snapped this.' She passed around a Polaroid photo of the barrels, which were apparently made from black plastic capped with a red screw top lid.

'How does this story end?' said Brendan. 'It's beginning to sound a bit like that bloody Snowtown bizzo. Is there a punch line?'

'Yeah, there is, drop kick,' said Gillian. 'It's in this lab report.'

Robin scanned the report before passing it around. It was an analysis of a liquid which Gillian had chanced on after the freezer truck left. On the floor where the barrels had been unloaded was a viscous pool which she managed to soak up with a hand towel from the bathroom. The liquid was a mixture of human blood and vinegar. The room was silent. Brendan's face was white.

'Are you sure?' asked Jack Dutton. 'That seems a little too easy and quite unbelievable. You're saying that Duffy, a successful businessman, is supplementing his pet food with human remains! Why? Did we run out of kangaroos?'

Robin was doodling on his writing pad, a large circle for Duffy's empire, a smaller circle for Vietnam, an even smaller circle for Lukashenko. The circles were separate, like lily pads in a pond. From Duffy's circle he extended tendrils attached to smaller pads. The funeral business. The funeral business! Fuck.

'Are you making the same connection I'm making, Gillian?' he asked. 'Funerals—human remains—pet food. Join the dots.'

'Excuse me,' said Brendan and left the room hurriedly.

'Delicate constitution,' said Gillian maliciously. 'Poor Brendan.'

The stayers attacked the puzzle. Why would Duffy choose to pollute his Hero brand in that way? What was the point? And if the funeral business was a front, as it appeared to be, what was behind it?

'All of this advances our case against Duffy,' said Robin. 'You remember at the first meeting of this little group we were sidetracked by Lukashenko.'

'Yes,' said Gillian. 'And I was appointed to lead the charge against child porn. What an exercise in futility that was.'

'You might also remember we were trying to link Duffy with the high-grade heroin finding its way onto the streets.'

'How long ago was that?' asked Jack. 'Seems like years.'

'I know,' said Robin. 'We are the collective incarnation of

Inspector Plod. But we have something new.' He unfolded an official looking report. 'I've just received this from the coroner. It may yet be the subject of an inquest. It concerns the death of two men in the sea rescue clubrooms at Windy Harbour.'

'Windy Harbour!' said Jack. 'I used to fish there with my father.'

'I've never been there, but I have a feeling that's going to change,' said Robin. This has Duffy's footprints all over it. His merry men have been seen around there, and I bet they weren't fishing. He was thinking of Renata. She had returned a week ago full of enthusiasm for the place, an emotion overshadowed by the explosion but bolstered by gladness that she had made a connection with her Uncle Peter. She had been urging Robin to take some time off and explore the place. Somehow work kept derailing the plan, but he knew it was important to her and was determined to do it. 'I'll read the findings, shall I?'

'What's the take home?' asked Jack. 'Those things are heavy going.'

'Ok,' said Robin. 'Here goes.'

Brendan returned and quietly took his seat, waving at the others.

'I tell you what boys and girls, this smells like Duffy. Just listen. The fire which destroyed the partially complete building began in an upstairs room which appeared to be secured more heavily than the rest of the building. Evidence collected by the forensic team included ... hmm, more words ... the remains of chemistry equipment: Bunsen burners, beakers and retorts. Traces of lithium and ephedrine, along with the scorched label from a bottle of ammonia. Also, a camp stove attached to a small tank of propane, which of course had blown up along with everything else. Witnesses reported a sizeable explosion, followed by tongues of red and green flames.' Robin said nothing about the fact that Renata was a witness. She was a complicating factor he could safely ignore, for now.

'Methamphetamine,' said Brendan. 'Highly volatile.'

'Right,' said Robin. 'They were making methamphetamine, or ice—the next big thing after heroin. Cheaper to make and much less complicated.'

'Have the bodies been identified?' asked Gillian.

'Yes and no. Oh boy, you're gonna love this. The first was our old friend Hugo, aka Niall Norman. His tatts gave him away. There wasn't a lot else, except for dental records. He'd spent a lot of money on his teeth—so he died pretty. The second body has not been identified. He wasn't so pretty. But they found him clutching a Zippo lighter.'

'You know about meth, Brendan?' asked Jack.

'Yeah, there was an in-service about it. The coming thing. As I said, it's highly volatile.'

'Do you have a theory about what caused the spark, if it was a spark, that set everything off?' asked Robin.

'What was the power source in the building?' asked Gillian. 'Do we know anything about that?'

'Solar electricity, according to this,' said Robin. 'But to cook the stuff, they would have had to use propane, wouldn't they?'

'Surely not,' said Gillian. 'Even Niall Norman wouldn't be stupid enough to have a naked flame to cook his ice?'

'Probably not,' said Brendan. 'It doesn't become volatile until you heat it up. So if they had a well-guarded propane camp stove and had lit it, say with the Zippo, no worries. Now, if they had reason to use the lighter when it was almost cooked... *Ka-boom*!'

'Why would they?' asked Gillian.

'The stove went out,' suggested Jack. 'You know what camp stoves are like.'

'There's one other possibility,' said Robin. 'It was a new building, not even complete at the time of the accident. These guys were very keen to get started. What if there was a power failure?'

'And?' asked Gillian.

'Right!' said Brendan. 'That's it. Mr Zippo wasn't thinking. The lights go out, and in a panic, he reaches for his lighter. Holy fuck! Can you imagine?'

Robin was scribbling furiously on his pad. Who did the wiring? Was it safety checked, or hadn't they reached that stage of completion? He knew who would know these things. But first of all. His last note to himself read: *Call Peter Duffy*.

CHAPTER 2

Twilight and Peter Duffy was mulling over the state of the world, in this case, his world. The steamer chair he'd found washed up on the beach supported him nicely, and the light beer he was sipping was just alcoholic enough to promote relaxation. There was one jarring note. He'd called Robin Edwards, the cop who was fast becoming a friend. Edwards had questions about the electrician who had wired the burnt-out sea rescue clubhouse. Peter had feigned innocence, said he would 'make enquiries'. Was he in trouble?

The strains of 'Amazing Grace' came wafting across the dunes. Fucking bagpipes, who plays the fucking bagpipes? he thought. Peter quite liked the song, but a little variety might have worked, and in any case, it was at odds with his mood. But of course, it was the dour Scot who lived two hundred metres away in the oldest cottage in the settlement. He tried to forget the din as he took another swig of his beer and focussed on the black and yellow honeyeaters feasting on the nectar from the red bottle brush at his front door. He knew the bagpipe player's name was Angus, owing to the crudely written and crudely expressed sign on the man's door: *If you're selling something, fuck off. Angus.*

The first time he'd seen Angus Buchanan, Peter had offered the man a friendly wave, after all this was a friendly place. Everyone knew everyone. They helped each other. This was a community. But not Angus. Friendly waves went unacknowledged.

Once Peter had followed the call of the pipes and found Angus on the platform overlooking Cathedral Rock. The vision of waves crashing over the rocks and the dopey Scotsman clad only in a flimsy torn singlet, thongs, and for Christ's sake, a kilt, was a strangely stirring sight. Angus was rock solid with brawny, hairy legs, thickly knotted arms and a broad chest. A man who needed no one and feared no one.

'Well, let him play his fucking pipes.'

Peter rose from his chair and stretched. The pipes abruptly stopped. Magic.

Next morning Peter packed his overnight bag and set out for the Green Activists Rally in Denmark, almost 190 kilometres from Windy Harbour, something he'd been anticipating for months. Even though the original purpose of joining—what to do about the Marine Rescue clubroom was no longer an issue, he pushed his Suzuki to the limit, the soft top flapping and the wind buffeting his rugged-up body. The tall trees never failed to settle Peter's darker emotions. *If only Dad would come down here and just see the beauty, maybe he'd stop seeing all this in dollars and cents.* Deep down, however he knew nothing could change his father's views.

Arriving at the big tent pitched opposite the Serendipity Gallery, he registered and joined the line of protesters ready to march.

The rally proceeded peacefully, if a little noisily, down the main street, the activists easy to recognise. Women with multi-coloured hair, long flowing dresses, broad brimmed hats, and beads pushed wide-eyed children in strollers. The exotic odour of patchouli oil permeated the staid Denmark street. The men were even more colourful, some with mohawk haircuts, multiple piercings and the gleam of activism in their eyes.

'Why don't you city faggots just fuck off? Go on, piss off.'

The screamer looked like he may have been a shearer. Surrounded by his mates, they stood on the veranda of the Denmark Pub, their uniform khaki trousers or shorts, T-shirts and Blundstone boots.

The procession moved inexorably to the stage in the main street, where Bob Brown himself was due to speak. Whistles blew and the repetitive chants bellowed their irresistible message, 'What do we want? Green space! When do we want it? Now!'

Peter's whole being soaked up the sights, the sound, the fervour. He gazed happily at the sea of humanity, united in a noble cause. He strode steadfastly down the street.

A tall man in jeans and a tight black T-shirt emblazoned with the word 'Everlast' blocked his way. The man held up a hand. 'What are you staring at, dipshit?'

Peter believed the crowd would protect him but sadly, his fellow activists scuttled away. The man exuded aggression and carried not an ounce of fat. 'Sorry, mate. Nothing,' he mumbled. 'I'm staring at nothing. I come in peace.' He managed a weak smile and tried to sidestep.

'Oh, right. I see. I'm nothing. Is that what you're saying?'

'I'm sorry mate. I meant no offence.'

The man grabbed Peter by the shirt front and pulled him in close. Peter could smell beery breath. Spittle flew from the man's mouth. Two police officers grinned as they leaned against a post at the front of the newsagents.

'Hey, laddie. Try picking on someone more your size.'

Peter hadn't noticed Angus as he quietly stepped up. No kilt, just everyday jeans, plaid shirt, and tennis shoes. The man let go of Peter's shirt and moved close to Angus.

'What do you know, a fucking pom.'

Angus winked at Peter before turning his attention back to the man.

'A fucking pom, is it? Actually, laddie, I'm a *Scot*. And guess what?'

The man now seemed a little uncertain. Angus had an air of confidence about him that was hard to argue with.

'Aye, sunshine. I'm from Glasgow. And here comes the kiss.'

Blood erupted from the man's shattered nose. He screamed and dropped to the ground, knelt for a moment, then fell flat on his face, unconscious.

'English. My fucking arse.' Angus chuckled as he regarded the prostrate figure, then grabbed Peter by the arm. 'C'mon, laddie. Out of here, the coppers aren't our friends.'

The march ended, speeches were delivered, and the protesters dispersed. Rainbow people were off to a full moon rave in the forest. Serious policy makers were meeting with Bob Brown at the Environment Centre. Peter found himself following Angus, who seemed to have his own ideas about the next thing.

CHAPTER 3

On the long drive back to his Windy Harbour refuge, Peter had much to reflect on. Uppermost in his mind was his encounter with Angus. The Scot had impressed him like no other person in his memory, male or female. He wondered if it would be possible to resume his everyday life, the humdrum rhythm of existence, with a force of nature like Angus living so close.

After the rally they had bought a bottle of Scotch and driven down to Ocean Beach in Peter's Suzuki, the sea breeze sluicing through the open side curtains.

'It's a quaint wee car you have, laddie,' shouted Angus.

'It's called a Samurai,' yelled Peter.

They both laughed at this, the pretentious name for the puny car and perhaps the idea of Peter being connected in any way with a Japanese warrior. And yet his warrior potential had already been proven—he had removed the blot on the Windy Harbour landscape that had so incensed him and now linked up with a movement that stood against those who would despoil the natural environment for profit. The two dead men he'd shoved firmly into 'the too hard basket'.

They parked on the dune overlooking the surf club and walked to where they could see the estuary and beyond that the Southern Ocean. Angus produced two small glasses from the deep pockets of his parka and poured a measure of Scotch into each glass. 'The elixir of the gods,' he said, and downed his in one gulp.

Peter sipped his carefully. Each taste burned his throat, but he tried not to cough. The wind was up, sand tearing off the top of the dune. He supposed that the Scotch warmed a person up, but it was the time of evening when he would have been lighting his fire and sealing up the windows of his shack. He turned up the collar of his donkey jacket and shivered.

'You're cold, laddie. I can see that. Shuffle back a bit and I'll warm ye.'

Peter moved his body so it was leaning against Angus's folded knees. He felt awkward, unsure of himself.

'You need another shot, man.' Angus poured him a second glass and Peter could feel it going down, down his throat and into his blood stream. He pushed his back into Angus's knees but now the big man had opened his legs, allowing Peter to snuggle into his embrace. They sat like that, both looking out to sea as the gulls busied themselves with the last catch of the day. A new moon had appeared from behind the headland to the east, its cold light bathing the scene in its glow. 'Are you comfortable?' Angus asked.

Peter gave him a thumbs up. No words were needed.

'There's no need to worry, man. I'm not a poof!' The Scottish burr extended the sound for a few beats.

Peter felt safer than he had ever felt in his life, safe from the taunts he had once collected from his schoolmates and safe from his father's judgements. He was warm and protected, and he wished for it never to end.

'Tell me about your life, laddie,' Angus said softly.

Peter told him—how growing up he had gradually learned

that his father could not be relied on, that despite his war service and the image of a respectable businessman which he projected, there was something underhand about him which seemed to seep into the big house in Jutland Parade like rising damp. And then there was his treatment of Peter's mother, the unbearable way he demeaned and insulted her.

'He sounds like a right feckin eejit' said Angus.

They had stayed talking, murmuring really, until finally the night had closed in, and it was time to leave. Peter had dropped Angus back at his tent in the sportsground and unrolled his swag next to it. By morning, Angus had cleared out. How many men were sure enough of their masculinity to do what the Scot had done, to embrace another man out of pure regard? Peter wondered.

The morning light was pouring through the trees as he drove into Walpole and found a parking space by the bakery. He would go in and order eggs and toast and coffee and count the blessings in his life: his life at Windy Harbour, his niece Renata, and his new friend and protector, Angus. He had reason to feel cautious optimism about the future, an unusual position for him. He could see a future of activism, growth and expansion, free of the black hat of his father's greed.

By the time he reached Windy Harbour it was after midday. He rounded the last bend, coasted downhill to the campground, and turned left. Outside his shack was a totally unexpected sight: a police cruiser and green Commodore. Renata was sitting on the veranda, next to a uniformed cop and another man he guessed was Detective Robin Edwards. None of them looked happy.

CHAPTER 4

Alan Duffy limped back and forth across the expanse of his carpet, his cane tapping out the rhythm of his steps. McBain, had just reported the latest on the Marine Rescue headquarters at Windy Harbour. The fire was being investigated as an insurance fraud, and with two bodies thrown into the mix which automatically meant police involvement and possible discovery of the burnt-out meth lab. The fire itself had been reported on the Channel 9 news the night before. Two dead, which probably meant Hugo and that idiot Doc. No great loss—that was his first thought—but it meant that he was going to have to lean on Grantley and Joey for muscle, two individuals who shared between them the brain of a flea.

He needed time to think. Later in the day he was due to talk to yet another bunch of schoolchildren out at Bull Creek. The talk was wearing thin. Each time he delivered it he tried to embellish it a little, add another touch of invention to a story that was deader than the crew he had bailed out on. Sandy's obituary should have been the end of it. No more war stories. But then Renata had turned up and the whole sorry business of shtupping the Nazi's wife ... he was tired of it. What had happened to the dream of easy money, a life of luxury, exotic holidays and fine foods? He even missed his wife some days.

The intercom sounded from downstairs.

'This a good time, boss?'

Duffy walked over to the French doors and took up a pose that he hoped exuded importance. Grantley entered, out on bail, wearing trackpants and a sleeveless body shirt. During his time inside he had acquired a mullet haircut and some amateurish tatts on his upper arms. He had turned the corner into Downhill Road, thought Duffy, and was heading for the dead end.

'Joey couldn't make it,' said Grantley. 'Had to go see his woman, urgently.'

When he said this Grantley reached down and cupped one hand around his groin. He grinned oafishly.

As a bodyguard for an important man, he just didn't cut it. 'Grantley, I'm afraid we are going to have to review your employment,' Duffy said.

'How do you mean, review?'

'We are looking at integrating some of our activities into a larger entity, resulting in economies of scale for head office.'

'Come again?'

'We're going to have to let you go.'

Grantley moved closer, staring hard into Duffy's flinty old eyes. 'Come again?'

'I think you heard me the first time,' said Duffy. 'There'll be severance pay of course. Just pack up any personals you've left in the house and off you go, there's a good man.'

Grantley snorted, then with a hand on his chest pushed Duffy out through the French doors onto the balcony. Outside it was a sunny Spring morning. A brisk easterly breeze bent the potted shrubs. Duffy reached for a tighter grip on his cane, but Grantley got to it first, wrenching it out of his hands and casting it aside.

'What are you doing?' cried Duffy.

For an answer, Grantley pushed him further back till he was bent over the balcony rail, then grabbed his ankles and tipped him backwards so he was dangling in space, the same airy space his wife once breathed before her untimely death. 'I'm thinking of letting you go,' said Grantley, and laughed.

Duffy's first thought concerned how he might look, smashed up and dead on the driveway like Annette, blood seeping onto the concrete and a look of surprise on her face. He yelled hoarsely, hoping the neighbours would hear, but in Jutland Parade you minded your own business. Nobody heard; nobody came. Grantley shook him a couple of times, his spine bashing against the slab and his head flopping around painfully.

'How do I contact Renata?' Grantley demanded.

'You can't,' said Duffy.

'Where?' Grantley demanded, shaking the old man some more.

'Fuck you!' said Duffy.

Grantley let go of his ankles for a split second, before regaining his vice-like grip.

'Fair Dinkum Backpackers will know,' he rasped. 'In Northbridge.'

Grantley pulled him up and dropped him back on the balcony. With another round of mocking laughter, he left. Duffy stood up painfully and searched for his cane. A broad patch of damp had appeared on his fawn trousers. He had pissed himself.

CHAPTER 5

Peter greeted his visitors in a quiet voice. After all the excitement of the rally, and the tender moments he had spent with Angus at Ocean beach, he was in no mood for an inquisition.

'Peter Duffy?' said the cop, as he flashed his badge. 'I'm Sergeant Barter. This is DS Edwards—'

'No need for all that,' said Peter. 'This isn't Hollywood. It's Windy Harbour. Both these people know who I am. Ask them.'

'We just need to have a word about the fire in the sea rescue building,' said Barter.

'Hi, Peter,' said Renata. 'You want a cup of tea? I can make a pot. Maybe we all need one.'

Peter unlocked the door and ushered them inside. Robin dragged some chairs into a rough semi-circle while Peter helped Renata locate the tea things and fire up the gas burner. Robin heard the pop of the burner as it lit. Everyone down here relied on bottled gas for their cooking, including the meth lab, apparently. Renata brought in the cups and Peter followed with an ancient brown teapot that looked like it might have been rescued from a Country Women's Association fete.

'Before we start,' said Peter, 'I just want to say that you don't have to rely on my version on any of this. Renata, my niece, was by my side when it happened.' While it was true, he hoped she'd said nothing about his quick visit to the toilet.

'You don't need to be so defensive, Peter,' said Robin. 'We're just trying to establish what happened.'

'As I said, Renata knows it all. You could have saved yourself a trip.'

'What she doesn't know, Peter, is who owned the Holden HSV that was left unclaimed in the car park, and what it was doing here.'

'You must have tracked down the registered owner, surely,' said Peter.

'We did,' said Robin. 'Of course. His name was Niall Norman. He used the name Hugo and he worked for your father. And this is why I'm involved. It's not necessarily just a local police matter. I'm not really at liberty to say more on the subject.'

Peter nodded.

'So my question is, do you have any idea why someone working for your father would be cooking, or trying to cook, methamphetamine in a half-finished building five hours drive south of Perth?'

Peter blinked. Why not tell them what he knew, up to a point? Except for Renata— and he wasn't even sure about her—they would never understand nor approve of the green warriors and their march through Denmark.

'I thought it must be something like that,' he said. 'I had a sniff around a few weeks before when they unloaded a whole lot of crates full of glassware and so on. It looked like a chemistry lab, but I couldn't really make sense of it. The car was familiar to me. Two of my father's thugs paid me a visit at the golf club, where I work, earlier in the year. They tore up one of my greens— maybe out of spite, or maybe my father had told them to.'

'Why would your father tell them that?' asked Peter.

'We don't get on,' said Peter. The understatement of the year. But I do have an idea why the club could become a meth lab?'

'Oh' Robin glanced at the at the sergeant.

Peter hesitated. 'I know that my father knows Dougal McBain. They go back years. I remember Mc Bain coming to the house when I was a kid. It's common knowledge he virtually controlled the local council. He could have easily allowed my father exclusive access, maybe not forever, but long enough to turn out a lot of drugs. I'm sure Dad would have realised that no drug manufacturing site could ever be permanent.'

'Yep. That makes sense. What do you know about Alf, the electrician?' asked Sergeant Barter. Peter guessed he was based at Pemberton.

'Not much,' said Peter. 'He told me the developer had ordered some fail-safe mechanisms for the room upstairs, including a generator. Why not ask him?'

'We tried,' said Robin dryly. 'He was incompetent by midday.'

'You mean drunk?'

'Exactly.'

'You know the slogan,' said Peter. 'Windy Harbour is a small drinking village with a fishing problem.'

The men laughed. Renata looked puzzled.

'How can there be a fishing problem?' she asked. 'Peter and I caught one easily.'

'It's a joke,' said Peter. 'I wish I could translate it for you.'

Renata shrugged. The men stood up. 'You've been a great help, Peter. Thank you,' said Robin.

'Let's take a walk up to the site,' said Barter. 'One last look before I make my report.'

'I'll stay here,' said Renata. 'Come and get me, Robin.'

They left Peter and Renata in awkward silence. Finally, Renata spoke.

'Is there anywhere we can stay down here for the night? *Ein gasthaus*? Anything. I don't fancy that long drive back tonight.'

Peter grinned. 'You would be wanting Mandy Tapioca.'

'Is that a name?'

'She's New Age. She keeps Windy Harbour's only bed and breakfast. I can't guarantee it will be clean. I hear she'd a bit slovenly. It may offend your German instinct for...'

'Instinct nothing,' said Renata. 'We'll take it. Can we walk there?'

'Sure, let's go.'

They walked east in the direction of the fishing co-op, past tumble-down houses with quaint names. They passed Angus's place, but there was no sign of the man. Peter realised he was missing him, that he wanted to see him urgently and tell him what? That he loved him? That was a bit extreme. That he cared for him? That he had saved his life in more ways than one? None of these words would cover how he felt, possibly because the society didn't allow straight men to express affection towards each other outside of standard mateship rituals.

In an overgrown lane behind the main track Peter located Mandy's place, once a grand two storey beach house, now weathered and showing its age. Mandy emerged, a head full of tangled curls followed by a bulbous body which, like her house, had once seen better days. Peter introduced Renata and the two women quickly made the arrangements. There was an upstairs room, but they would have to share the bathroom downstairs because the toilet upstairs was blocked.

'A strange woman,' said Renata on the way back to Peter's. 'We have women like that in Germany, *hausfrau*, who let themselves go.'

Peter laughed. They were passing Angus's house. The door opened and the Scot emerged.

'Laddie, wee laddie,' he said, barrelling down the steps. 'Give me a hug, do.' He wrapped Peter in his great arms, squeezing all the breath from his lungs. 'And who would your lassie be?'

'This is my niece, Renata. She's from Germany, out here to trace her grandfather, who just happens to be my father.'

'Well then you'd better come in and join me in a wee dram of Laphroaig,' he said. 'I have just invested in a bottle, which entitles me to a square yard of real estate in the peat bogs of Islay. All I must do is go there and claim it!'

By the time they reached Peter's place both Renata and Peter were feeling the effects of the smoky brew. It was dusk and Robin was pacing the veranda.

'I thought you'd got lost,' he said.

'No darling,' said Renata. 'Come with me. We are found.'

CHAPTER 6

Next morning Renata and Robin woke early. The strange bed and the even stranger landlady had invigorated their love life. In the darkened room, with the sound of the sea so strong it might have been lapping at the front door, they had reached and found each other, stripped off and gone at it so vigorously that the bed threatened to roll across the room on its castors.

Now they were on the road, trying to make up time for Robin's early afternoon meeting.

'You say it's at our place? Sorry, your place?'

'Our place, honey. I love it that you think it's our place.'

'But why? Don't you have meeting rooms?'

'We do, but the Commissioner thinks it's best to keep our meetings secret, just the small group. The gang of four: Gillian, Brendan, me, and Jack. Big stuff is unfolding.'

They made it to Maylands by midday. Renata showered and dressed, then announced she would go shopping in the city and maybe take in a movie. She called her mother in Germany and had a long chat. She'd decided to message Trung to see if he was available to pick her up. Robin, drained from the journey but re-energized. He had a quick tidy up of the kitchen, and was ready to greet the team at 1 pm.

Brendan arrived first with some meat pies, then Jack with a carton of beer and finally Gillian with the salad she'd promised.

By mid-afternoon they were well into it. A collection of empty Swan Lager cans was now scattered across Robin's kitchen table. Jack Dutton leaned forward, carefully making a triangular stack of the empties.

'Jack, could you please focus on things. I think you've been watching too much play school,' said Gillian.

'There's a bear in there.' Brendan chortled.

'Guys, c'mon this is serious.' Robin glanced at his watch. They all had work the next day. Robin had told the team about Vietnam, Baumann, the drugs in the coffins, in fact everything, including his meeting with Commissioner Bruce. Lukashenko was the wild card, hence the need to meet in secret.

'Robin, I'm still a bit nervous. You've told the Commissioner the whole story?' Gillians brows furrowed.

Brendan took a generous swig from the red, white and gold can with its distinctive black swan emblem. Robin nodded.

'Well, how the fuck do we know he isn't on the take? How do we know we aren't going to be set up? Jesus, Lukashenko is capable of just about anything. We haven't heard a peep out of the top brass. How long has it been?'

'Weeks, I guess.'

Robin shared his uneasiness. The commissioner had suggested the four officers stay under the radar, meeting in secret. Robin believed the Commissioner was an honest cop, and the idea the head of the union, Walter Jessup could be corrupt also, was simply unthinkable. 'Let's just focus, please. Do you all agree the human remains going into cans of Hero dog food simply have to be from the bodies in the coffins?'

The detectives glanced at each other, murmuring their assent.

Robin spoke. 'Ok, that's a given. We are going to avail ourselves of this, this, what do they call it? DNA technology. That will take time, but I think we know what the results will be. But the thing is, why on earth would he do that? It's not as if there are enough bodies to fill any more than a fraction of the pet food cans he churns out.'

Gillian shuddered. 'God this is awful. Macabre. It's like a cheap horror movie.'

'Anyone see *The Texas Chainsaw Massacre*?' Jack Dutton asked.

Gillian picked up an empty can, hurling it at Jack's pyramid. It fell to the floor in a deafening clatter.

'Why did you do that?' Jack Dutton scowled.

'Now I know why I don't want children,' Gillian muttered.

Robin pushed his chair back. Climbing to his feet, he stretched, lacing his hands behind his head. 'I think I have it. Yep. I've got it figured.'

The others sat up a little. They were all ready for some logic.

'Trung the taxi driver couldn't understand why Vietnamese people would send family members back to Perth to be buried. He said it just didn't make sense. The Vietnamese have their own burial customs. All this time I simply accepted everything at face value. Vietnamese people with family here died in Vietnam and Duffy was legitimately filling a need and exporting their remains here for burial.'

'Hang on.' Brendan spoke, 'what are you talking about? We know, the bodies are Vietnamese, albeit with a snazzy bit of organ removal. So, what's your point? Obviously for whatever reason their family wanted them sent back home to Perth. Perhaps Trung simply got it wrong. I mean cultural things do change. They are bloody Vietnamese, they are dead. So, what exactly are you getting at? I'm confused.'

'So am I 'growled Jack.

Gillian jumped to her feet, punching Robin playfully on the shoulder. 'Oh boy, I get it. Wow. This is a doozy. Bloody hell, this is worse than a bit of heroin importation. Shall I tell them, or should you?'

Robin grinned. 'Go ahead.'

'Here it is. The bodies aren't related to anybody in Perth.'

'No?' Jack asked.

'No. Baumann has acquired these stiffs.' Gillian was grim faced.

'How the fuck do you ... acquire dead bodies?' Jack asked.

'These bodies are simply murder victims. Baumann has selected them. God knows how, or what criteria he applied.' Gillian scanned their faces.

'Apart from organ removal,' Robin interjected.

Gillian nodded. 'Yep, the organ removal was simply a bit of extra cash for Baumann.'

'Hang on.' Brendan held up a hand. 'So why didn't Duffy just proceed with a burial here in Perth? I mean it's hardly as if a few dozen corpses are going to affect the bottom line of his pet food business.'

'My turn.' Robin grinned at Gillian. 'Well, here's the thing. Obviously, Duffy has a very streamlined operation getting bodies into Perth. But ... then what? Think about it. Funerals are an expensive business. There's a lot of records. A lot of official procedure. Clearly Duffy has figured out a great angle. Nobody in Perth is going to enquire about the bodies, because they don't have any rellies here. So ... the bodies simply disappear, and the evidence becomes dog poo. How good is that?'

'So,' Brendan said slowly, 'using the cadavers as pet food was simply expediency?'

'Got it in one' Robin beamed. 'Nobody was going to miss them. A proper burial service is expensive. On top of which, sooner or later the crematorium people, the cemetery people, or whoever, would start to ask questions. If Satinwood kept having funerals with no bloody mourners it was going to look a little suspicious. The reality is, getting rid of bodies is a tricky business. How many murderers have been put away because they didn't manage to hide the corpse? I tell you this is sheer brilliance. It could have gone on forever.'

'Except?' Gillian murmured.

'Yes, well ... Trung, bless his heart. And of course, my dearly beloved Renata who helped get us out of Vietnam.'

There was a moment of silence as they digested the appalling story of possible multiple murders and drug importation. The phone rang. Robin grabbed it. 'Yes?'

'It's Len, Robin. I'm about to leave a function just down the road from your place. I'd quite like to drop in if that's ok. I know it's late in the day.'

'Yes, sir. Fantastic. The rest of the team is here. And we have some things to tell you.'

'Likewise. Ten minutes.'

The sprawling Police Academy, originally Perth's first aerodrome, lay at the end of Robin's Street, Peninsula Road. His passing out ceremony was there just a few short years ago. There was a short break for Jack to pick up his toys before the lights from the Commissioners Statesman Caprice pierced the room. Len Bruce, clad in his impressive full-dress uniform, bounded up the stairs to Robin's door. Three coppers stood nervously to attention.

'Oh, for Christ's sake you lot, sit down. Now, where's that cold beer I was promised?' He found a seat and began.

'Robin has told me all about his team. You can't imagine just how pleased and proud I am of all of you. Corruption is somewhat of a problem in most police forces around the world. Robin has explained how Lukashenko uses and abuses his power to snare good officers and turn them into bad ones.' Len Bruce smiled like a proud father. 'I'd like to think of you four as my untouchables. Now, down to business. I know you haven't heard a peep from me since Robin and Renata spilled the beans but believe me we've been busy. We plan to swoop on Lukashenko, the other crooked officers and of course Alan Duffy and his bully boys, just as soon as the next lot of heroin laden coffins arrive.'

Perched on a lounge chair, Commissioner Bruce was like one of the boys. Everything about the man exuded a tough confidence. With his jutting chin, blonde greying hair with its boyish cowlick and the footballer physique running ever so slightly to fat, he had the persona designed to instil confidence. Brendan offered him another beer.

'Good man.' Len jerked back the ring pull and drank. 'We have some very interesting developments. All confidential. Recently I was at a law-and-order conference in Singapore. I had a long chat with my opposite number from Vietnam, Pham. Nice chap. In the way that Vietnamese police can be nice when they choose to be. He is going to take out Gunther Baumann.'

'Take out?' Robin echoed. Len Bruce chuckled.

CHAPTER 6

'Pham is determined to clean up corruption in the Hanoi Police. They don't have the same problem with due diligence that we have here. I reckon Baumann is, as they say in the classics, fucked.'

CHAPTER 7

Tok-tok-tok-tok, the terrifying sound of machine gun rounds echoed through the jail. Was the executioner a good shot, or were the Government swine just trying to save money on ammunition?

Gunter Baumann knew this was the day. The time he'd spent in the general prison population had been unpleasant. It had been a relief to reach the condemned man's cell, even though he knew his stay would be short. The dirty camp stretcher in the cell was not designed for Westerners; his feet dangled over the end. Yet he had found his new accommodation quite spacious. The rough-hewn bricks of the cell walls rose up a good twenty feet. A small, barred window allowed the tantalising sounds of busy street life to penetrate. There was a bucket and rolls of grubby toilet paper. Neatly laid orange and black floor tiles stretched out into the prison corridor and then abruptly stopped, as if the tiler had suddenly run out of materials.

The taciturn guard seemed to take perverse pleasure in telling him that he was probably going to be the last to be executed in Hoa Lo known as the Hanoi Hilton. It was to become a museum.

He noticed the food had improved. He no longer needed to poke and prod the predominately rice dishes, searching for the animal or human faeces placed there by sadistic guards. The knife wound he'd sustained in the first ten minutes of his prison life had been swift, executed with all the precision of a skilled surgeon. Non-fatal but very bloody. He remembered the man approaching and he remembered his foul breath, his rotten teeth. He also remembered the man whispering, 'She was my sister, you pig.'

The problem for Gunther Baumann was he really had no idea which woman the man was referring to. He thought perhaps she was the one he'd executed in Sapa. For God's sake, she'd been caught stealing. Or maybe it was that prostitute? Pretty girl. What was her name? Again, hardly his fault. He reflected on the unfairness of it all. It wasn't as if he killed for pleasure. They had all died for good reason. The problem with these people was they lacked discipline. If they just did what they were told!

Tok-tok-tok-tok-tok-tok. A longer burst. *I hope I get someone who's a good shot.* He remembered when he'd executed some Jews all those years ago in Poland. Some had screamed after being hit in the stomach instead of the chest. He'd had to finish them off with a shot to the head from his pistol.

Baumann had been stunned by just how quickly it had all unravelled. The Australian cop who'd escaped had told his story to a high-ranking superior. Then, unbelievably, that cop had spoken to Pham Van Duc, the head of the PPF, The People's Police Force. Gunther had been aghast. His bribes had made Pham Van Duc a wealthy man. Duc's wife and Gunther's wife, Bertha, had become the best of friends.

His reverie was interrupted by screaming in the corridor. A man pleading, wailing, begging for mercy. The scraping sound of the man's sandals as he was dragged across the flagstones. Bloody fool, did he think his screams would save him? *Tok-tok-tok-tok.*

Gunther Baumann had accepted the inevitability of his death. There was only one item of unfinished business. She had not visited him once. This was to be his last day on earth. Surely, she would come. Wouldn't she?

'We missed a slam there.'

Bertha Baumann, cards in hand, smiled consolingly at her three Bridge partners. The Sheraton Hanoi had been their choice of venue for their club for the last fifteen years.

Sandra Butler was the wife of the CEO of the Asian KPMG office. Yvonne Maltravers, apparently, was a minor British aristocrat. Her husband did something in government. And June Cawley just had a lot of money and a succession of young male lovers. Today the atmosphere was heavy; the usual pre-game chitchat had been forced and stilted. Bertha Baumann's husband was to be executed today. The ladies were still reeling at the shock of it all. Surely there must have been a mistake? Jovial Gunther; charming, urbane Gunther? Never a breath of scandal. He doted on his wife. The ladies marvelled at Bertha's stoicism, her courage, her fortitude, carrying on as if today were just another day.

'Bertha,' Sandra had asked, a sympathetic hand on her arm, 'are you sure you want to play? Today of all days?'

Bertha dabbed a lace handkerchief at a dry eye. 'It's what Gunther wanted. He even insisted I not visit him. I mean, that prison is a horrible place, and he didn't want that to be my last memory of him. He loved me so much; he was always so considerate.' She paused for effect. 'Junie dear, did you order the cakes and coffee? I do hope they have some of those cinnamon thingies, they really are something else.'

CHAPTER 8

Angus's shack at Windy Harbour had once been owned by a fisherman, and still displayed signs of that history. Glass floats festooned the walls, fragments of nets hung from the veranda rafters, and flotsam discarded from a thousand catches littered the front yard. Inside, it was a different story. Angus had lined the walls with wood panelling, installed pressed metal sheets over the old ceiling panels and fitted lamps where the strip lighting used to hang. In a word, it was cosy, and Peter loved to visit. He had learned that Angus, like many bachelors, valued his privacy. You didn't just drop in—you were invited. But ever since the rally in Denmark, the invitations had come regularly enough, and tonight was such an occasion.

'Bring some fish to cook, I'll supply the drinks,' Angus had said.

Now they were at the rough wooden table the fisherman had left behind, mopping up the juices of whiting cooked in butter, with pieces of chunky bread. Each man had a glass of whisky before him; Peter's diluted with rainwater, Angus's straight.

'Cheers, laddie,' said Angus. 'That was outstanding.'

'Here's to ush,' said Peter.

He was already feeling the effects of the single malt The big man opposite exceeded his capacity for Scotch by reason of his bulk, but Peter also imagined it was in his genes. If he was aware of his own intolerance for more than a glass, he didn't show it. He felt warm inside, expansive. The fire crackling in the stove, the wind outside, the sound of the sea and the company of Angus—it all added up his newfound feeling of wellbeing. His life, he believed, was proceeding on an upwards trajectory.

'I had a call from the Great White Chief,' he said, a new name for his father, coined by Angus.

'I see,' said Angus. 'And what did his eminence have to say this time?'

'He wants me to take over the running of Satinwood Funerals, his principal business.'

Angus guffawed. 'And that would involve...?'

'Just about everything I hate,' said Peter, grabbing the whisky bottle and topping himself up. 'Cheers!'

Angus didn't laugh. 'Perhaps you should consider it, laddie. It might mean a lot of money. Your birthright, do ye ken?'

'My birthright was obliterated when my mother died.'

Angus nodded. 'Come on, we'll sit closer to the fire. Tell me about it. All about it.'

Peter couldn't remember walking home that night, but somehow, he did. They'd knocked off the rest of the bottle, with Angus leading the drinking but Peter close behind. Angus had talked about his childhood in Glasgow, the brutality of the street gangs and the outright callousness of his father's desertion when he was ten. Peter had never heard of the Glasgow smile before, and when Angus explained it—hacking into the corners of the victim's mouth all the way to the ears, leaving a permanent grin—he had felt ill.

'They got my mate, a wee chap called Dudley, because he was gay. You couldn't fight them, there was too many of them.

I was fourteen. My mother was an alcoholic by then. I left her with my sister and sent money from London, where I worked as a builder's labourer. I never went back.'

Much later, the conversation moved back to Peter's mother, the fall from the balcony, the failure of police to do anything about it.

'I hate that bastard and all his medals and his suits and his plummy accent and his moustache,' Peter had said, referring to his father. 'I can't believe he had the gall to call me and offer the business as if it was some great act of generosity. I wanted to tell him to jack it up his arse!'

'That's it, laddie! Spit it all out,' said Angus.

'The long and short of it? He's a murderer. My niece Renata told me about another murder he committed when he was on the run, in wartime Germany. After he'd fucked Renata's grandmother, he decided he needed to "borrow" the motorbike he'd spotted next door. The German men were all away at the front, and so it was fair game, or at least my father the hero thought so. But the neighbour didn't agree, folded her arms, and said no. So, my very brave father took off his scarf and strangled her. As Renata told it, there was no blame. It was wartime and such behaviour was justified. Even her grandmother thought so. The murder was blamed on Franz Wagner, Renata's German grandfather, who was found guilty of war crimes and hauled off sometime in the 1980s. But my father gets away with murder. And somehow, he wakes up every day and looks in the mirror and tells himself that he is right.'

'He's a psychopath, laddie,' said Angus gently. 'And I'm sorry.'

The last thing before Peter staggered off out the door was

a decision. Angus and Peter would drive up to Perth and visit Duffy senior in his lair. Peter had seen what Angus could do with his enemies, and over the course of the night it seemed that Alan Duffy had become the class enemy for Angus. He tried to imagine the scene: a very large Scot and his frail father, his empire recently depleted by the meth lab explosion. It was no contest really. Peter went to sleep with a grin on his face and a belly full of single malt. His fathers dead goons gone and forgotten.

CHAPTER 9

'Can you run that past me again? You've been seconded because...'

Robin shrugged. 'Hey, sir, your guess is as good as mine.'

'Well, I'm not fucking having it.' Spittle flew from Lukashenko's mouth as mottled splotches spread like a red algal bloom across his face. Robin flinched.

'You saw who the letter was from?' Robin said.

Lukashenko waved the letter from the Assistant Commissioner Clarence Cassidy under Robin's nose. 'That slimy weasel. We did our training together. Brown nosed little cunt. But the prick outranks me. Looks like I don't have a choice.'

Robin nodded, wearing what he hoped was a sympathetic expression. 'Sir, you'll notice he also wants Dutton, O'Brien and Mortlock.'

'Yes, I noticed. Any idea why those officers were requested?' Lukashenko's eyes narrowed. The three hadn't ever been on his payroll. He leaned forward, his eyes boring into Robin's. 'I don't know what the fuck's going on, but I'm not happy. Of course, we really don't want people to know about your little escapade in Gookland, do we?' Relenting a little, Lukashenko placed a fatherly hand on Robin's shoulder. 'As soon as you know what the fuck this is all about, I want to know. All right?'

'I may be sworn to secrecy ...sir.'

'Listen, DS Edwards. You don't have any secrets from me. Understand?'

Robin managed a thin smile. 'Yes sir, I understand. But now I need to go. A meeting with...'

'Let me guess, that little shit, Hopalong?'

'Yes sir, Assistant Commissioner Cassidy. Look, I don't know for sure, but I have heard rumours illegal firearms are being smuggled in by a group associated with Jack Van Tongeren. That's the rumour anyhow.' Robin smiled to himself; he was slandering the name of a vicious white supremacist currently doing time for racist attacks on Asian businesses.

'Van Tongeren, eh? Yeah, well that makes sense. I could understand the need for secrecy if that's the case. But I still need to know. Got it?'

Robin watched Lukashenko stride back down the corridor. It was probably the last time he would ever have to call him sir or suffer the hated hand-on-shoulder routine.

Robin was chilled to the bone. '*Christ*, it's bloody Baltic. Any more coffee there?' It was cold and damp, the sort of night you wished you worked a sensible job.

Two unmarked police Falcons, hidden away like a couple of mad relatives, sat parked between two fire trucks. In full view of the detectives, the Qantas 747 squatted insolently in its bay, lights on but nobody home. The pungent smell of avgas filled the air.

Arms folded against the cold, Gillian chortled. 'No shit, Robin, and you an acting Detective Inspector. Doesn't seem fair, does it? Sadly, no more coffee. Would you care for a mint ... sir?'

CHAPTER 9

In the second car, Jack and Brendan were slumped down like a pair of drunks. Their wagon gleamed with a fine dew, which made it seem even colder.

'Jesus, it's like a freezer in here. Any more coffee in that thermos, Brendon?' Jack didn't want to be there. He had a new girlfriend and he'd been looking forward to a night with her, certainly not spending it with flatulent Brendon Gill.

'That bloody plane's been sitting there for twenty minutes,' Brendan said. 'The passengers have long gone. I reckon this could be an all-nighter.'

'I don't think so. Buckle up, oh smelly one.'

Jack poured the last trickle of coffee down his throat and screwed the top on the thermos. The black Satinwood Mercedes rolled silently across the runway and in a practised motion, reversed up to the cargo hold. A uniformed customs officer with a clipboard collected a signature and retreated to his warm office.

Jack glanced sideways at the other Ford. Robin gave him a thumbs up. Two coffins slid down a conveyor and were loaded into the van. The rear door of the Mercedes clicked shut, an innocent sound that carried easily across the silent runway. Both Falcons followed the slow-moving Mercedes as it turned onto the exit road. The police radios crackled with chatter but as far as Robin and his team were concerned, this was the main game.

'We stand out like the proverbials, I'm afraid,' Gillian grumbled.

There was no reply from Robin, concentrating fiercely on staying back. The Reid Highway curved its way to the Indian Ocean. Sparse, late-night traffic moved lazily along the artery.

'I think I know where the bastards are going,' said Robin. 'I'm going to shoot ahead. If I'm wrong, Jack or Brendan can radio.'

Twenty minutes later they were snaking through the ghostly-quiet industrial centre of Osborne Park. Robin made a tight turn into Carbon Court and floored it. Tyres screeched as the Falcon bounced over speed bumps. Robin squeezed the car in between two Toyota Land Cruisers and switched the motor off. The Allstar Entertainment sign beamed its incongruous message: Excellence in Event Management.

'That was a bit dramatic, DI Edwards,' said Gillian.

'I just wanted to park before the Mercedes arrived. If they see another vehicle drive in, they'll be suspicious.'

Headlights flashed up and down the wall as the Mercedes crawled over the speed bumps, then quietly reversed up to the Satinwood factory unit. Two men in dark coveralls sprung out. The roll-a-door clanged as it rattled skywards. Funereal decorum was dispensed with as the coffins were manhandled inside. Robin and Gillian heard muffled voices. The roll-a-door bounced shut.

'The cavalry should be here about now,' Robin murmured. 'With luck we'll have two warrants first thing and Duffy and Lukashenko will be done for.' As if programmed, the grey Falcon was cautiously negotiating the speed bumps. Robin flashed his lights.

'Do you reckon the four of us will be enough? Maybe we need backup?' Gillian peered nervously at the silent factory unit.

'Nah, we're super cops,' said Robin. 'We're ready to rock and roll.'

Brendon opened the boot of his car and grabbed the enforcer, the chunky steel battering ram that made keys redundant. The front door to the factory unit exploded in a shower of glass and the four were inside, weapons drawn.

'Armed police raise your hands.' Brendon's voice roared the loudest, followed by Jack and Robin's in discordant unity. The shrill screams from Gillian rounded off the a cappella quartet.

Four men in white coveralls stared in disbelief. Harsh lights from fluorescent tubes made the whole scene look like a '40s black and white noir movie. Grey metal coffins, rested on black steel benches. One casket was already sliced open, its contents not quite visible. The man doing the cutting held a whirring angle grinder on a long lead as it ripped into metal. A rainbow of sparks leaping into the air.

'What the fuck?' the man with the angle grinder, thrust his protective goggles high onto his forehead with one hand. With another curse, his face contorted into a snarl, he launched himself at the detectives, the howling angle grinder still spinning.

All guns were trained on the thug, fingers tightening on the triggers, when the angle grinder fell silent. It had run out of cord.

'What a wanker,' Brendon chortled.

'Anyone else want to play games?' Robin yelled. 'Now face the fucking wall. Hands behind your back. Do it now.'

***

'Point car on the Wesley.'

'Don 82.'

'Ah, Trung me old mate. You're back?'

'You bet, Barnsey.'

'Pick up at the Maj. Mr Oswald going to the domestic. M11 on pickup.'

Reluctantly Trung closed the novel he was reading, The Bruce Lee story. He thought, I could do that. Taekwondo, karate, jujitsu. I'm not a big guy. Neither was Bruce. He remembered seeing Lee in some Chinese action movies. *The man's a hero*. He thought about the thugs who'd roughed him up last year. *Yeah, I can do it.*

Trung had spent the last twenty minutes at the head of the line of cabs on the taxi rank on the corner of William and Hay Street, opposite the venerable old Wesley Church. Built of brick laid in Flemish bond in a gothic style and featuring a landmark spire, it was a beautiful old structure, an oasis of peace in the busy city.

Trung heard the clunk as the rear door of the Falcon taxi opened. He pressed his mike button. 'Sorry Barnsey I've got a walk up.'

'Where to, sir?' Trung started the engine and adjusted his wing mirror. He glanced at the passenger in his rear vision. His blood ran cold. Fuck. Of all people, it was Grantley, carrying a long cardboard box. 'What are you up to, Grantley? I've got witnesses. I can send a distress call. Leave me alone. C'mon fuck off outa my cab. I'm calling the coppers.' Trung's mouth was dry, his heart thumped against his rib cage.

'What do you know? My favourite little slope. I don't have a problem with you no more. My beef is with fucking Duffy. Now if you want to take me to his place, fine. If not, I'll take the cab behind. It's up to you.' Grantley pulled a twenty out of his top pocket. 'All yours, pal, and you can keep the change.'

Something about Grantley's manner soothed his nerves. 'Ok, Jutland Parade.'

Trung's mind ran at a hundred miles an hour. Why had he agreed to this fare? The cab crawled through the busy lunchtime traffic. Passing His Majesty's Theatre on the corner of King and Hay, a young guy in jeans and a West Coast Eagles T-shirt, a suitcase by his side, waved and smiled. That'll be Mr Oswald off to the airport. It's not too late. I haven't left the city. Trung knew all he had to do was press the mike button and say M99, the cabbie distress call. Barnsey would rally every cab in the CBD. Trung also knew cabbies protected their own, when the taxis arrived, they'd haul Grantley out of the car and administer some rough justice. His finger snaked to the mike button.

'Hey, you're reading that book about Bruce Lee. I've read it? Bloody fantastic.'

Trung's hand dropped to his side. The idea of Grantley reading a book was a bit hard to grasp. 'You read it. Really?'

'Oh yeah. He's, my hero.'

'But he's Asian?'

'Look actually I don't mind slant eyes. After I saw the movie, *Dragon*, I decided to learn karate.'

'Oh really?'

'Do you mind?' Grantley grabbed the book from the armrest and flicked through it. Just look at these photos. Bloody hell! What a guy.' Grantley placed the biography back on the armrest. 'I'm sorry about everything that happened. I didn't have a choice.'

Trung wasn't entirely sure what he was apologising for, but he smiled hesitantly 'Yeah, sure, Grantley.'

'Duffy isn't going to be a problem again. Just one thing?'

Trung's heart missed a beat.

'Don't tell anyone that you took me to Jutland Parade. Ok?'

Trung glanced again at the cardboard box Grantley nursed on his lap, this time with a little more interest.

CHAPTER 10

Peter decided that driving for half a day with a hangover was not to be recommended. At Pemberton they decided to stop at a new place up on the ridge behind the rail for a much-needed coffee. Angus lingered over the shrubs in the garden shop before joining him on the terrace, where Peter was tucking into an apple pie with cream.

'You're heading for an early death, laddie,' he said. 'All that cream!'

Every time Angus came into view, Peter experienced a rush of affection. This was a man he admired, a man he wanted to spend time with. Did that make him queer? His father, a noted homophobe, would have thought so. But Peter didn't much care what his father thought anymore. The purpose of their trip was to have it out, once and for all. Was he a coward for enlisting Angus to help? Peter didn't think so. With a lifetime of bullying and intimidation, and maybe much worse, behind him, Alan Duffy was not to be trifled with.

'Your coffee's coming,' said Peter. 'Mate.'

'Och now, don't be calling me mate,' said Angus. 'It's a term of abuse.'

'How do you mean?'

'Ok, probably not abuse. But it's the Australians' way of

pretending that everyone is equal, that this is an egalitarian society with no class distinction.'

Peter grunted. With the whisky still in his bloodstream, he wasn't in the mood for semantics. 'Your coffee is coming, Angus.'

They made good time after that, grabbed a sandwich at Donnybrook and were in Crawley by early afternoon. The closer they came to Dalkeith the more reluctant Peter felt to perform what he and Angus had cooked up the night before – an intervention in what had seemed the inevitable arc of Peter's life. Was it possible to change something so well established? All his life Peter had bitten his tongue, or else vainly tried to make peace. But his father's tyranny had continued unabated.

They parked in the driveway and rang the bell. After a wait, his father's voice came over the intercom. *'Who is it?'*

'It's Peter.'

'Come up, I'm in my study.'

The lock buzzed and the two men entered the vestibule, lined with paintings and tapestries. Angus looked around, shaking his head. 'Jesus Christ,' he said. 'Eat the rich!'

They climbed the stairs to find Duffy standing at the top, his cane propping up his left side, which seemed to Peter to have slumped. The Great White Chief was getting old, he thought. Soon he would be moving on to the happy hunting ground. The thought made him giggle, but he recovered in time to introduce Angus.

Angus took the hand that Duffy held out.

'I thought we would meet in the Lancaster Room,' said Duffy.

Really? There was a Lancaster Room? This was news to Peter. When they reached the open door after a short walk across the landing, he realised it was his mother's old sewing room, now repainted and bedecked with trophies and framed photographs. A model of the famous bomber hung from the ceiling. There were images of Duffy in his uniform, Duffy high up in the pilot's seat giving a thumbs up, and Duffy with his crew clustered around a 4000lb bomb the size of three or four oil drums. Another shot of the same crew in front of their plane emphasized the size of the thing, its Perspex flight deck pointing skywards and the bomb aimer's bubble hanging beneath it. A kangaroo on top of an inverted boomerang left no doubt as to the crew's origin.

'What's your poison?' asked Duffy, closing the door. Both men declined the offer.

Angus inspected the photographs. There were watercolour renderings of the bombers in flight, medals framed and on display and a shop dummy in full uniform, the cap worn jauntily on one side of the head and the distinctive wing insignia pinned just under the collar on the left side of the regulation woollen jackets. Angus turned around to face Duffy. Was the old man expecting to be admired, Peter wondered? Or was he looking for a fight?

'We used to have a saying when I went to school in Glasgow,' said Angus. 'If anyone was boasting, we'd say "so what do you want, a medal?" But it seems you already have plenty of those.'

'I'm proud I was able to serve my country,' said Duffy.

'Well, I guess you did,' said Angus. 'But we only have your word for that.'

'Well, I think you can go beyond my word,' Duffy countered. 'More than half of the flyers in Bomber Command gave their lives. It was no picnic.'

'That's right, sir,' said Angus. 'On the other hand, six hundred thousand German civilians died because of Allied bombing in the last two years of the war. Is that something to be proud of?'

Peter held his breath. He had never heard anyone challenge his father's heroic version of the war. Duffy shrugged. 'It was war,' he said. 'People die in wartime. Or maybe you are just reciting things you read in a book?'

'Your son was telling me that your plane crashed, but that you survived,' said Angus.

'True,' said Duffy. 'Although I was under the impression, he had no interest in my war stories.'

'Oh, he is interested,' said Angus. 'Just as he is interested in your peacetime stories.'

'Meaning?'

Peter had taken a seat on the sofa in the corner. Any minute now he expected his father to press the alarm which would summon one of his goons. Although two of them had perished in the meth lab explosion, he was sure there'd be replacements. Angus turned his way. 'Peter?' he said.

Peter reached inside his jacket and found what he was looking for. He unfolded it carefully and began to read. '*Historical War Crimes Charge for WWII Bomber Pilot. Alan Duffy DSO, who piloted a Lancaster bomber during the Second World War, has come under scrutiny by the RAAF for his alleged part in the murder of a German female on a farm near Freiburg in 1942 ... The charges arise from historic photographs of the murder scene together with testimony gathered from the late Sandy Tuckwell—*'

'That old fraud,' Duffy exploded. 'Ever wondered why

nothing more was written about that? My lawyer warned *The West Australian* of the consequences of publishing rumours and gossip.'

'*Gossip* which is backed up at the source,' said Peter. 'I've met your granddaughter, Renata, my niece. She heard it from her grandmother, you know, the one you fucked when you were on the run.'

Duffy raised his cane and waved it close to Peter's face. 'You think you can bring your big boyfriend here and insult me? You watch your language in this house. I don't care how old you are...'

Peter said nothing. For the first time, he had his father on the defensive.

Angus moved a step closer to the old man, his arms folded. 'If you threaten Peter, I will have to break your cane,' he said.

Duffy looked up at the bulk of the Scotsman and retreated to an office chair pulled up to a roll-top desk. 'I'm sorry,' he said softly. 'But I do have something that will refute these foul accusations. Let me show you both.'

He rolled up the wooden shutter and swivelled back on the chair holding an impressively aged handgun, which he pointed at Angus. 'Another one of my mementoes. It's the weapon that German bitch pulled out to discourage me from taking her precious BMW motor bike. She made a big mistake. Had no idea how to handle a gun, that was clear. If she had, it would have been all over for me. See? It's a Luger P08. Quite lethal. Would you like to test that statement out?'

Both Peter and Angus recoiled. It was all Peter could do not to put his hands up. There was a long silence, broken by a creak from the wooden stairs loud enough to alert all three people in the room. Heavy footsteps crossed the landing to the front lounge, which overlooked the river. A door slammed and the footsteps approached the Lancaster Room. As Duffy was standing unsteadily from his swivel chair, still holding the Luger, the door burst open and Grantley entered, a sawn-off shotgun levelled and cocked.

'Grantley, how in hell...' Duffy's eyes bulged.

'You stupid old prick. I still have my fucking key.' He aimed at Duffy and fired at his chest, bringing the old man down in a heap on the rug.

Grantley turned to face the other two, but Angus was quicker. With deadly aim he kicked the shotgun out of Grantley's grip and smashed him in the face with his fist. Grantley replied with a blow to the heart, which left the big Scot winded. Grantley stooped quickly to retrieve the shotgun, but Peter kicked it out of the way. Grantley, enraged, picked Peter up by the collar with his left hand and drew back his other arm, fist clenched.

The counterattack from Angus was something Peter would never forget. Angus grabbed Grantley from behind in a stranglehold. Grantley turned white, flailing about to try and escape. Very slowly Angus pulled Grantley's head the other way, his great paw splayed across the man's face like a blanket. Peter heard the crack as Grantley's top two vertebrae gave way. Grantley's head flopped forward, unsupported now and unable to perform the executive functions the rest of his body required. Angus let the dead man down slowly to the floor and walked out of the room, beckoning Peter to come with him.

They cleared the driveway and set off in the direction of the city, which stood gleaming in the afternoon light. Neither spoke for some minutes. Passing Matilda Bay, Angus broke the silence. 'That should give the forensic team something to puzzle about,' he said. 'It's clear what killed the old man, but how about the goon? Maybe it was the Abominable Snowman, or the Dalkeith yeti.'

Peter tried to laugh through his tears. The Great White Chief was dead.

CHAPTER 11

It hardly seemed necessary, but Robin decided to ask for backup for his arrest of Duffy. Gillian clutched the warrant, although neither of them were too concerned about the paperwork. A squad car loomed in the rear-view mirror, its blue light flashing but no siren sounding.

'Good not to alarm the genteel people of Jutland Parade,' said Robin.

'Alan Duffy, DSO,' said Gillian. 'Distinctly Shitty and Odorous.'

'His goose is cooked this time,' said Robin.

'Better than what he's been putting in his pet food,' said Gillian.

They were both packing weapons, although nobody expected Duffy to resist. He was a white-collar criminal, with fingers in every sort of vice. Robin had a strong aversion to heroin dealers and now they'd cornered one of the kingpins— not exactly a death blow to the trade in Perth, he thought, but an important strike. The only resistance might come from bodyguards if he still had any. Duffy was more likely at this stage to have surrounded himself with lawyers.

They turned into Broadway and made their way to the river. Whenever he saw Steves Hotel, he was reminded of student days, long nights at the pool tables or in summer around wooden benches in the beer garden. He was one of the new guard, as Lukashenko had known and despised: the young cops who got a degree before attending the Academy. With his degree came campus life, the same university Bob Hawke had attended. It was what had made him dare to think he could relate to a woman like Renata, who had just had her article published in Germany and was contemplating a life in academia.

They pulled into Duffy's driveway and left one of the squaddies standing guard. Robin drew his weapon and approached the door. It was half open. A robbery? He took the stairs with Gillian behind him and the second squaddie behind her. They searched the front sitting room and then backtracked along the landing to a smaller room. Inside were two bodies, one with a shotgun blast in his chest and the other lying prone, his head at a peculiar angle. Robin quickly identified Duffy and called Forensics. Gillian took pictures of both corpses where they lay, something to show Brendan and Jack. As delicately as possible, Robin retrieved a diary he had spotted on the open roll-top desk.

'Really?' asked Gillian.

'You know what will happen if I don't. Forensics will dust it, bag it, and then lose it.'

They left the way they had arrived, without fanfare, and instructed the two squaddies to wait for the white overall brigade. It was time for coffee, self-congratulations, and some speculation about the manner of Grantley's death. Also, thought Robin, for a quick squiz at Duffy's diary. He did that while Gillian was ordering the coffee. The last entry in the diary was: *MC arrives*. It meant less than any cryptic crossword clue, thought Robin. Or maybe it meant everything.

Gillian returned with the croissants, the coffee still to come. 'What do you make of this?' asked Robin. Gillian peered at it.

'Elementary, my dear Watson. Something went wrong and MC turned on the Sky Pilot.'

'Ok, but why a shotgun? Isn't that a bit crude and unnecessary?'

'Low life,' said Gillian. 'With low life, you never can tell.'

Renata surveyed her meagre possessions. Robin had offered her an array of baggage options. 'You don't have to be a backpacker for this trip,' he'd said on the way out the door that morning. 'You're a serious journalist now.'

She had been in Perth almost a year, she reflected. In that time, she had tracked down her *opa*, fallen in love with a cop, rescued him and Trung from a nest of vipers in Vietnam, and planted some seeds in the publishing world back in Germany. She had even adopted the West Coast Eagles football team, watching their star player Chris Mainwaring, spellbound by his prowess. But all in all, it had been a whirlwind, almost too much to take in. She was looking forward to some time on her own, time to reflect and get clear. In Germany she would stay with her mother. Perhaps sharing stories in her native language would help her to clear her mind and make some decisions about the future. Most importantly, with all she had learnt in Perth she was going to get her German Opa's murder conviction overturned.

Robin wanted to marry her. She wasn't sure she was ready for that. At 22, she could afford to wait. But not too long! After their romantic night at Windy Harbour, she was once again in love with her man. It was a happy state. In a few days' time she'd be winging her way to Germany, but she knew she would return. Australia was going to be her home.

She began to pack her warmest clothes. Germany would be cool, going on cold, by the time she arrived. Her best woollen jacket was beginning to look frayed at the cuffs. She would find a new one back home, maybe take a shopping trip to Munich with her mother.

What was she to do about her *opa*? Nothing, she supposed. He had made it clear that he wanted nothing to do with her. But she would enjoy telling her mother about the meeting, what the brave Aussie pilot had made of his life—and how he had turned a respectable family business into a network of criminal enterprises. And then there was her Uncle Peter, and the wonderful wildness of the D'Entrecasteaux.

Robin had come in late the night before, but not too late to convey the news: for Alan Duffy, the game was up. They had tracked down the source of his heroin imports, his method of operation, the lot. In the morning they would arrest him. She had to admit a tinge of disappointment at the news. The chase had been thrilling, but some perverse part of her wanted the rogue to elude them, at least for a while. She shook her head. She would never really understand all the warring parts of herself. And now Robin's car was in the driveway. She put aside her packing and walked to the door to welcome him. He smiled sadly; his arms open as he walked up the steps.

'I'm sorry, love,' he said. 'Your *opa* is dead.'

CHAPTER 12

The view from the eighth-floor reception of Commissioner Bruce's offices was spectacular. Mid-afternoon traffic snaked silently along Riverside Drive and a flotilla of yachts scudded along the Swan River, their colourful mainsails billowing.

This is quite a love-in, Robin thought. Walter Jessup the union man and Assistant Commissioner Clarence Cassidy were waiting to offer their congratulations. Robin's head was still in a whirl at the speed of change. Detective Inspector at his age? This was really their day, all of them. Robin, Jack, Brendan, and Gillian were about to be escorted into the office of the king. Carol Wilkins, often referred to as the power behind the throne, was all smiles.

'Good morning, you can all come on through. I'll be bringing coffee in shortly.

The gang of four trooped into Len Bruce's office and sat down. Commissioner Bruce looked like the cat that got the cream. He introduced Gillian, Jack and Brendan to Assistant Commissioner Clarence Cassidy, and Walter Jessup, union rep. Robin shook Cassidy's hand and quickly appraised the man that Lukashenko had so vehemently despised. His impression was of a shrewd, observant cop who missed nothing. The next commissioner he thought.

'Sit down, sit down.' Len Bruce was beaming from ear to ear. 'First of all, congratulations Robin. You are now Detective Inspector Edwards. How does that feel?'

Robin grinned. 'Thank you, sir, I couldn't be happier.'

'Look, to all of you: this has been an outstanding success. We are only missing Renata Schmidt, who really was the catalyst for all this. She was invited today?'

Robin nodded and offered a mumbled excuse. He couldn't say that Renata had refused, using some colourful German oaths to emphasise her view that the police force in WA was a nest of vipers.

'Just to recap, your team has destroyed a vicious international heroin smuggling operation,' said Bruce. 'As I mentioned before, our counterparts in Vietnam have done their job to close down and arrest the kingpin in that organization. For all I know, he may already have been executed. They don't muck around over there.'

The Commissioner paused for effect, wearing his best made-for-television 'aren't I sincere' expression. 'As you all know there have been accusations of corruption made against certain officers. A number of arrest warrants have been issued. We've flushed out some detective constables, detective sergeants and sadly, one detective superintendent.'

Robin glanced guiltily at the Breitling on his wrist. He'd held off dropping the bombshell about the bodies in the pet food, until DNA results were confirmed. *The press is going to have a field day with that one.*

'We do have some rather extraordinary loose ends. Robin, as I understand it, Alan Duffy was found shot and killed in his Jutland Parade mansion. The supposed killer was found in the same room, dead from a broken neck. Can you throw any light on this?'

Suddenly Robin didn't care what he said. The grand office, the uniforms, the pomp and ceremony could have come from a Gilbert and Sullivan operetta he had seen once with his aunt, a satire about ambition.

'Well, sir, it seems as if Rodney Chamberlain, aka Grantley, entered the house with a shotgun and executed Alan Duffy.'

The Commissioner sat with his hands steepled. 'And how did Rodney Chamberlain die?'

'Well, sir, at this stage we can only assume after killing Mr Duffy he was filled with remorse and broke his own neck.'

Len Bruce stared at Robin and then shifted his gaze to Walter Jessup and Clarence Cassidy. Cassidy jumped to his feet, red-faced.

'I am really very surprised to hear that from the mouth of a newly appointed Detective Inspector. I would like to remind DI Edwards—'

Carol burst into the room and approached the Commissioner. 'Sir, I need to see you outside.'

Gillian seemed to get the joke. She grinned at Robin. Jack and Brendon kept mum, although Jack had a smile playing on his mouth. Cassidy and Jessup conducted a muttered conversation at their end of the circle. The hiatus ended with Commissioner Bruce's return.

'Vincent Lukashenko has been discovered in his car, at the front of one Malcom Farrand's mansion in Swan View, with what appears to be a self-inflicted gunshot wound to the head. I'm sorry to close the meeting on that note. Thank you for coming.'

The gang of four shuffled down the corridor, like children told to go to bed early. As soon as the lift door closed, they erupted in disbelieving joy.

'Very soon,' intoned Jack, 'we are going to have one hell of a party.'

CHAPTER 13

Mike Cornish cleared Perth Airport without fuss. He was travelling light and by 8am was sitting atop a red double-decker bus destined for the city, via the Swan River, Kings Park, and Northbridge. The driver was droning on about the Swan River Colony, as if the white people's flimsy settlement was the only thing worth noting. From Kings Park the bus coasted down the hill to the CBD, took a left into William and crossed the Horseshoe Bridge into Northbridge.

'This is Northbridge,' said the driver, 'and the end of our journey this morning. We hope you enjoyed ... *drone, drone, drone.*'

Mike climbed stiffly down the stairs from the top deck of the bus. His gammy leg had all but seized up on the long flight from Hanoi. He would be glad to walk around and explore, then back to the Mantra for a sleep and some dinner. The tour had terminated outside the museum in Beaufort Street. He walked along the pedestrian path skirting the museum and down into the heart of Northbridge. At a pub called the Brass Monkey he ordered a schooner of Swan Lager and looked around. The morning punters were mostly male, slow drinkers who studied the horse racing form guide, peering occasionally at the sports broadcasts beamed into every corner on the hotel's array of screens.

A young, muscular type in a T-shirt and jeans sat next to him, ordered a vodka and coke, was served, paid up.

'Fuck me,' he said. 'These drink prices are over the top, aren't they?'

Mike nodded and smiled. He wasn't getting involved. Nothing about this trip was unplanned. There were to be no casual encounters, no side trips, no smelling the roses. If they even had roses in this desert, that is. He unfolded the single sheet of notes Baumann had sent him, just days before his demise. All it contained were names and a single piece of information. Robin Edwards and Peter Duffy. The information was in Baumann's native tongue. Mike had translated it the day he got it. *The cops you need to meet all drink at the Queens in Mount Lawley.*

He folded the paper and returned it to the pocket of his jacket. Baumann had made it clear that he was not to contact old man Duffy, who was feeling the heat. Baumann himself knew that the Australian cop who got away was making waves back home, waves that threatened to engulf the Hanoi operation and perhaps Duffy's business as well. If nothing else, Baumann had emphasized, it would be a revenge killing. The emphasis had come in the form of a lucrative contract, three times Mike's usual rate.

Mike had been stunned when Baumann was arrested and then executed. He had briefly considered not fulfilling the contract, but it was a point of honour, and he'd been quite fond of the old kraut. *Yes, those bastards will pay. The son included, piece of shit. Mike Cornish doesn't welch.*

'Say, buddy,' he said to the muscle man. 'Is Mount Lawley close to here?'

'Just up the road,' the man said.

'Ever heard of a place called the Queens?'

'Sure. It's another old pub with jacked up prices, just like this one. It's in Beaufort Street, next street that way.' He pointed in the direction Mike had come.

'Cheers, buddy,' said Mike, draining his beer with a grimace. The so-called lager had none of the freshness of its European counterparts. A lesson learned. He walked out into William Street and turned left. A stroll through Northbridge would almost certainly yield what he was after. A little further up William Street he came to 'Periscope'. In the window was displayed a range of women's fashions, perfect.

CHAPTER 14

Friday night at the Queens and the place was jumping. Renata had arrived early to reserve a large table in the lounge bar and now they were gathering: Peter and Angus, who had driven up from Windy Harbour together; Trung, and the rest of the Gang of Four, Gillian, Brendan and Jack. Robin, who was feeling proud enough for all of them, had claimed a seat at the top of the table next to Renata.

He had cautioned his team not to discuss the Duffy case. Apart from the confidential nature of the matter, they were to respect Renata's feelings for her *opa*. The warning hadn't quelled their exuberance. Brendan had struck up a conversation with Angus. Gillian was listening to Renata's travel plans. Jack sat drinking steadily and appreciating the parade of young women, all of whom were pleasingly underdressed for a cool night. Peter was staring into space, perhaps waiting to catch up with Renata. Robin approached Trung, who was hanging back from the crowd.

'No more threats, Trung?' he asked.

'All good, Robin. I hope you have locked up all those bastards,' he said.

'Let's say we have dealt with them,' said Robin. 'You won't hear from them again. Did you move back into your apartment?'

'No, boss. I bought a little cottage for me and Lily.'

CHAPTER 14

'Your girlfriend?'

'My mistress, boss. What about you and Renata? Good?'

'She's off to visit her mother back in Germany,' said Robin. 'But she'll be back. Ask me in six months.'

Trung smiled into his beer. 'That was one big fucking time we all had in Vietnam,' he said. 'She saved our bacon. Isn't that right?'

The expression sounded so quaint coming out of Trung's mouth, Robin roared laughing. He clinked glasses with Trung and then ordered more jugs of Swan Lager for the table. Angus was following his beers with shots of Scotch, but that was his business. Peter seemed cut off, and a bit wobbly on his pins. The noise level elevated a few decibels with each round. Unlawful acts were probably occurring in most corners of the pub: drug deals, drunken drivers staggering out to their cars, and underage kids drinking. One couple was doing the wild thing against the wall. Robin was off duty.

An overdressed woman with a too-short skirt walked in, looked around, and headed for the back bar. She looked awkward in her heels. Maybe it was her limp. Robin took in the visual impression and tried to process it. He needed to piss. Walking past Angus and Brendan on the way to the toilets, he overheard Brendan discussing the mysterious death of Grantley. He didn't use his name, but he might as well have. Angus had a huge smile on his face and was shaking his head.

'That certainly is a mystery, Brendan,' he said. 'A definite mystery.'

'Have you seen Peter?' asked Renata when he returned.

'No,' said Robin. 'I'll go find him up after I grab the next round.'

Robin ordered more jugs of Swan. Something was troubling him, relaxed as he was after a couple of beers. The last entry in Duffy's diary was turning in his mind like a disco ball. He moved next to Trung, claimed his attention through all the noise and happy confusion. 'Hey, Trung,' he said. 'You remember that guy working for Baumann who liked karaoke so much?'

'Yeah, Mike,' said Trung. 'Nice guy. Very good at singing. And at drugging people.'

'Do you remember his second name?'

'Yeah, never forget a name. I'm a cabbie, remember? It was Cornish.'

Mike ... Cornish. The jugs arrived and Robin signed the tab. Renata was right. Peter was missing. *Mike Cornish, it is fucking Mike Cornish.* He grabbed Jack Dutton's arm.

'What's up, boss?' asked Dutton.

'Are you armed?'

'Affirmative,' said Dutton.

'We're looking for an American, possibly in drag. And we're looking for Peter. High risk. Cover my tracks.'

The two of them began to scour the outer reaches of the big room, now full to capacity.

Peter pulled his stool closer to the dimly lit back bar, parked his feet on the rung and breathed a sigh of relief. Ever since his father's execution he had wanted to be alone, to digest the sight of the old man with blood gushing out of his chest, pooling on the white rug of the Lancaster Room. The man who had survived seventeen raids on enemy territory in a bomber, then crashed it and endured a flight through wartime Germany, had died like a cheap crim. And his father's death changed everything, Peter thought. Now, he could be whoever he wanted to be.

He wasn't even sure he needed to be a recluse anymore. What did he want? To be more adventurous, for sure. And to shape his own life, not in reaction to his father's oppression but as his own, authentic creation.

The barman offered him a cocktail list, which he studied carefully. Reading something meant that he didn't have to feel self-conscious about drinking alone. The bar was almost deserted—a pair of lovebirds on the far side and a blonde woman with strong features and a body-hugging sequinned dress sitting a few seats away. She too, was studying the cocktail list, but she had something to say about it.

'Wadda they think we are? Millionaires?' She turned to Peter with a smile. 'Name's Michelle,' she said. Her voice was low pitched, her accent American.

'Peter Duffy,' said Peter automatically.

'You with a group, or are you a loner like me?' asked Michelle.

'I'm with a group, but I decided to take a rest from the beer and try something different.'

'In that case, to hell with the prices. My shout. Isn't that what you Aussies say? What'll it be?'

Peter smiled and apologetically asked for a classic old-fashioned daiquiri. He had no idea what it was, but it seemed to fit his new goal, to move away from the defensive and conservative man he had grown up to be. It seemed as if his lefty anarchist ways dissipated with the acquisition of wealth. He noticed that Michelle ordered a coke. Peter's inexperience with women was beginning to surface. He liked her hair, and her shaven legs, on show because she had had to hitch up her dress to sit on the bar stool. He tried to keep his eyes away from her breasts, which lit up the sequined bodice every time she moved.

The drinks arrived and she talked about her travels, her stopover in Singapore and how much she was looking forward to catching up with her brother in Bunbury. Peter told her about Windy Harbour, and in a conversational flourish that surprised him as it rolled off his tongue, mentioned his recent meeting with Renata, his niece. Michelle nodded and smiled.

Peter felt glad to be away from Robin and the other cops, who made him feel guilty. Not only that, but they had wolfed down the bar snacks and chips that were supposed to mop up the alcohol. He hoped Angus was being careful. After all, the Scot had killed a man with his bare hands. In the macho atmosphere of cops socialising, he needed to be careful not to brag. Robin had assured him the police weren't interested in delving any deeper; they were in panic mode. 'You have nothing to worry about Peter. They just want the whole business to go away.'

They finished their drinks and Michelle looked around the bar, which was filling up with giggling girls from a hens' party. 'Say, Peter,' she said. 'There's a great little bar across the road where we can talk. Why don't we head over there?'

Peter was openly staring at her bosom now. Michelle was leaning towards him, her mouth glossy with lipstick, her blue eyes half closed. There was something magnetic about her, Peter thought. And something repellent. He reached down to stroke her thigh, imagined being held by her somewhere safe, the way Angus had held him after the rally but with the added dimension of sex. She brushed his hand away.

'Not yet, darling,' she said. Her voice was husky, almost masculine.

She picked up her clutch bag, grabbed Peter's hand and stood up. They strolled confidently past the mob in the front bar and out through the door. Surely no one would miss him for a little while, thought Peter. He averted his eyes, as if no one was there, and held on.

'Peter!'

It was Robin's voice, shouting over the din. Peter ignored it. He was with Michelle. A man should follow his instincts, he thought. He wasn't a baby. He could do what he wanted.

Outside in Beaufort Street the Friday night traffic was building. Michelle stood on the kerb, Peter just behind her. Peter turned to see Robin burst out the door, his face contorted. Jack Dutton followed; gun drawn. Holding Peter's hand tightly now, Michelle looked left and stepped out. It was all wrong. Peter let go.

The van that collected her, a battered Ford Transit, didn't even slow as her shattered body flew into the air, before disappearing into the night. Peter crouched down, the daquiri pumping through his veins, and dragged the broken body onto the pavement. He left her blonde wig where it lay, bloodied and muddy.

CHAPTER 15

POLICE CORRUPTION, the headline of The West Australian screamed.

Liv topped up her chardonnay and pored over the story. Everything Sandy had spoken of or alluded to, was there. Her mind reeled. His old captain, Alan Duffy, a drug smuggler had been murdered. And Police Superintendent Lukashenko allegedly committing suicide. He was obviously a part of it. Alan Duffy's accomplices dying in mysterious explosions. Drug labs, bribes, numerous crooked cops. 'No wonder you were scared, Sandy.' Was Sandy the catalyst? Liv wondered. Did he set all or some of this in motion?

She remembered that walk home and his clumsy attempts at romance: 'Olivia Bayliss you are a very attractive woman, and I would like to officially announce my intentions, which I can assure you are honourable.' She remembered his voice had trailed off, but there was a definite twinkle in his eye. A tear slid down her face 'Oh Sandy, it would have been nice, but it was not meant to be.' She gazed at the old photo she'd filched from his home; Sandy, standing young and proud in front of a Lancaster bomber.

Liv raised a glass. 'To you Sandy, and what might have been.'

CHAPTER 16

Jack Sprague was in his corner office when Trung arrived, looking spruced up and ready for anything.

'What are you on, Trung? It's Sunday morning, it's still early, and you look like the man who has everything.'

'I do, boss. I have a new car.'

'And a new taxi plate. What did you do, rob a bank?'

'No need, boss. Used the family bank. Vietnamese families stick together.'

'Good for you, hot shot,' said Jack. 'Wish I could say the same about Australians.'

'More good things too, boss. I have a new woman—well, same woman, new arrangement—and some people who were giving me grief in my life have been terminated.'

'Ah, I see. You've been reading Jack Reacher again.'

'No, boss. You are wrong.'

'By the way, how about you stop calling me boss? You're an owner driver. You are your own boss!'

'True, boss,' said Trung.

'Should I ask you to say more about these terminations?'

Trung shrugged. 'Let me put it this way. The hitman has been hit. The sky pilot has been grounded. And the muscle man has been snuffed.'

'Ok ... whatever you say. I don't want to know. You want to

pay me something for Friday night?'

'Oh yeah, sorry, boss. I forgot. Too much monkey business.'

Sprague shook his head and held out a pay envelope for Trung to complete. Trung did the arithmetic, peeled off the money from the wad in his pocket and went to work. His first job of the day felt more like pleasure: pick up Renata and take her to the airport.

In Peninsular Road, Robin Edwards was stacking Renata's luggage in the driveway. Trung sounded his horn, backed in and began to load the boot. He could see it was tender moment, so he pretended to busy himself with car stuff—cleaning the glove box that was already spotless, wiping the windscreen and re-reading the owners' manual. When Renata joined him in the front, he could see she'd been crying. Robin came to the driver's window, putting on a good imitation of a man who wasn't feeling emotional.

'All good, Trung?'

'Never better, Robin,' said Trung.

On Guildford Road he twiddled with the dials of his new radio and found the classical station. Renata smiled weakly and looked straight ahead. As they passed the old brickworks, she turned to Trung.

'Here we are again, Trung,' she said. 'Another adventure.'

'So, goodbye to Perth?'

'*Wiedersehn*,' she said. 'Till we meet again.'

'You're coming back?'

'I will put it this way. I left my best dress and my best sandals and all my books and some CDs at Robin's. That's what I tried to tell him. He thinks I am making a runner.'

'We say, *doing* a runner.'

Renata laughed. They had reached the International Terminal and Trung pulled up as close as he could to the Lufthansa check-in. When she was on the footpath and surrounded by baggage, Renata reached out and gave Trung a hug. She was crying again and Trung saw no reason to stop her.

Back in the car he turned on the Swan Taxis network. The despatcher's voice had taken on a desperate note. *Anyone at all on the Domestic?*

It was the familiar voice of Barnsey. 'Don 82 at the International,' said Trung.

'Trung. What a treat! You know how to get to the Domestic from there, don't you, driver?'

'Me not know, boss. Where is, please?' asked Trung, in his best impression of a green recruit.

The day was opening before him and the shiny bonnet of his new Holden Commodore led the way.

MESSAGE TO THE READER

Dear reader, I hope you have enjoyed Birthright.

This novel is a very different genre from my previous novels, The Singapore Saga and The Hawaiian Intervention.

I am grateful for the kind reviews I have received on Amazon and Goodreads for those two "Spencer Marlowe" stories.

Once again, I would ask any reader who enjoys Birthright to be so kind as to consider placing a review. They are vitally important and are much appreciated.

BIOGRAPHY

KELVIN WHITE

I am a Western Australian author, having been born in Perth and living in WA for most of my life. Like so many authors, my background is littered with many and varied careers; taxi driver, musician, roof tiler, shoe salesman and a plethora of others I attempted when young.

Being an avid reader prompted my desire to put pen to paper. I have three self-published novels, the first being 'Oh, How We Rocked', my musical memoir published 2021. This sold quite well in local Perth and Fremantle bookshops, as well as internationally on Amazon and other on-line sales outlets.

My 'Spencer Marlowe' adventure stories, 'The Singapore Saga' and 'The Hawaiian Intervention', published in 2021, have sold in twelve countries as well as Perth and Albany bookshops. They have received excellent reviews on Amazon and Goodreads.

I have a fan base for my Spencer Marlowe series, encouraging me to write sequels. The next novel in the series, 'The Manhattan Sting', has reached copyedit stage and will be published early 2024.

My latest story 'Birthright', a crime novel, is a change of direction and draws on my experience as a taxi driver in Perth in the 1990's.

BIOGRAPHY

BRUCE RUSSELL

Bruce Russell's first novel, Jacob's Air, won the T.A.G. Hungerford Award in 1995 and was published by Fremantle Arts Centre Press in 1996. He published two more novels with the Press, The Chelsea Manifesto (1999) and Channelling Henry (2003). Since then, he has published Reunion (2013) with Vivid Publishing and three commissioned biographies, "Blackie", "Under the Radar", and "Il Capitano".

Over the years he has mentored many individuals, the most notable being Sheryl McCorrey, who wrote Diamonds and Dust (Pan Macmillan, 2007).

He currently teaches Creative Writing with OOTA.